Praise for *Forever, Interrupted*

"Touching and powerful . . . Reid masterfully grabs hold of the heartstrings and doesn't let go. A stunning first novel."

—*Publishers Weekly*, starred review

"You'll laugh, weep, and fly through each crazy-readable page."

—*Redbook*

"A moving novel about life and death."

—*Kirkus*

"A poignant and heartfelt exploration of love and commitment in the absence of shared time that asks, what does it take to be the love of someone's life?"

—Emma McLaughlin and Nicola Kraus,
#1 *New York Times* bestselling authors

"Moving, gorgeous, and at times heart-wrenching."

—Sarah Jio, *New York Times* bestselling author

"Sweet, heartfelt, and surprising. These characters made me laugh as well as cry, and I ended up falling in love with them, too."

—Sarah Pekkanen, internationally bestselling
author of *The Opposite of Me*

"This beautifully rendered story explores the brilliance and rarity of finding true love, and how we find our way back through the painful aftermath of losing it. These characters will leap right off the page and into your heart."

—Amy Hatvany, author of *Safe with Me*

ALSO BY TAYLOR JENKINS REID

Forever, Interrupted

AFTER I DO

~ *A Novel* ~

TAYLOR JENKINS REID

WASHINGTON SQUARE PRESS

New York London Toronto Sydney New Delhi

W

Washington Square Press
A Division of Simon & Schuster, Inc.
1230 Avenue of the Americas
New York, NY 10020

First Washington Square Press trade paperback edition July 2014

WASHINGTON SQUARE PRESS and colophon are registered
trademarks of Simon & Schuster, Inc.

For information about special discounts for bulk purchases,
please contact Simon & Schuster Special Sales at 1-866-506-1949
or business@simonandschuster.com.

The Simon & Schuster Speakers Bureau can bring authors to your live
event. For more information or to book an event, contact the Simon &
Schuster Speakers Bureau at 1-866-248-3049 or visit our website at
www.simonspeakers.com.

Manufactured in the United States of America

Cover design © Connie Gabbert Design and Illustration LLC

40 39 38 37 36 35 34

Library of Congress Cataloging-in-Publication Data

Reid, Taylor Jenkins.
  After I do : a novel / Taylor Jenkins Reid.
    pages cm
  1. Marriage—Fiction. 2. Separation (Psychology)—Fiction. 3. Self-
realization—Fiction. 4. Domestic fiction. 5. Psychological fiction. I. Title.
  PS3618.E5478A69 2014
  813'.6—dc23
                                          2013046056
  ISBN 978-1-4767-1284-0
  ISBN 978-1-4767-1285-7 (ebook)

To Mindy Jenkins and Jake Jenkins
(May this serve as the final word that I
have the best feet in the family.)

flagrant, *adj*

I would be standing right there, and you would walk out of the bathroom without putting the cap back on the toothpaste.

The Lover's Dictionary

part one

WHERE DOES THE GOOD GO?

We are in the parking lot of Dodger Stadium, and once again, Ryan has forgotten where we left the car. I keep telling him that it's in Lot C, but he doesn't believe me.

"No," he says, for the tenth time. "I specifically remember turning right when we got here, not left."

It's incredibly dark, the path in front of us lit only by lampposts featuring oversized baseballs. I looked at the sign when we parked.

"You remember wrong," I say, my tone clipped and pissed-off. We've already been here too long, and I hate the chaos of Dodger Stadium. It's a warm summer night, so I have that to be thankful for, but it's ten P.M., and the rest of the fans are pouring out of the stands, the two of us fighting through a sea of blue and white jerseys. We've been at this for about twenty minutes.

"I don't remember wrong," he says, walking ahead and not even bothering to look back at me as he speaks. "You're the one with the bad memory."

"Oh, I see," I say, mocking him. "Just because I lost my keys this morning, suddenly, I'm an idiot?"

He turns and looks at me; I use the moment to try to catch up to him. The parking lot is hilly and steep. I'm slow.

"Yeah, Lauren, that's exactly what I said. I said you were an idiot."

"I mean, you basically did. You said that you know what you're talking about, like I don't."

"Just help me find the goddamn car so we can go home."

I don't respond. I simply follow him as he moves farther and farther away from Lot C. Why he wants to go home is a mystery to me. None of this will be any better at home. It hasn't been for months.

He walks around in a long, wide circle, going up and down the hills of the Dodger Stadium parking lot. I follow close behind, waiting with him at the crosswalks, crossing at his pace. We don't say anything. I think of how much I want to scream at him. I think of how I wanted to scream at him last night, too. I think of how much I'll probably want to scream at him tomorrow. I can only imagine he's thinking much of the same. And yet the air between us is perfectly still, uninterrupted by any of our thoughts. So often lately, our nights and weekends are full of tension, a tension that is only relieved by saying good-bye or good night.

After the initial rush of people leaving the parking lot, it becomes a lot easier to see where we are and where we parked.

"There it is," Ryan says, not bothering to point for further edification. I turn my head to follow his gaze. There it is. Our small black Honda.

Right in Lot C.

I smile at him. It's not a kind smile.

He smiles back. His isn't kind, either.

ELEVEN AND A HALF YEARS AGO

It was the middle of my sophomore year of college. My freshman year had been a lonely one. UCLA was not as inviting as I'd thought it might be when I applied. It was hard for me to meet people. I went home a lot on weekends to see my family. Well, really, I went home to see my younger sister, Rachel. My mom and my little brother, Charlie, were secondary. Rachel was the person I told everything to. Rachel was the one I missed when I ate alone in the dining hall, and I ate alone in the dining hall more than I cared to admit.

At the age of nineteen, I was much shier than I'd been at seventeen, graduating from high school toward the top of my class, my hand cramping from signing so many yearbooks. My mom kept asking me all through my freshman year of college if I wanted to transfer. She kept saying that it was OK to look someplace else, but I didn't want to. I liked my classes. "I just haven't found my stride yet," I said to her every time she asked. "But I will. I'll find it."

I started to find it when I took a job in the mailroom. Most nights, it was one or two other people and me, a dynamic in which I thrived. I was good in small groups. I could shine when I didn't have to struggle to be heard. And after a few months of shifts in the mailroom, I was getting to know a lot of people. Some of them I really liked. And some of those people really liked me, too. By the time we broke for Christmas that year, I was excited to go back in January. I missed my friends.

When classes began again, I found myself with a new

schedule that put me in a few buildings I'd never been in before. I was starting to take psychology classes since I'd fulfilled most of my gen eds. And with this new schedule, I started running into the same guy everywhere I went. The fitness center, the bookstore, the elevators of Franz Hall.

He was tall and broad-shouldered. He had strong arms, round around the biceps, barely fitting into the sleeves of his shirts. His hair was light brown, his face often marked with stubble. He was always smiling, always talking to someone. Even when I saw him walking alone, he seemed to have the confidence of a person with a mission.

I was in line to enter the dining hall when we finally spoke. I was wearing the same gray shirt I'd worn the day before, and it occurred to me as I spotted him a bit farther up in the line that he might notice.

After he swiped his ID to get in, he hung back behind his friends and carried on a conversation with the guy running the card machine. When I got up to the front of the line, he stopped his conversation and looked at me.

"Are you following me or what?" he said, looking right into my eyes and smiling.

I was immediately embarrassed, and I thought he could see it.

"Sorry, stupid joke," he said. "I've just been seeing you everywhere lately." I took my card back. "Can I walk with you?"

"Yeah," I said. I was meeting my mailroom friends, but I didn't see them there yet anyway. And he was cute. That was a lot of what swayed me. He was cute.

"Where are we going?" he asked me. "What line?"

"We are going to the grill," I said. "That is, if you're standing in line with me."

"That's actually perfect. I have been dying for a patty melt."

"The grill it is, then."

It was quiet as we stood in line together, but he was trying hard to keep the conversation going.

"Ryan Lawrence Cooper," he said, putting his hand out. I laughed and shook it. His grip was tight. I got the distinct feeling that if he did not want this handshake to end, there was nothing I could do about it. That's how strong his hand felt.

"Lauren Maureen Spencer," I said. He let go.

I had pictured him as smooth and confident, poised and charming, and he was those things to a certain degree. But as we talked, he seemed to be stumbling a bit, not sure of the right thing to say. This cute guy who had seemed so much surer of himself than I could ever be turned out to be . . . entirely human. He was just a person who was good-looking and probably funny and just comfortable enough with himself to seem as if he understood the world better than the rest of us. But he didn't, really. He was just like me. And suddenly, that made me like him a whole lot more than I realized. And that made me nervous. My stomach started to flutter. My palms started to sweat.

"So, it's OK, you can admit it," I said, trying to be funny. "It's *you* who have actually been stalking *me*."

"I admit it," he said, and then quickly reversed his story. "No! Of course not. But you have noticed it, right? It's like suddenly you're everywhere."

"*You're* everywhere," I said, stepping up in line as it moved. "I'm just in my normal places."

"You mean you're in *my* normal places."

"Maybe we're just cosmically linked," I joked. "Or we have similar schedules. The first time I saw you was on the quad, I think. And I've been killing time there between Intro to Psych and Statistics. So you must have picked up a class around that time on South Campus, right?"

"You've unintentionally revealed two things to me, Lauren," Ryan said, smiling.

"I have?" I said.

"Yep." He nodded. "Less important is that I now know you're a psych major and two of the classes you take. If I was a stalker, that would be a gold mine."

"OK." I nodded. "Although if you were any decent stalker, you would have known that already."

"Regardless, a stalker is a stalker."

We were finally at the front of the line, but Ryan seemed more focused on me than on the fact that it was time to order. I looked away from him only long enough to order my dinner. "Can I get a grilled cheese, please?" I asked the cook.

"And you?" the cook asked Ryan.

"Patty melt, extra cheese," Ryan said, leaning forward and accidentally grazing my forearm with his sleeve. I felt just the smallest jolt of electricity.

"And the second thing?" I said.

"Hm?" Ryan said, looking back at me, already losing his train of thought.

"You said I revealed two things."

"Oh!" Ryan smiled and moved his tray closer to mine on the counter. "You said you noticed me in the quad."

"Right."

"But I didn't see you then."

"OK," I said, not clear what he meant.

"So technically speaking, you noticed me first."

I smiled at him. "Touché," I said. The cook handed me my grilled cheese. He handed Ryan his patty melt. We took our trays and headed to the soda machine.

"So," Ryan said, "since you're the pursuer here, I guess I'll just have to wait for you to ask me out."

"What?" I asked, halfway between shocked and mortified.

"Look," he said, "I can be very patient. I know you have to work up the courage, you have to find a way to talk to me, you have to make it seem casual."

"Uh-huh," I said. I reached for a glass and thrust it under the ice machine. The ice machine roared and then produced three measly ice cubes. Ryan stood beside me and thwacked the side of it. An avalanche of ice fell into my glass. I thanked him.

"No problem. So how about this?" Ryan suggested. "How about I wait until tomorrow night, six P.M.? We'll meet in the lobby of Hendrick Hall. I'll take you out for a burger and maybe some ice cream. We'll talk. And you can ask me out then."

I smiled at him.

"It's only fair," he said. "You noticed me first." He was very charming. And he knew it.

"OK. One question, though. In line over there," I said as I I pointed to the swiper. "What did you talk to him about?" I was asking because I was pretty sure I knew the answer, and I wanted to make him say it.

"The guy swiping the cards?" Ryan asked, smiling, knowing he'd been caught.

"Yeah, I'm just curious what you two had to talk about."

Ryan looked me right in the eye. "I said, 'Act like we are having a conversation. I need to buy time until that girl in the gray shirt gets up here.'"

That jolt of electricity that felt small only a few moments earlier now seared through me. It lit me up. I could feel it in the tips of my fingers and the furthest ends of my toes.

"Hendrick Hall, tomorrow. Six P.M.," I said, confirming that I would be there. But by that point, I think we both knew I was dying to be there. I wanted *then* and *there* to be *here* and *now*.

"Don't be late," he said, smiling and already walking away.

I put my drink on my tray and walked casually through the dining hall. I sat down at a table by myself, not yet ready to meet my friends. The smile on my face was too wide, too strong, too bright.

• • •

I was in the lobby of Hendrick Hall by 5:55 P.M.

I waited around for a couple of minutes, trying to pretend that I wasn't eagerly awaiting the arrival of someone.

This was a date. A real date. This wasn't like the guys who asked you to come with them and their friends to some party they heard about on Friday night. This wasn't like when the guy you liked in high school, the guy you'd known since eighth grade, finally kissed you.

This was a date.

What was I going to say to him? I barely knew him! What if I had bad breath or said something stupid? What if my mascara smudged and I spent the whole night not realizing I looked like a raccoon?

Panicking, I tried to catch a glimpse of my reflection in a window, but as soon as I did, Ryan came through the front doors into the lobby.

"Wow," he said when he saw me. In that instant, I was no longer worried that I might be somehow imperfect. I didn't worry about my knobby hands or my thin lips. Instead, I thought about the shine of my dark brown hair and the grayish tint to my blue eyes. I thought about my long legs as I saw Ryan's eyes drift toward them. I was happy that I'd decided to show them off with a short black jersey dress and a zip-up sweatshirt. "You look great," he continued. "You must really like me."

I laughed at him as he smiled at me. He was wearing jeans and a T-shirt, with a UCLA fleece over it.

"And you must be trying really hard to not show how much you like *me*," I said.

He smiled at me then, and it was a different smile from earlier. He wasn't smiling at me trying to charm me. He was charmed *by* me.

It felt good. It felt really good.

• • •

Over burgers, we asked each other where we were from and what we wanted to do with the rest of our lives. We talked about our classes. We figured out that we'd both had the same teacher for Public Speaking the year before.

"Professor Hunt!" Ryan said, his voice sounding almost nostalgic about the old man.

"Don't tell me you liked Professor Hunt!" I said. No one liked Professor Hunt. That man was about as interesting as a cardboard box.

"What is not to like about that guy? He's nice. He's complimentary! That was one of the only classes I got an A in that semester."

Ironically, Public Speaking was the only class I got a B in that semester. But that seemed like an obnoxious thing to say.

"That was my worst class," I said. "Public speaking is not my forte. I'm better with research, papers, multiple-choice tests. I'm not great with oral stuff."

I looked at him after I said it, and I could feel my cheeks burning red. It was such an awkward sentence to say on a date with someone you barely knew. I was terrified he was going to make a joke about it. But he didn't. He pretended not to notice.

"You seem like the kind of girl who gets straight As," he said. I was so relieved. He had somehow managed to take this sort of embarrassing moment I'd had and turned it around for me.

I blushed again. This time for a different reason. "Well, I do OK," I said. "But I'm impressed you got an A in Public Speaking. It's actually not an easy A, that class."

Ryan shrugged. "I think I'm just one of those people who can do the public speaking thing. Like, large crowds don't scare me. I could speak to a room full of people and not feel the slightest bit out of place. It's the one-on-one stuff that makes me nervous."

I could feel myself cock my head to one side, a physical indication of my curiosity. "You don't seem the type to be nervous talking in any situation," I said. "Regardless of how many people are there."

He smiled at me as he finished his burger. "Don't be fooled by this air of nonchalance," he said. "I know I'm devilishly handsome and probably the most charming guy you've met in your life, but there's a reason it took me so long before I could find a way to talk to you."

This guy, this guy who seemed so cool, he liked *me*. *I* made him nervous.

I'm not sure there is a feeling quite like finding out that you make the person who makes you nervous, nervous.

It makes you bold. It makes you confident. It makes you feel as if you could do anything in the world.

I leaned over the table and kissed him. I kissed him in the middle of a burger place, the arm of my sweatshirt accidentally falling into the container of ketchup. It wasn't perfectly timed, by any means. I didn't hit his mouth straight on. It was sort of to the side a bit. And it was clear I had taken him by surprise, because he froze for a moment before he relaxed into it. He tasted like salt.

When I pulled away from him, it really hit me. What I had just done. I'd never kissed someone before. I had always *been* kissed. I'd always kissed *back*.

He looked at me, confused. "I thought *I* was supposed to do that," he said.

I was now horribly, terribly mortified. This was the sort of thing I'd read about in the "embarrassing moments" section of *YM* magazine as a girl. "I know," I said. "I'm sorry. I'm so . . . I don't know why I—"

"Sorry?" he said, shocked. "No, don't be sorry. That was perhaps the single greatest moment of my life."

I looked up at him, smiling despite myself.

"All girls should kiss like that," he said. "All girls should be exactly like you."

When we walked home, he kept pulling me into doorways and alcoves to kiss me. The closer we got to my dorm, the longer the kisses became. Until just outside the front door to my building, we kissed for what felt like hours. It was cold outside by this point; the sun had set hours ago. My bare legs were freezing. But I couldn't feel anything except his hands on me, his lips on mine. I could think of nothing but what we were doing, the way my hands felt on his neck, the way he smelled like fresh laundry and musk.

When it became time to progress or say good-bye, I pulled away from him, leaving my hand still in his. I could see in his eyes that he wanted me to ask him to come back to my room. But I didn't. Instead, I said, "Can I see you tomorrow?"

"Of course."

"Will you come by and take me to breakfast?"

"Of course."

"Good night," I said, kissing his cheek.

I pulled my hand out of his and turned to leave. I almost stopped right there and asked him to come up with me. I didn't want the date to end. I didn't want to stop touching him, hearing his voice, finding out what he would say next. But I didn't turn around. I kept walking.

I knew then that I was sunk. I was smitten. I knew that I would give myself to him, that I would bare my soul to him, that I would let him break my heart if that's what it came to.

So there wasn't any rush, I told myself, as I got into the elevator alone.

When I got to my room, I called Rachel. I had to tell her everything. I had to tell her how cute he was, how sweet he was. I had to tell her the things he said, the way he looked at me. I had to relive it with someone who would understand just how exciting it all was.

And Rachel did understand; she understood completely.

"So when are you going to sleep with him? That's my question," she said. "Because it sounds like things got pretty steamy out there on the sidewalk. Maybe you should put a date on it, you know? Like, don't sleep with him until you've been dating this many weeks or days or months." She started laughing. "Or years, if that's the way you want to play it."

I told her I was just going to see what happened naturally.

"That is a terrible idea," she told me. "You need a plan. What if you sleep with him too soon or too late?"

But I really didn't think there *was* a too soon or too late. I was so confident about Ryan, so confident in myself, that something about it seemed foolproof. As if I could already tell that we were so good together we couldn't mess it up if we tried.

And that brought me both an intense thrill and a deep calm.

• • •

When it did happen, Ryan and I were in his room. His roommate was out of town for the weekend. We hadn't told each other that we loved each other yet, but it was obvious that we did.

I marveled at how well he understood my body. I didn't need to tell him what I wanted. He knew. He knew how to kiss me. He knew where to put his hands, what to touch, how to touch it.

I had never understood the concept of making love before. It seemed cheesy and dramatic. But I got it then. It isn't just about the movement. It's about the way your heart swells when he gets close. The way his breath feels like a warm fire. It's about the fact that your brain shuts down and your heart takes over.

I cared about nothing but the feel of him, the smell of him, the taste of him. I wanted more of him.

Afterward, we lay next to each other, naked and vulnerable but not feeling as if we were either. He grabbed my hand.

He said, "I have something I'm ready to say, but I don't want you to think it's because of what we just did."

I knew what it was. We both knew what it was. "So say it later, then," I said.

He looked disappointed by my answer, so I made myself clear.

"When you say it," I told him, "I'll say it back."

He smiled, and then he was quiet for a minute. I actually thought he might have fallen asleep. But then he said, "This is good, isn't it?"

I turned toward him. "Yeah," I said. "It is."

"No," he said to me. "This is, like, perfect, what we have. We could get married someday."

I thought of my grandparents, the only married couple I knew. I thought of the way my grandmother cut up my grandfather's food sometimes when he was feeling too weak to do it himself.

"Someday," I said. "Yeah."

We were nineteen.

ELEVEN YEARS AGO

Over summer break, Ryan went home to Kansas. We talked to each other every day. We would send e-mails back and forth in rapid fire, waiting impatiently for the other to respond. I would sit on my bed, waiting for him to get home from his internship and call me. I visited him early in the summer, meeting his parents and sister for the first time. We all got along. They seemed to like me. I stayed for a week, the two of us hanging on each other's every word, Ryan sneaking into the guest room to see me every night. When he drove me to the airport and walked me up to the security gate, I thought someone was ripping my heart out of my chest. How could I leave him? How could I get on the plane and fly so many miles away from the other half of my soul?

I tried to explain all of this to Rachel, also home for the summer after her freshman year at USC. I complained to her about how much I missed him. I brought him up in conversation more often than he was really relevant. I had a one-track mind. Rachel mostly responded to these overdramatic testaments of my love by saying, "Oh, that's great. I'm really happy for you," and then pretending to vomit.

My brother, Charlie, meanwhile, had just turned fourteen and was about to enter high school, so he wanted nothing to do with Rachel or me. He didn't even pretend to listen to anything I had to say that summer. The minute I started talking, he would put on his headphones or turn on the TV.

A few weeks after I got home from visiting him, Ryan insisted that he visit me. It didn't matter that the tickets were expensive or that he wasn't making any money. He said it was worth it. He had to see me.

When he arrived at LAX, I watched him come down the escalator with the other passengers. I saw him scan the crowd until he saw my face. I saw it register. I saw in that moment how much I was loved, how relieved he was to have me in his eyesight. And I could recognize all of those emotions because I felt the same way about him.

He ran to me, dropping his bag and picking me up in one fell swoop. He spun me around, holding me tighter than I had ever been held. As devastated as I'd been to leave him weeks ago, I was that thrilled to be with him again.

He put me down and grabbed my face in his hands, kissing me. I opened my eyes finally to see an older woman with kids watching us. I caught her eye by accident, and she smiled at me, shyly looking away. The look on her face made it clear that she had been me before.

My family caught up to us then, finally done parking the car. They had all insisted on coming, in part, I think, because it was so clear that I did not want them to come.

Ryan dried his sweaty hand on the back of his jeans and offered a handshake to my mother.

"Ms. Spencer," he said. "It's nice to see you again." They had met once before, only briefly, when Mom came to move me out of the dorms.

"Ryan, I told you to call me Leslie," my mom said, laughing at him.

Ryan nodded and gestured to Rachel and Charlie. "Rachel, Charlie, nice to meet you. I've heard a lot of good things."

"Actually," Charlie said, "we prefer to be called Miss and Mr. Spencer."

Ryan chose to take him seriously. "Excuse me, Mr. Spencer, my mistake. Miss Spencer," he said, tipping his imaginary hat

and bowing to Rachel. Then he extended his hand in a firm
handshake to Charlie.

And maybe because someone was taking him seriously,
Charlie chose to lighten up.

- "OK, fine," Charlie said. "You can call me Charles."

"You can call him Charlie," Rachel interjected.

We all headed to baggage claim. And as much of a spoil-
sport as Charlie wanted to be, I couldn't help but notice that
he talked Ryan's ear off the entire way home.

NINE AND HALF YEARS AGO

Spring break of our senior year, Ryan and I both decided to stay in Los Angeles. But at the last minute, my mom found a deal on flights to Cabo San Lucas and decided to splurge. That's how the five of us—my mom, Rachel, Charlie, Ryan, and I—found ourselves on a flight to Mexico.

Oddly enough, Charlie was perhaps the most excited about this idea. As we took our seats on the plane—Mom, Ryan, and I on one side of the aisle, Rachel, Charlie, and a strange bald man on the other—Charlie kept reminding my mom that the drinking age was eighteen.

"That's nice, sweetheart," she said to him. "That doesn't change the fact that you're still sixteen."

"But it would be less illegal," he said, as he clipped in his seat belt and the flight attendants walked up and down the aisles. "It's less illegal for me to get drunk in Mexico than here."

"I'm not sure there are degrees of illegal," Rachel said, scrunching herself tightly in the middle seat so as not to touch the bald man. He had already fallen asleep.

"Although I think prostitution is legal in Mexico," I said. "Right? Is it?"

"Well, not for minors," Ryan said. "Sorry, Charlie."

Charlie shrugged. "I don't look sixteen."

"Is weed legal in Mexico?" Rachel asked.

"Excuse me!" my mom said, exasperated. "This is a *family* vacation. I didn't bring you all to Mexico to get high and hire hookers."

And of course, all of us laughed at her. Because we had all been joking. At least, I thought we had all been joking.

"You're too gullible, Mom!" Rachel said.

"We were kidding," I added.

"Speak for yourself!" Charlie said. "I was serious. They might actually serve me alcohol at this place."

Ryan laughed.

It really struck me then just how different Charlie was from Rachel and me. It wasn't just in the superficial stuff, either, like the difference between brothers and sisters, high-schoolers versus college students. He was markedly different from the two of us.

Rachel and I were a little more than a year apart. We experienced things together, through a similar lens. When our dad left, I was almost four and a half years old, and Rachel had just turned three. Mom was still pregnant with Charlie. Rachel and I may not really remember our dad, but we had time with him. We knew his voice. Charlie entered this world with only my mother to hold him.

I sometimes wondered if Rachel and I were so close, if we meant so much to each other, that it prevented us from really letting Charlie in. By the time he was born, we had our own language, our own world. But the truth was, Charlie simply wasn't that interested in us. As a little kid, he did his own thing, played his own games. He didn't want to do the kind of stuff Rachel and I were doing. He didn't want to talk about what Rachel and I talked about. He was always forging his own path, rejecting the one we had laid out for him.

But as much as we had our differences, it was staggering how the three of us had grown up to look exactly alike. Charlie may not have been similar to Rachel and me in temperament or personality, but he couldn't distance himself from us genetically.

We all shared the same high cheekbones. All three of us got our dark hair and blue eyes from our mother. Charlie was taller and lankier, Rachel was petite and daintier, and I was broader, curvier. But we belonged together, that much was clear.

The plane took flight, and we started talking about other things. When the seat-belt sign went off, my mom got up and went to the bathroom. That's when I saw Ryan lean over the aisle to whisper something to Charlie. Charlie smiled and nodded.

"What did you just say to him?" I asked. Ryan smiled wide and refused to tell me. "You're not going to tell me?"

"It's between Charlie and me," Ryan said.

"Yeah," Charlie piped in. "It's between us."

"You can't buy him alcohol at this place," I said. "Is that what you were talking about? Because you can't." I sounded like a narc.

"Who said anything about anyone buying anyone alcohol?" Ryan said, perhaps a bit too innocently.

"Well, then, why can't I know what you're talking about?"

"Some things don't involve you, Lauren," Charlie said, teasing me.

My jaw dropped. Mom was on her way toward us, back from the bathroom.

"You are!" I said, somehow yelling and whispering. "You are going to get my sixteen-year-old brother drunk!"

Rachel, finally having enough of all this, said, "Oh, Lauren, cut it out. Ryan leaned over and said, 'Let's see if I can get your sister to freak out over nothing.'"

I looked at him for confirmation, and he started laughing. So did Charlie.

"I swear," Rachel said. "You're as gullible as Mom."

A LITTLE MORE THAN NINE YEARS AGO

I graduated magna cum laude. I missed summa cum laude by a fraction, but Ryan kept telling me not to worry myself over it. "I'm just graduating," he said. "Not a single Latin word after it, and I'm going to be fine. So you're going to be better than fine."

I couldn't argue about my prospects. I already had a job. I had accepted a position in the alumni department of UCLA. I wasn't sure what I wanted to do with my psychology degree, but I figured it would come to me in due time. The alumni department seemed like an easy, reliable place to start out.

On graduation day, Ryan and I were at opposite ends of the auditorium, so we only spoke in the morning and then made faces at each other during the ceremony. I spotted my mom in the audience with her huge camera, Rachel and Charlie next to her. Rachel was waving at me, giving me a thumbs-up. A few rows back, I saw Ryan's parents and his sister.

As I sat there, waiting for the moment when they called my name, it occurred to me that this was the end of so many things, and more to the point, it was the beginning of my adult life.

Ryan and I had rented a studio apartment in Hollywood. We were moving in the next week, on the first of the month. It was an ugly little thing, cramped and dark. But it would be ours.

The night before, Ryan and I had fought about what furniture to buy. He thought all we needed was a mattress on the floor. I figured that since we were adults, we should have a bed frame. Ryan thought all we needed were a few cardboard boxes for our clothes; I was insistent that we have dressers. It got heated. I said he was being cheap, that he didn't understand how to be an adult. He said I was acting like a spoiled brat, expecting money to grow on trees. It got bad enough that I started crying; he got upset enough that his face turned red.

And then, before we knew it, we were at the part where we both admitted we were wrong and begged each other's forgiveness with a passion unlike anything since the last time we'd fought. That was always the way it was with us. The *I love you*s and *I'm sorry*s, the *I'll never do that again*s and the *I don't know what I'd do without you*s always eclipsed the thing we were fighting about in the first place.

We woke up that morning with smiles on our faces, holding each other tight. We ate breakfast together. We got dressed together. We helped each other put on our caps and gowns.

Our life was starting. We were growing up.

I stood up with my row and followed the path up to the podium.

"Lauren Spencer."

I walked up, shook the chancellor's hand, and took my diploma. Out of the corner of my eye, I saw Ryan. He was holding a sign so small only I could see it. "I Love You," it said. And at that moment, I just knew adulthood was going to be great.

SEVEN AND A HALF YEARS AGO

For the fourth anniversary of when we met, Ryan and I went camping in Yosemite.

We had been out of school for a year and a half. I was making a decent salary in the alumni department. Ryan was doing OK himself. We were just starting to get ahead of our bills a bit, starting to save, when we decided that a trip to Yosemite wouldn't put us back too much. We had borrowed camping equipment from my mom and packed food from home.

We got there late Friday afternoon and pitched our tent. By the time it was properly set up, the sun was setting and it was getting cold, so we went to bed. The next morning, we woke up and decided that we should hike up Vernal Fall. The visitor's guide said that Vernal Fall was a hard hike but that the view from the top was like nothing you could imagine. At that, Ryan said, "I'm in the mood to see something I could never imagine." So we put on hiking boots and got into the car.

I knew that he had called my mother the week before our trip and asked for her blessing. I knew that he had told her he had a ring picked out. My family doesn't keep secrets. We try to, but we're all too excited to keep anything good to ourselves. It bursts out of us, overflowing like a ruptured pipe. So on some level, I was expecting to get to the top of Vernal Fall and find him on one knee.

However, the guidebook was pretty misleading. Vernal Fall wasn't just a hard hike. It felt impossible. I kept thinking it would end, that we were close to the top. But the way the path snaked up the mountain, you'd turn a corner and realize

you had hours more work ahead of you. There were treacher-
ous paths, steep climbs, areas where you couldn't rest. At one
point, I cut myself on one of the rocks, a deep gash torn into
my ankle. Despite the fact that it was bleeding into my sock,
there was nothing I could do. I just had to keep moving.

And yet somehow during this entire hike, there were
groups of people ahead of us and behind us who seemed to
be doing just fine. There were even people coming down the
mountain with smiles on their faces, proud of themselves for
making it up there. I wanted to grab their shirts and demand
that they tell me what lay ahead. But what was the point?
Maybe if I didn't know what I was in for, I wouldn't know to
give up.

By the second hour, Ryan and I were standing on stairs
built into the mountain, stairs so rickety and steep that you
couldn't fit your whole foot on them at once. There was a
waterfall nearby, and I remember thinking to myself, *This
is a beautiful waterfall, but I don't even care because I'm so
exhausted.* I felt as if I'd never get up that mountain, and this
view that I supposedly couldn't imagine, well, I didn't care
to imagine it anymore. My hair was sticking to my forehead.
My shirt was soaked through with sweat. My face was as red
as a tomato. This wasn't the way to get engaged. And I wasn't
even sure that was Ryan's intention. It was starting to seem
that maybe it wasn't.

I figured I'd ask Ryan if he wanted to turn around, and if
he said yes, I probably wasn't spoiling anything anyway. If he
said no, I'd do it. I'd climb the rest of the mountain, and I'd
see what happened.

"Wanna turn around?" I said. "I don't know if I can do this."

Ryan could barely catch his breath. He was a few stairs behind me. He was more fit than I was, but he insisted on staying
behind so he could catch me if I slipped.

"Sure," he said. "OK."

Suddenly, I was crestfallen. I didn't realize how much I'd been waiting for him to propose to me until I heard him say we could turn back. It was like when you aren't sure what you want for dinner and someone suggests Chinese, and only then do you realize how badly you wanted a burger.

"Oh, OK," I said, starting slowly to back my feet up and turn my body back. This moment felt like a failure on two accounts. I thought of all those people I had seen making their way down the mountain. They seemed victorious. As I started to turn down the mountain, I knew that I would seem victorious to all the people I would pass on the way down. It just goes to show how alike failure and success can appear. Sometimes only you know the truth.

"Oh, wait," Ryan said. He bent down to readjust his backpack, and I got scared because he was so perilously close to the edge of the stairway. He looked as if he could slip right into the waterfall.

But he didn't. He reached his hand out and carefully rested one knee on an unreliable stair. He looked at me and said, "Lauren, I love you more than I've loved anything in my life. You are the reason I was put on this earth. You make me happier than anything I've ever known. I cannot live without you." He was smiling, and yet the edges of his mouth were starting to pull in and quiver. His voice started to lose its confidence. It became shaky. I noticed the group ahead of us had turned around. The pack of kids a few stairs behind Ryan had stopped and were waiting.

"Lauren," he said, now barely hiding his emotion, "will you marry me?"

That waterfall suddenly felt like the most gorgeous waterfall I'd ever seen in my life. I ran down the steps to him and whispered "Yes" into his ear. There wasn't a moment of hesitation. There was nothing except my absolute and irrevocable answer. *Yes. Yes. Yes. Are you crazy? Yes.*

Ryan hugged me, and I wept. I suddenly had the energy of ten men. I knew if we kept going, I could get up those stairs. I could make it to the top of that damn mountain.

Ryan turned and yelled, "She said yes!" People started clapping. I could hear Ryan's voice echoing through the canyon. A woman shouted, "Congratulations!" I swear it felt as if all of Yosemite was in on it.

We pushed forward, and within an hour, we had made our way to the top. Vernal Fall was more gorgeous than anything I could have imagined. Ryan and I stayed up there, putting our feet in the wide stream, letting the rushing water clean us, watching the squirrels eat nuts and the birds soar overhead. We talked about the future as we ate the sandwiches we had packed for ourselves. We talked about potential wedding dates, about when we'd have kids, if we'd buy a house. The wedding, we figured, could be in a year or so. The kids could wait until we were thirty. The house we'd have to play by ear. Maybe it was because I was high up in the clouds physically, or figuratively, but I felt that the sun shone brighter that afternoon, that the world was mine for the taking. The future seemed so easy.

When we finally left, it was with heavy hearts. This thing that I felt I couldn't do, this thing that wasn't worth it, had started to feel like the only important thing I'd ever done.

A LITTLE MORE THAN SIX YEARS AGO

Two months before the wedding, we went shopping for a new bed. We intended to get a queen-size. With the mattress, box spring, bed frame, and sheets, a queen was cheaper. It was practical. But when we got to the mattress store and started to look at the beds, we were tempted to go for broke. We were looking at two mattresses set up next to each other, one king, one queen. Ryan was standing behind me, his arms wrapped around my shoulders, and he whispered into my ear, "Let's spring for the big one. Let's make all of our sex hotel sex." My heart fluttered, and I blushed, and I told the man we'd take the king.

SIX YEARS AGO

We had a July wedding. It was outdoors on the wide lawn of a hotel just outside of Los Angeles. I wore a white dress. I threw my bouquet. We danced all night, Ryan spinning me around, holding me close, and showing me off. The morning after the festivities were over, we got into the car and headed out for our honeymoon. We had considered places like Costa Rica or Paris, maybe a cruise through the Italian Riviera. But the truth was, we didn't have that kind of money. We decided to take it easy. We'd drive up to Big Sur and stay in a cabin in the woods, where no one could find us for a week. A fireplace and a beautiful view seemed like all the luxury we needed in the world.

We got on the road early in the morning, hoping to make good time by beating midday traffic. We stopped for breakfast and again later for lunch. We played Twenty Questions, and I fiddled with the radio, tuning in to local stations as we passed through towns. We were in love, high on the novelty of marriage. The words *husband* and *wife* felt as if they had a shine to them. They were simply more fun to say than all the other words we knew.

We were two hours outside of Big Sur when the tire blew. The loud bang scared us both out of our newlywed daze. Ryan quickly pulled over to the side of the road. I hopped out first; Ryan was a second behind me.

"Fuck!" he said.

"Calm down," I told him. "It's going to be OK. We just

have to call Triple A. They will come out here and solve the whole thing."

"We can't call Triple A," he said.

"Sure we can," I told him. "I have the card in my wallet. Let me get it."

"No," he said, shaking his head and pulling his hands up onto the back of his neck in a resigned position. "I forgot to pay the renewal fee."

"Oh," I said. The disappointment was clear in my voice.

"It came last month, and it said on it that we had to pay it by the fifteenth, and . . . with the wedding and everything going on at work, I just . . ." He shrugged, and his voice got defensive. "I forgot, OK? I'm sorry. I forgot."

I wasn't mad at him. He made a mistake. But I was very concerned with what we were going to do about it. I was frustrated that I was in this position. If you do not have the ability to call Triple A, how do you fix a tire? We were not the sort of people who knew how to do that on our own. We were the sort of people who needed Triple A. I didn't like that about us at that very moment. In fact, I was starting to think we were two useless idiots on the side of the road.

"You don't know how to fix a tire, right?" I asked him. I knew he didn't. I shouldn't have asked.

"No," he said. "I don't. Thank you for highlighting that."

"Well, shit," I said, the polite cushion around my voice fading and exposing my irritation. "What should we do?"

"I don't know!" he said. "I mean, it was an accident."

"Yeah, OK, so what do we do? We're on the side of the road in the middle of nowhere. How are we going to get to the cabin?"

"I don't know, OK? I don't know what we're gonna do. I think there is a spare tire in the trunk," he said, walking back there to confirm it. "Yeah," he said as he lifted the bottom out. "But there's no jack, so I don't know what we would even do."

"Well, we have to think of something."

"You could think of something, too, you know," he said to me. "This isn't only up to me."

"I never said it was, all right? Geez."

"Well? What's your bright idea, then?"

"You know what?" I said. "I . . . Why are we even fighting right now? We're on our honeymoon."

"I know!" he said. "I know that! Do you have any idea how upset I am that this is happening on our honeymoon? Do you have any idea how heartbroken I am that I fucked up this thing that we have been looking forward to for months?"

I found it completely impossible to be angry with Ryan when he was angry at himself. I melted like a popsicle the minute I suspected he might blame himself for anything. It was part of the impracticality of fighting with him. I would fight until he admitted he'd done something wrong, and then I'd spend the entire rest of the night trying to take it all away, trying to convince him he was nothing short of perfect.

"Baby, no," I said. "No, you didn't mess anything up. This is going to be fine. I swear. Totally fine." I hugged him, burying my head in his chest and holding his hand by the side of the road.

"I'm sorry," he said, meaning it.

"No!" I said. "Don't be sorry. It's not just your job to pay the Triple A bill. It could have happened to either of us. We had so much stuff going on with the wedding. C'mon," I said, lifting his chin. "We're not gonna let this get us down."

Ryan started laughing. "We aren't?"

"Hell no!" I said, trying to cheer him up. "Are you kidding? I, for one, am having a great time. As far as I'm concerned, the honeymoon has already started."

"It has?"

"Yep," I said. "We'll make it a game. I'll try to flag down the next car that comes down the road, OK? If they stop and they have a jack and they let us borrow it, I win. Next car, you go. Whoever gets the jack wins."

Ryan laughed again. It was so nice to see him laugh.

"Neither of us knows how to use a jack," he pointed out.

"Well, we'll figure it out! How hard could it be? I'm sure we can Google it."

"OK, you're on, sweetheart," he said.

But he never got a chance. I flagged down the first car that came down the road, and they let us use their jack. They even taught us what to do and helped us get the donut on.

We were back on the road in no time, no trace of anger or frustration. I buried my head in his shoulder, my back bent awkwardly over the center console. I just wanted to be near him, touching him. It didn't matter if it wasn't comfortable.

The donut got us all the way to the lodge in Big Sur. Trees surrounding us to our right, massive cliffs dropping off into the Pacific to our left. The sky above us was just turning from blue to a rosy orange.

We checked in, yet another honeymooning couple in the cabins of Big Sur. The woman at the front desk looked as if she'd seen it all before. There was nothing new about us to her, and yet everything about this was new to us.

Our hotel room was small and cozy, with a gas fireplace on the far wall. When we put our bags down, Ryan joked that our bed at home was bigger than the bed in the cabin. But everything felt so intimate. He was mine. I was his. The hard part was over: the wedding, the details, the planning, the families. Now it was just us, starting our life together.

We were on the bed before our bags were unpacked. Ryan slid on top of me. His weight pressed against me, weighing me down, pushing me further into the mattress. I had chosen a masculine man, a strong man.

"Baby, I'm so sorry," he said to me. "I'll renew the Triple A membership as soon as we get home. Now, even! I can do it now."

"No," I said. "Don't do it now. I don't want you to do it now. I don't want you to ever leave this spot."

"No?"

"No," I said, shaking my head.

"Well, what should we do, then?" Ryan asked. He used to ask this when he wanted to have sex. It was his way of making me say it. He always loved making me say the things he wanted to say.

"I don't know," I teased him. "What *should* we do?"

"You look like you have something on your mind," he said, kissing me.

"I have nothing on my mind. My mind is blank," I said, smiling wide, both of us knowing everything that wasn't being said.

"No," he said. "You're thinking about having sex with me, you perv."

I laughed loudly, so loudly it filled the tiny room, and Ryan kissed my collarbone. He kissed it tenderly at first and then started to lick further up my neck. By the time he reached my earlobe, nothing seemed funny anymore.

THREE YEARS AGO

I had just started a new job, still in the alumni department but now at Occidental College.

My former coworker, Mila, recommended me for the position. We'd worked together in the alumni department at UCLA, and she'd left for Occidental the previous year. I was excited by the idea of working with her again and eager to branch out. I loved UCLA, but I'd been there my entire adult life. I wanted to learn a new community. I wanted to meet new people. Plus, it didn't hurt that Occidental's campus was breathtaking. If you're looking for a change of scenery, choose beautiful scenery.

And since I was making more money, Ryan and I decided to find a new place. When we saw a house for rent in Hancock Park, we pulled over. Sure, it looked too big for us. It looked too expensive for us. And we technically didn't need a second bedroom or a yard. But we wanted it. So Ryan picked up the phone and dialed the number on the sign.

"Hi, I'm standing outside your property on Rimpau. How much are you renting it for?" Ryan said, and then he listened intently.

"Uh-huh," he said. I couldn't hear what the other person was saying. Ryan was pacing back and forth. "And is that including utilities?"

I was eager to hear what number this person had given him.

"Well, we can't do that," Ryan said. I sat on the hood of our car, disappointed. "I've noticed, though, that this sign has been out for a while." He was bluffing. Ryan knew no such thing. "So I'm wondering what your wiggle room is." He listened and then looked at me, and I smiled at him. "OK, is it open now? Can my wife and I take a look?"

Ryan directed his eye to a drainpipe. "Yeah, I see it. We'll take a look, and I'll call you back." He hung up, and we ran to the front door. Ryan got the key from the drainpipe and let us in.

While so much of Los Angeles is crowded roads and cramped buildings, Hancock Park is almost entirely residential, full of long, wide streets and houses set far back from the curb. Most of the neighborhood was built in the 1920s, and this place was no exception. The house was old, but it was gorgeous. Rough stucco exterior, dramatic interior archways, hardwood floors, checkered tile kitchen. The rooms were small and tight but perfect for us. I saw my life in there. I saw where our couch would go. I saw myself brushing my teeth over the prewar porcelain sink.

"We can't afford this, can we?" I asked him.

"I will make this work, if you want it," Ryan said to me, standing in the middle of the house. It was so empty that his voice traveled quickly, finding its way into the farthest corners of the room. "I will get this woman down to something we can afford."

"How?" I asked. I wasn't sure what the starting number was, and Ryan wasn't telling, which said to me that it was much higher than the figure we had in mind.

"Just . . . Do you want it?" he asked me.

"Yes, I want it. Bad."

"Then I'm gonna get it for you." Ryan left the house through the front door and walked back to the sidewalk. I walked through the kitchen and opened the sliding glass doors that led to the backyard. It was small and useless, a patch of grass and a few bushes. But there was an old lemon tree in the corner. Lemons were scattered around the trunk, most of them rotting where the peel touched the earth. It looked as if no one had taken care of the lemon tree. No one had watered it or pruned it. No one cared about it. I walked out and reached high above my head to a lemon still on the branch. I twisted it off the tree and smelled it. It smelled fresh and clean.

I took it out to the front yard to show Ryan. He was still on the phone, pacing up and down the sidewalk. I stared at him, trying to decipher how the conversation might be going. Finally, he looked up at the sky and smiled, pumping his fist into the air and looking at me as if we'd won the lottery. "September first? Yeah, that works."

When he hung up the phone, I ran into his arms, jumping up and wrapping my legs around his waist. He laughed.

"You did it!" I said. "You got me the house!" I handed him the lemon. "We have a lemon tree! We can make fresh lemonade and lemon bars and . . . other lemon stuff! How did you do it?" I asked him. "How did you talk her down?"

Ryan just shook his head. "A magician never tells."

"No, but seriously, how did you?"

He smiled, evading me. For some reason, I liked it better not knowing. He had made the impossible possible. And I liked that I didn't know his secret. It made me think that maybe other impossible things were possible. That maybe all I needed was to want it badly enough, and I really could have it.

That night, I was already looking at paint colors and thinking about packing up our stuff. I was so committed to our new house that I could no longer stand the sight of our current apartment.

I was on my computer, mentally decorating and online shopping, when Ryan walked over to me and closed my laptop.

"Hey!" I said. "I was looking at that!"

He smiled. "Well, looks like you can't use the computer anymore," he said. "So what should we do to pass the time?"

"Huh?" I asked. I knew what he was getting at.

"I'm just saying . . . it's late, and we should probably get into bed. What should we do when we get in there?" He wanted to have sex. He wanted me to say it.

"I was looking at that, though!" I told him. My voice had bounce to it, but the truth was, I really wasn't in the mood.

"You sure you don't have anything on your mind? Anything you want to do?"

Maybe if he'd said what he wanted, I might have given it to him. But it wasn't what I wanted to do. And I wasn't going to pretend it was.

"Yeah, I know exactly what I want to do," I said. "I want to continue looking at curtains!"

Ryan sighed and opened my computer back up. "You are no fun," he said, laughing and kissing me on the cheek before leaving the room.

"But you still love me, right?" I joked, calling out to him in the other room.

He popped his head back in. "Always will," he said. "Until the day I die." Then he threw himself onto the floor, lying on the ground with his tongue out and his eyes shut, pretending to be dead.

"Are you dead?" I teased him.

He was silent. He was freakishly good at remaining perfectly still. His chest didn't even rise and fall with his breath.

I got on the floor next to him and playfully poked at him.

"Looks like he's really dead," I said out loud. "Ah, well." I sighed. "That just means more time for me to look at curtains."

That's when he grabbed me and pulled me toward him, burying his fingers into my armpits, making me laugh and scream.

"So how about now, huh?" he said, when he was done tick-
ling me. "What do you want to do now?"

"I told you," I said, standing up and smiling at him. "I want
to look at curtains."

● ● ●

The day after we moved in, I was still unpacking boxes and
considering painting the bedroom when Ryan came in and
said, "What would you say if I told you I think we should get
a dog?"

I threw the clothes that were in my hand back into their
box and started walking into the hallway to get my shoes. "I'd
say it's Sunday morning, there might be dog adoptions right
now. Get your keys."

I was half joking, but he didn't stop me. We got into the
car. We drove around looking for signs. We came home with
Butter, a three-year-old yellow Lab. He peed and pooped all
over the house, and he kept us up all night scratching his neck
with his hind leg, but we loved him. The next morning, we
renamed him Thumper.

Ryan and I installed a doggie door a few weeks later, and
the minute we were done, Thumper jetted into the backyard.
We watched as he ran around and around, jumped on the
fence, and then settled on a spot to lie out in the sun.

I was sitting on the floor, stretching, when he finally came
back into the house. He walked right in and sat in my lap. He
was done playing outside. He wanted to be near me.

I cried for a half hour because I couldn't believe I could
love a dog so much. When I finally gathered myself, I noticed
there was sticky dirt in my lap and all over his paws. He
smelled clean and sweet.

It turned out Thumper liked playing with lemons.

TWO YEARS AGO

I was washing the sheets one evening and decided that it was probably time to wash the mattress pad. So I pulled everything off the bed and threw it all in the laundry.

When I went to put the mattress pad back on the bed, I noticed a huge, well-worn, darker spot in the middle. It was oblong and graying where everything else was bright white.

I laid it on the bed and showed it to Ryan.

"Weird, right?" I said. "What is that from?"

Ryan gave it a good look, and as he did, Thumper came into the room. He hopped onto the bed and fit his furry tan body right into the faded gray stain, his big, dirty paws crossed over his black nose, his big, dark eyes looking at the two of us. Mystery solved. We had found the culprit.

We looked at each other and started laughing. I loved watching Ryan laugh that hard.

"That's how dirty he is," Ryan said. "He can permanently stain layers of fabric."

Thumper barely looked at us. He wasn't concerned with being laughed at. He was blissfully happy in the middle of the bed.

We kicked him off briefly so we could put the sheets on. We gathered the pillows and blankets. We got into bed, and then we told Thumper he could get back in.

He jumped right back into his spot.

Ryan turned out the light.

"I feel like this," I said, as I gestured to Ryan and me with Thumper in the middle, "is enough. Is that bad? I mean, I feel like the three of us, you and me and this dog, are all we need. I don't feel like I'm aching to add a kid to this. That's bad, right?"

"Well, we always said thirty," Ryan said, as if thirty was decades away.

"Yeah, I know," I said. "But you're twenty-eight. I'll be twenty-eight soon, too. We're two years from thirty."

Ryan thought about it. "Yeah, two years doesn't really seem like a long time."

"Do you really think we'll be ready for kids in two years? Do you feel like we are there yet?"

"No," he said plainly. "I guess I don't."

It was quiet for a while, and since we'd already turned out the lights, I wasn't sure if maybe we were done talking, if we were on our way to falling asleep.

I had started to fade a bit, started to dream, when I heard Ryan say, "That was just a guess, though, when we said thirty. We could do thirty-two, maybe. Or thirty-four."

"Yeah," I chimed in. "Or thirty-six. Plenty of people have kids when they are past forty, even."

"Or not at all," Ryan said. It wasn't loaded. His voice wasn't pointed. It was just a fact. Some couples don't have kids at all. There's nothing wrong with that. There's nothing wrong with not being ready, not knowing if you are up for it.

"Right," I said. "I mean, we can just play it by ear. Doesn't have to be thirty just because we planned on thirty."

"Right," he said. The word hung in the air.

We had plenty of time to decide what we wanted. We were still young. And yet I couldn't help but feel a type of disappointment that I'd never felt before: a sense that the future might not turn out exactly the way we pictured it.

"I love you," I said into the darkness.

"I love you, too," he said, and then we fell asleep, Thumper in between us.

A YEAR AND A HALF AGO

I was reading a magazine in bed. Ryan was watching television and petting Thumper. It was almost midnight, and I was tired, but something was nagging at me. I put my magazine down.

"Do you remember the last time we had sex?" I asked Ryan.

He didn't look over from the television, nor did he turn it down or pause it.

"No," he said, not giving it another thought. "Why?"

"Well, don't you think that's . . . you know . . . not great?"

"I guess," he said.

"Can you pause the TV for a second?" I asked him, and he did, begrudgingly. He looked at me. "I'm just saying, maybe it's something we should work on."

"Work on? That sounds awful." Ryan laughed.

I laughed, too. "No, I know, but it's important. We used to have sex all the time."

He laughed again, but this time, I wasn't sure why. "When was this?" he teased.

"What? All the time! You know, there were times we would do it, like, four times a day."

"You mean, like the time we did it in the laundry room?" he asked.

"Yes!" I said, sitting up, excited that he was finally agreeing with me.

"Or the time we did it three times in forty-five minutes?"

"Yes!"

"Or the time we had sex in the backseat of my car parked on a side street in Westwood?"

"This is exactly what I'm talking about!"

"Baby, those all happened in college."

I looked at him, keeping his gaze, trying to remember if that was true. Was all of that in college? How long ago was college, anyway? Seven years ago.

"I'm sure we've done crazy stuff since then, haven't we?"

Ryan shook his head. "Nope, we haven't."

"Surely we have," I said, my voice still sounding upbeat.

"It's not a big deal," he said, grabbing the remote and turning the TV back on. "We've been together for almost ten years. We were bound to stop having sex all the time."

"Well," I said, talking over the TV, "maybe we should spice it up."

"OK," he said. "So spice it up, then."

"Maybe I will!" I said, joking with him and turning off the light. But . . . you know, I never did.

A YEAR AGO

It was a Friday night in the middle of the summer. We were in the height of long, sunny days. I knew Ryan was meeting a few friends after work and wouldn't be home for a while, so instead of going straight home, I drove into Burbank and went to IKEA. I had been meaning to buy a new coffee table. Thumper had chewed through a leg on our old one.

After picking out a new table and paying for it, it was later than I thought. I got on the freeway to head home and found that it was backed up for what looked like miles. I flipped through the talk-radio stations until one of them announced that there was a three-car accident on the 5. That's when I knew I'd be there for a while.

It was about forty-five minutes until traffic started to pick up, and when it did, I felt my mood markedly improve. I was flying across the freeway when I saw a number of cars in front of me hit their brakes. Once again, traffic came to a complete stop.

I slowed down just in time, and then, instantaneously, I felt something slam into me. The entire car lurched forward.

My heart started to race. My brain started to panic. I looked in my rearview mirror and saw, in the twilight, a dark blue car veering away.

I started to pull over to the side of the freeway, but by the time I got there, the car that hit me had sped down the shoulder, out of sight.

I called Ryan. No answer.

I got out and stood on the shoulder, slowly maneuvering

my way to look at the back of my car. The entire back right half had been smashed. My brake lights cracked, my trunk crumpled in.

I called Ryan again. No answer.

Frustrated, I got back into the car and drove home.

When I got there, Ryan was sitting on the couch, watching television.

"You've been here the whole time?" I asked.

He turned off the TV and looked at me. "Yeah, we rescheduled drinks," he said.

"Why didn't you answer the phone when I called you? Twice?"

Ryan made a vague hand gesture to his phone across the room. "Sorry," he said. "I guess the ringer must be off. What's the matter?"

I finally put my purse down. "Well, I was hit in a hit-and-run," I said. "But I'm fine."

"Oh, my God!" Ryan said, running toward the window to take a look at the car. I'd said I was fine. But it still bothered me that he didn't run to take a look at *me*.

"The car is in bad shape," I said. "But I'm sure insurance will cover it."

He turned to me. "You got the license plate of the person who hit you, right?"

"No," I said. "I couldn't. It all happened too fast."

"They aren't going to cover it," Ryan said, "if you can't tell them who did it."

"Well, I'm sorry, Ryan!" I said. "I'm sorry someone slammed into me and didn't bother to hand me their license-plate number."

"Well, you could have gotten it as they sped away," Ryan said. "That's all I meant."

"Yeah, well, I didn't, OK?"

Ryan just looked at me.

"I'm fine, by the way. Don't worry about me. I was in a car accident, but who cares, right? As long as I can square it all with the insurance company."

"That's not what I meant, and you know it. I know you're OK. You said you were OK."

He was right. I did say that. But I still wanted him to ask. I wanted him to hug me and feel bad for me. I wanted him to offer to take care of me. And also, deep down, I was truly, truly pissed off that he had been sitting there watching a movie while I stood on the shoulder of the 5 South, not knowing what I should do.

"OK," I said, after it was quiet for a while. "I guess I'll call the insurance company."

"Do you want me to do it?" he asked.

"I got it, thanks," I said.

The woman I filed the claim with asked me how I was. She said, "Oh, you poor baby." I'm sure that's just what they say to everyone in an accident. I'm sure they are taught to act very concerned and understanding. But still, it felt nice. After I reviewed all of the information with her, she told me that the insurance company would cover it after all. We just had to pay the deductible.

When I got off the phone, I walked into the living room and joined Ryan.

"They will pay for it," I said. I was trying to keep my tone polite, but the truth was, I wanted him to know that he had been wrong.

"Cool," he said.

"We just have to pay a deductible."

"Got it. Sounds like it would have been better if we'd gotten the license plate. I guess we know for next time."

It took everything I had not to call him an asshole.

SIX MONTHS AGO

"Where do you want to go for dinner?" I asked Ryan. He was twenty minutes late coming home from work. He seemed to always be late coming home from work. Sometimes he'd call, sometimes he wouldn't. But regardless, I was always starving by the time he got home.

"I don't care," he said. "What do you want to eat? I just don't want Italian."

I groaned. He would never just pick a place. "Vietnamese?" I said, standing by the front door, grabbing my coat. As soon as we agreed on a place, I wanted to get moving.

"Ugh," he said. His voice was grumpy. He didn't want Vietnamese.

"Greek? Thai? Indian?"

"Let's just order pizza," he said. He took off his jacket when he said it. He was deciding that we would stay home. But I wanted to go out.

"You just said you didn't want Italian," I said.

"It's pizza." His tone was a little bit pointed. "You asked me what I wanted. I want pizza."

"Sorry, did I do something?" I asked him. "You seem frustrated with me."

"I was going to say the same to you."

"No," I said, trying to back off, trying to seem pleasant. "I just want to eat dinner."

"I'll get the pizza menu."

"Wait." I stopped him. "Can't we go out? I feel like I've been eating such junk lately. I'd love to go out someplace."

"Well, call Rachel, then. I'm sorry. I've had a long day at work. I'm exhausted. Can't I sit this one out?"

"Fine," I said. "Fine. I'll call Rachel."

I picked up my phone and walked out the door.

"Do you want to get dinner?" I asked her before she said hello.

"Tonight?" Rachel asked me, surprised.

"Yeah," I said. "Why not tonight?" Sure, I had seen her for lunch the day before, and we went out for drinks two nights before that, but c'mon. "I can't see my own sister three times in four days?"

Rachel laughed. "Well, no, I mean, you know very well I'd see you *seven* times in four days. *Eight. Nine. Ten* times in four days. I just mean, it's Valentine's Day. I assumed you and Ryan had plans."

Valentine's Day. It was Valentine's Day. I found myself unable to admit, even to my own sister, that Ryan and I had forgotten.

"Right, no, totally, but Ryan has to work late," I said to her. "So I thought maybe we could get dinner, you and me."

"Well, obviously, I'm up for it!" she said. "I am, as always, sans Valentine. Come on over."

FOUR MONTHS AGO

Ryan was supposed to go to San Francisco for work one week. He was going to be gone from Monday night to Saturday morning.

He asked me if I wanted to go with him.

"No," I said, without hesitation. "Better to save the vacation time."

"Got it," he said. "I'll tell the travel department it's just me, then."

"Yeah, sounds good."

The weeks went by, and I found myself desperately looking forward to time alone. I thought about it the way I thought about going to Disneyland as a kid.

And then a week before he was supposed to leave, he called me at work and told me the trip was canceled.

"Canceled?" I asked.

"Yeah," he said. "So I'll be home all next week."

"That's great!" I said, hoping my voice was convincing.

"Yeah," Ryan said. His voice was not.

THREE MONTHS AGO

I lost my wallet. I'd had it when we were at the store. I remembered pulling my credit card out to pay for the dress I was buying. Ryan was in the men's section at the time.

Then we walked around a bit more, got into the car, and came home. And that's when I realized it was gone

We searched the living room, the couch cushions, the car, and the driveway. I knew I had to go back to the mall. I had to retrace our steps from the store to the car.

"I guess we have to go back to the store," I said. My voice was apologetic. I felt bad. This wasn't the first time I'd lost my wallet. In fact, I probably lost it about once every six months. Only three times had I never found it again.

"You go," Ryan said, heading back into the house. We had just finished checking the car. "I'm going to stay here."

"You don't want to come?" I said. "We could get dinner while we are out."

"No, I'll just grab something here."

"Without me?" I asked.

"Huh?"

"You're gonna eat dinner without me?"

"I'll wait, then," he said, as if he was doing me a favor.

"No, it's OK. You seem mad, though. Are you mad?"

He shrugged.

I smiled at him, trying to warm him up. "You used to think it was cute, remember? How I always lost my wallet? You said my lack of organization was endearing."

He looked at me, impatient. "Yeah, well," he said to me, "it gets old after eleven years of it."

And then he went inside the house.

When I got into the car and started driving away, my wallet slid out from underneath the passenger's seat.

Didn't matter, though. I cried anyway.

SIX WEEKS AGO

It was Ryan's thirtieth birthday. We spent the night out with his friends, going from sports bar to sports bar.

When we got home, Ryan started undressing me in the bedroom. He unbuttoned my shirt, and then he took the tie out of my hair, letting it fall onto my shoulders. I had a flash of how this would all go. He would kiss my neck and push us onto the bed. He would do the same things he always did, say the same stuff he always said. I'd stare up at the ceiling, counting the minutes. I wasn't in the mood. I wanted to go to sleep.

I held on to the sides of my open shirt and pulled them closer. "I'm not up for it," I said, moving away from him toward my pajamas.

He sighed. "It's my birthday," he said, keeping his hands on my shirt, staying close to me.

"Just not tonight, I'm sorry, I'm just . . . my head hurts, and I'm so tired. We've been out at the smoky bar all night, and I'm feeling . . . not very sexy."

"We could get in the shower," he said.

"Maybe tomorrow," I offered, putting on my sweatpants, ending the discussion. "Would that be OK? Tomorrow?"

"Lauren, it's my birthday." His tone wasn't playful or pleading. He was letting me know he expected me to change my mind. And suddenly, that enraged me.

I looked at him, incredulous. "So what? I owe you or something?"

LAST WEEK

Ryan asked me where his leftover burger was from the night before.

"I fed it to Thumper for dinner," I said. "I added it to his dog food."

"I was going to eat that," he said, looking at me as if I'd stolen something from him.

"Sorry," I said, laughing at how serious he was being. "It was pretty nasty, though," I added. "I don't think you would have wanted it."

"Like you have any idea what I want," he said, and he grabbed a bottle of water and walked away.

RIGHT NOW

The ride home from Dodger Stadium is cold and lonely despite it being eighty degrees out and that there are two of us in the car. We use the radio to gracefully ignore each other for a little while, but it eventually becomes clear that there is nothing graceful about it.

When we pull into the driveway, I am relieved to be able to get away from him. By the time we get to the front of our house, we can hear Thumper whimpering at the door. He is fine being alone, but the minute he can hear us, and I swear he can hear us from blocks away, he suddenly becomes overtaken with dependence. He forgets how to live without us the minute he knows we are there.

Ryan puts his key in the lock. He turns toward me and pauses. "I'm sorry," he says.

"No, me, too," I say. But I don't really know what I am even sorry for. I feel as if I've been sorry for months now without a reason. What am I really doing wrong here? What is happening to us? I've read books on it. I've read the articles that show up in all the women's magazines about marital ruts and turning the heat up in your marriage. They don't tell you anything real. They don't have any answers.

Ryan opens the door, and Thumper runs toward us. His excitement only highlights our own misery. Why can't we be more like him? Why can't I be easy to please? Why can't Ryan be that happy to see me?

"I'm going to take a shower," Ryan says.

I don't say anything back. He heads to the bathroom, and

I sit down on the floor and pet Thumper. His fur soothes me. He licks my face. He nuzzles my ear. For a minute, I feel OK.

"Goddammit!" Ryan calls from the bathroom.

I close my eyes for a moment. Bracing myself.

"What?" I call to him.

"There is no fucking hot water. Did you call the landlord?"

"I thought you were calling the landlord!"

"Why do I always have to do that stuff? Why is it always up to me?" he asks. He has opened the bathroom door and is standing there in a towel.

"I don't know," I say. "You just normally do. So I assumed you were going to be the one to handle it. Sorry." It is clear by the way I say it that I am not sorry.

"Why don't you ever do what you say you're going to do? How hard is it to just pick up the goddamn phone and call the landlord?"

"I never said I was going to do it. If you wanted me to do it, you should have said something. I'm not a mind reader."

"Oh, OK. Got it. My apologies. I thought it was clear that if we have no hot water, someone needs to call the landlord."

"Yeah," I say. "That is obvious. And it's normal for me to assume that you will do it. Since you are the person who normally does that. Just like I am the one who does all the fucking laundry in this house."

"Oh, so you do the laundry, and that makes you some sort of saint?"

"Fine. You can do your laundry, then, if it doesn't matter who does it. Do you know how to use the washing machine?"

Ryan laughs at me. No, he scoffs at me.

"Do you?" I say. "I'm not being funny. I'll bet you a hundred bucks you don't know how it works."

"I'm sure I could figure it out," he says. "I'm not as much of a complete moron as you make me out to be."

"I don't make you out to be anything."

"Oh, yes, Lauren. Yes, you do. You act like you're the most perfect person in the whole world and you're stuck with your stupid husband who can't do a damn thing but call the landlord. You know what? I'll be the one who gets the hot water fixed. Since you do all the complicated stuff for smart people, like the laundry." He starts angrily putting his clothes back on.

"Where are you even going?" I say to him.

"To see if I can fix the fucking thing!" he says, putting on his shoes with equal parts anger and haste.

"Now? It's almost midnight. You need to stay here and talk to me."

"Let's drop it, Lauren," Ryan says. He walks to the front door. His hand is on the doorknob, getting ready to leave. Thumper is resting at my feet, no idea what he's in the middle of.

"We can't drop it, Ryan," I say. "I'm not going to drop it. We've been 'dropping it' for months now."

That's what's really concerning about all of this. We aren't fighting about the hot water or the Dodger Stadium parking lot. We aren't fighting about money or jealousy or communication skills. We are fighting because we don't know how to be happy. We are fighting because we are not happy. We are fighting because we no longer make each other happy. And I think, at least if I'm speaking for myself, I'm pretty pissed off about that.

"We have to deal with this, Ryan. It's been three straight weeks of bitching at each other. Out of the past month, I think we have spent maybe one evening in a good mood. The rest of it has been like this."

"You think I don't know that?" Ryan says, his hand gesticulating wildly. When he gets angry, his normally confident and controlled demeanor becomes unrestrained and forceful. "You think I don't know how miserable I am?"

"Miserable?" I say. "Miserable?" I can't argue with what he is saying. It's really about how he says it. He says it as if I'm the one making him miserable. As if I'm the one who's causing all of this.

"I'm not saying anything you didn't just say yourself. Please calm down."

"Calm down?"

"Stop repeating everything I say as a question."

"Then try being a bit more clear."

Ryan sighs, moving his hand to his forehead, covering it with his thumb and fingers as if they were the brim of a baseball cap. He's rubbing his temples. I don't know when he became so dramatic. Somewhere along the way, he went from being this super calm, collected person to being *this* guy, this guy who sighs loudly and rubs his temples as if he's Jesus on the cross. It's as if the world is happening *to* him. I can tell he wants to say something, but he doesn't. He starts to, and he stops himself.

I'm not sure what it is about me that insists that he say every little thing in his head. But when we fight like this, I can't stand to see him hold back. You know why? I know why. It's because if you're really holding back, you don't even start to say it. But that's not what he does. He does this little song and dance where he pretends he's not going to say something, but it's clear that eventually, he's going to say something.

"Just say it," I say.

"No," he says. "It's not worth it."

"Well, clearly, it is. Because you can barely stop yourself. So get on with it. I don't have all fucking night."

"Why don't you take it down a notch, OK?"

I shake my head at him. "You are such a dick sometimes."

"Yeah, well, you're a bitch."

"Excuse me?"

"Here we go. Her Royal Highness is offended."

"It's not hard to be offended by being called a bitch."

"It's no different from you just calling me a dick."

"It is, actually. It's much different."

"Lauren, get over it. OK? I'm sorry I called you a bitch. Pretend I called you whatever you want to be called. The point is, I'm sick of this. I'm sick of every little thing being a disaster of epic proportions. I can't even go to a goddamn Dodgers game without you moping through every inning." Thumper moves from my feet and heads toward Ryan. I try not to worry that he's choosing sides.

"If you don't want me to be upset, then stop doing things to upset me."

"This is exactly the problem! I'm not doing things to upset you."

"Right. You just get tickets to the Dodgers game even when I tell you I don't feel like going. That's not to upset me, that's because . . . why, exactly?" I move toward the dining-room table, getting a better angle at him, looking at him even more directly, but I'm not doing a great job of paying attention to the speed and force of my body. I hit the table so hard with my hip that I almost knock over the vase in the middle of the table. It wobbles, ever so slightly. I steady it.

"Because I want to see the Dodgers, and I really don't fucking care if you're there or not. I got the extra ticket to be nice, actually."

I cross my arms. I can feel myself crossing them. I know it's terrible body language. I know it makes things worse. And yet there is no other way for my arms to be. "To be nice? So you wanted to spend Friday night by yourself at the Dodgers? You didn't even want me to go with you?"

"Honestly, Lauren," Ryan says, his voice now perfectly calm, "I did not want you to go with me. I haven't wanted you to go someplace with me in months."

It's the truth. He's not saying it to hurt me. I can see that in his eyes, in his face, in the way his lips relax after he says it. He doesn't care if it hurts me. He's just saying it because it's true.

Sometimes people do things because they are furious or because they are upset or because they are out for blood. And those things can hurt. But what hurts the most is when someone does something out of apathy. They don't care about you the way they said they did back in college. They don't care about you the way they promised to when you got married. They don't care about you at all.

And because there is just the tiniest part of me that still cares, and because his not caring enrages that tiny part of me, I do something I have never done before. I do something I never thought I would ever do. I do something that, even as I'm doing it, I can't believe is actually happening.

I pick up the vase. The glass vase. And I throw it against the door behind him. Flowers and all.

I watch Ryan duck, yanking his shoulders up around his neck and ears. I watch Thumper jump to attention. I watch as the water flies into the air, the stems and petals disperse and fall to the ground, and the glass shatters into so many pieces that I'm not sure I even remember what it used to look like.

And when all of the shards have landed, when Ryan looks up at me stunned, when Thumper scurries out into the other room, the tiny part of me that cared is gone. Now I don't care anymore, either. It's a shitty feeling. But it beats the hell out of caring, even the tiniest bit.

Ryan stares at me for a moment and then grabs his keys off the side table. He swipes the water and glass out of his way with the shoes already on his feet. He walks out the front door.

I don't know what he's thinking. I don't know where he's going. I don't know how long he'll be gone. All I know is that this might, in fact, be the end of my marriage. It might be the end of something I thought had no ending.

• • •

I stare at the door for a while after Ryan leaves. I can't believe that I have thrown a vase at the wall. I can't believe that the crushed mess of glass on the floor is because of me. I wasn't intending to hurt him. I didn't throw it *at* him. And yet the violence of it startles me. I didn't know I was capable of it.

Eventually, I stand up and go to the kitchen and get the broom and the dust pan. I put on a pair of shoes. I start to sweep it all up. As I do, Thumper comes running into the room, and I have to tell him to stop where he is. He listens and sits, watching me. The *clink* of the pieces against one another as they hit the trash can are almost soothing. *Brush. Brush. Clink.*

I grab a few paper towels and run them over the area to mop up any remaining shards and water, and then I vacuum. I'm hesitant to stop vacuuming, because I don't know what I'm going to do after I'm done. I don't know what to do with myself.

I put everything away and lie down on the bed. I am reminded of when we bought it, why we bought it.

What happened to us?

I can hear a voice in my head, speaking crisply and clearly. *I don't love him anymore.* That's what it says. *I don't love him anymore.* And maybe more heartbreaking is the fact that I know, deep down, he doesn't love me, either.

It all clicks into place. That's what all of this is, isn't it? That's what the fighting is. That's why I disagree with everything he says. That's why I can't stand all the things I used to stand. That's why we haven't been having sex. That's why we never try hard to please each other. That's why we are never pleased with each other.

Ryan and I are two people who used to be in love.

What a beautiful thing to have been.

What a sad thing to be.

Ryan must have returned late at night or early in the morning. I don't know which. I didn't wake up when he came home.

When I do wake up, he is on the other side of the bed, Thumper in between us. Ryan's back is facing me. He is snoring. It scares me that we are able to sleep during this sort of turmoil. I think of the way it used to be, the way fights used to keep us up all night and into the morning. The way we couldn't sleep on our anger, couldn't put it on hold. Now we are on the verge of defeat and . . . he's snoring.

I wait patiently for him to wake up. When he finally does, he doesn't say anything to me. He stands up and walks to the bathroom. He goes to the kitchen and brews himself a cup of coffee and gets back into bed. He is next to me but not beside me. We are both in this bed, but we are not sharing it.

"We're not in love anymore," I say. Just the sound of it coming out of my mouth makes my skin crawl and my adrenaline run. I am shaking.

Ryan stares at me for a moment, no doubt shocked, and then he pulls his hands to his face, burying his fingers in his hair. He is a handsome man. I wonder when I stopped seeing that.

When we got married, he was almost prettier than I was on our wedding day. Our wedding pictures, where he is smiling like a young boy, his eyes crinkled and bright like stars, were beautiful, in part, because he was beautiful. But he no longer seems exceptional to me.

"I wish you hadn't said that," Ryan says, not looking up, not moving his head from his hands. He is frozen, staring at the blanket beneath him.

"Why?" I ask him, suddenly eager to hear what he thinks, desperate to know if maybe he remembers something I don't, to know if he thinks I am wrong. Because maybe he can convince me. Maybe I *am* wrong. I want to be wrong. It will feel so good to be wrong. I will wallow in my wrongness; I will swim in it. I will breathe it in and let it overtake my lungs and my body, and I will cry it out, heavy tears so full of relief they will be baptismal.

"Because now I don't know how we keep going," he says. "I don't know where we go from here."

He finally looks up at me. His eyes are bloodshot. When he pulls his fingers out of his hair, they leave it in disarray, scattered every which way across his head. I start to say, *What do you mean?* but instead, I say, "How long have you known?"

Ryan's face drops into an expression that isn't so much miserable but, rather, lifeless. "Does it matter?" he asks me, and honestly, I'm not sure. But I press on.

"I just figured it out," I say. "I'm just wondering how long you've known you weren't in love with me."

"I don't know. A few weeks, I guess," he says, staring back at the blanket. It is striped and multicolored, and for that, I am thankful. It will keep his attention. Maybe he won't look at me.

"Like a month?" I ask.

"Yeah." He shrugs. "Or like a few weeks, like I said."

"When?" I say. I don't know why I get out of bed, but I do. I have to stand up. My body has to be standing.

"I just told you when," he says. He doesn't move from the bed.

"No," I say, my back now up against our bedroom wall. "Like, what happened that made you realize it?"

"What happened that made *you* realize it?" he asks me. The blanket's stripes have failed to do their job; he looks at me. I flinch.

"I don't know," I say. "It just sort of flew into my head. One moment, I didn't know what was going on, and then suddenly, I just . . . got it."

"Same here," he says. "Same thing for me."

"But, like, what day? What were we doing?" I don't know why I need to seek this information out. It just feels like something I don't know—his side of this. "I'm just trying to get some context."

"Just lay off it, OK?" Back to the stripes.

"Just be honest, would you? We're clearing the air here. Just let it out. It's all about to come out anyway, every last ugly piece of this. Just let it out. Just let it—"

"I'm not in love with another woman, if that's what you're asking," he says.

That wasn't what I was asking at all.

"But I just . . ." He continues. "I noticed that I am seeing them differently."

"Women?"

"Yeah. I look at them now. I never used to look at them. I was looking at one of them, and I just . . . I realized that I don't think of you the way I think of them."

"Women?"

"Yeah."

I let it sink in. Thumper gets off the bed and walks over to me. Can he sense what's happening? He sits at the door by my feet and looks at Ryan. My heart starts to crack. This might all end in me losing Thumper.

"So what does this mean?" I ask quietly, gently. By saying

the words out loud, I have changed our fate. I have set us in motion. I am ripping us out of this comfortable prison once and for all. I am going to solve this problem. I have a lot of other problems, and I know this is going to cause a whole new set of problems, but living with someone I don't like isn't going to be one of them. Not anymore.

Ryan steps toward me, and he holds me. I want it to feel better than it does. His voice is just as quiet and calm as mine. "This can't be the end, Lauren. This is just a rough patch or something."

"But," I say, looking up at him, finally ready to say the last of what had been in my heart for so long, "I can't stand you."

It feels like such a sweet and visceral release, and yet the minute it comes out of my mouth, I wish I never said it. I wish I was the sort of person who doesn't need her pain to be heard. I want to be the type of person who can keep it to herself and spare the feelings of others. But I'm not that person. My anger has to take flight. It has to be set free and allowed to bounce off the walls and into the ears of the person it could hurt the most.

Ryan and I sink to the floor. We rest our backs against the wall, our knees bent in front of us, our arms crossed, our posture perfectly matched. We have spent enough years together to know how to work in sync, even if we don't want to. Thumper sits at my feet, his belly warming them. I want to love Ryan the way I love Thumper. I want to love him and protect him and believe in him and be ready to jump in front of a bus for him, the way I would for my dog. But they are two completely different types of love, aren't they? They shouldn't even have the same name. The kind that Ryan and I had, it runs out.

Eventually, Ryan speaks. "I have no idea what we are going to do," he says, still sitting with me, his back now slouched, his posture truly defeated, his gaze directed firmly at the wayward nail in our hardwood floor.

"Me, neither," I say, looking at him and remembering how much I used to melt when I smelled him. He is so close to me that I quietly sniff the air, seeing if I can inhale him, if I can feel that bliss again. I think maybe if I can breathe deeply enough, his scent will flow through my nose and flood my heart. Maybe it will infect me again. Maybe I can be happy again if I just smell hard enough. But it doesn't work. I feel nothing.

Ryan starts laughing. He actually manages to laugh. "I don't know why I'm laughing," he says, as he gains his composure. "This is the saddest moment of my life."

And then his voice breaks, and the tears fall from his eyes, and he truly looks at me for maybe the first time in a year. He repeats himself, slowly and deliberately. "This is the saddest moment of my life."

I think, for a moment, that we might cry together. That this might be the beginning of our healing. But as I go to put my head on his shoulder, Ryan stands up.

"I'm going to call the landlord," he says. "We need hot water."

I wrote down 'couple's counseling,' 'living separately,' and 'open marriage,'" I say, sitting at our dining-room table. I have a piece of paper in front of me. Ryan has a piece of paper in front of him. I am not open to the idea of open marriage. I am just spitballing. But I know, I am positive, that an open marriage is not on the table.

"Open marriage?" Ryan asks. He is intrigued.

"Ignore that last one," I say. "I just . . . I didn't have any other ideas."

"It's not a bad idea," Ryan says, and the minute he says it, I hate him. Of course, he would say that. Of course, that would be the one he jumped on. Leave it to Ryan to ignore that I said "couple's counseling" but jump at the chance to screw someone else.

"Just . . ." I say, annoyed. "Just say what you wrote down."

"OK." Ryan looks down at his paper. "I wrote 'date again' and 'trial separation.'"

"I don't know what those mean," I say.

"Well, the first one is kind of like your thing about living apart. We would just try to see if maybe we lived in different places and we just went on a few dates and saw each other less, maybe that would work. Maybe take some pressure off. Make it more exciting to see each other."

"OK, and the second one?"

"We break up for a little while."

"You mean, like, we're done?"

"Well, I mean," he starts to explain, "I move out, or you

move out, and we see how we do on our own, without each other."

"And then what?"

"I don't know. Maybe some time apart would make us . . . you know, ready to try again."

"How long would we do this? Like, a few months?"

"I was thinking longer."

"Like, how long?"

"I don't know, Lauren. Jesus," Ryan says, losing his patience at all of my questions. It's been a few weeks since we told each other we didn't love each other anymore. We've been tiptoeing around each other. This is the beginning of pulling the Band-Aid off. A very large, very sticky Band-Aid.

"I'm just asking you to clarify your suggestion," I say. "I don't think you need to act like this is the Spanish Inquisition."

"Like, a year. Like, we take a year apart."

"And we sleep with other people?"

"Yeah," Ryan says, as if I'm an idiot. "I think that's kind of the point."

Ryan has made it clear that he no longer thinks of me the way he thinks about other women. It hurts. And yet when I try to break down why it hurts, I don't have an answer. I don't really think of him in that way, either.

"Let's talk about this later," I say, getting up from the table.

"I'm ready to talk about this now," Ryan says. "Don't walk away."

"I'm asking you nicely," I say, my tone slow and pointed, "if we can please discuss this later."

"Fine," Ryan says, getting up from the table and throwing his sheet of paper into the air. "I'm getting out of here."

I don't ask him where he is going. He leaves often enough now that I know his answer will be harmless. I resent him so much for being predictable. He'll go to a bar and get a drink.

He'll go to the movies. He'll call his friends to play basketball. I don't care. He'll come back when he feels like it, and when he does, the air in the house will be sharpened and tightened, so much that I will feel I can barely breathe.

I lie on the couch for hours, contemplating a year without my husband. It feels freeing and terrifying. I think about him sleeping with another woman, but the thought quickly transforms into the thought of me sleeping with another man. I don't know who this man is, but I can see his hands on me. I can feel his lips on me. I can imagine the way he will look at me, the way he will make me feel like the only woman in the room, the most important woman in the world. I imagine his slim body and his dark hair. I imagine his deep voice. I imagine being nervous, a type of nervous I haven't been in years.

When Ryan finally does come home, I tell him I think he is right. We should take a year apart.

Ryan sighs loudly, and his shoulders slump. He tries to speak, but his voice catches. I walk over to him and wrap my arms around his shoulders. I start crying. Once again, finally, we are on the same team. We wallow in it for a while. We let ourselves feel the relief we have given each other. That's what it feels like, ultimately: immense relief. Like cold water on a burn.

When we disengage, Ryan offers to move out. He says I can keep the house for the year. I take him up on it. I don't argue. He's offering me a gift. I'm going to take it. We sit quietly next to each other on the sofa, holding hands, not looking at each other for what feels like hours. It feels so good to stop fighting.

Then we realize we both thought we were the one keeping Thumper.

We fight about the dog until five in the morning.

Most of Ryan's things are packed. There are boxes all over the living room and bedroom with words like "Books" and "Bathroom Stuff" scribbled in black Sharpie. The moving truck is on its way. Ryan is in the bedroom packing shoes. I can hear each one land on the cardboard as it is chucked.

I grab a few of my things and prepare to leave. I can't stay here for this. I can't watch it happen. I am glad he is leaving. I really am. I keep telling myself that over and over. I keep thinking of my new freedom. But I realize that I don't really know what it means—freedom. I don't know anything of the practical ramifications of my actions. We have covered only the basics in terms of our preparation. We haven't talked about what it would feel like or what our new life would look like. We've stuck to numbers and figures. We've talked about how to divide our bank account. We've talked about how to afford two rent payments. How to keep him on my insurance. Whether we need to file legally. "We'll cross that bridge when we come to it," Ryan said, and I let it go. That answer was good with me. I certainly don't want any of this in writing.

I told Ryan last night that I didn't want to be here to see him leave. He agreed that it might be best if I left for the weekend and gave him his space to move out as he wished. "The last thing I need is you critiquing the way I pack my toothbrush," Ryan told me. His voice was jovial, but his words were sincere. I could feel the tension and resentment underneath. The smile on his face was the sort of smile car salesmen have, pretending everybody's having a good time when, really, you're at war.

I pick up my deodorant and my face wash. I pick up only the most necessary pieces for my makeup bag. I grab my toothbrush and put it in my travel case, snapping the tooth-brush cap over the bristles so they won't get dirty. Ryan usu-ally stuffs his in a plastic bag. He is right to be defensive about the way he packs toothbrushes. He does it wrong. I put all of it in my bag and zip it up. For better or worse, I am ready to go.

My plan is to drive straight to Rachel's house. Rachel knows that things with Ryan and me aren't going well. She has noticed how tense I've been. She has noticed how often I criticize him, how rarely I have anything nice to say. But I have been insisting that things were fine. I don't know why I've had such a hard time admitting it to her. I think, in some ways, I hid it because I knew telling Rachel made it real. I had already told Mila about all of this. The tension, the fighting, the loss of love, the plan to separate. For some reason, in my mind, Mila could know, and that didn't seem tantamount to carving it in stone. But with Rachel, it would be official. A witness. I can't turn around and pretend it never happened. Maybe that's the difference between a friend and a sister: a friend can just listen to your problems in the present, but your sister remembers and reminds you of everything in the past. Or maybe it's not a difference between friends and sisters. Maybe it's the differ-ence between Mila and Rachel.

But this really *is* happening. The moving truck is coming. And if I am going to deal with this, I need Rachel. Rachel, who will hold my hand and tell me it is going to be OK. Rachel, who will believe in me. I have to admit to her that my mar-riage is failing. That *I* am failing. That I am not the successful and together older sister I have been pretending to be. That I am no longer the one with her shit together.

I find Ryan in the bedroom, grabbing boxes of clothes. We have already split up the furniture. We are both going to have to go shopping on our own. I now need a new TV. Ryan is going to need pots and pans. What had seemed like a whole is now two halves.

"OK," I say. "I'm going to go and leave you to it." Ryan has friends coming over to help. He doesn't need me.

He doesn't need me.

"OK," he says, looking into the closet. Our closet. My closet. He finally looks up at me, and I can see he has been crying. He breathes in and out, trying to control himself, trying to take control of his feelings. Suddenly, my heart swells and overtakes me. I can't leave him like this. I can't. I can't leave him in pain.

He does need me.

I run to him. I put my arms around him. I let him bury his face in me. I hold him as he lets it out, and then I say, "You know what? This is stupid. I'm going to stay." This whole idea has been far-fetched and absurd. We just needed a wake-up call. And this is the wake-up call. This is what we needed to see how foolish we've been. Of course, we love each other! We always have. We just forgot for a little while but we are going to be OK now. We have pushed ourselves to the brink and learned our lesson. We don't have to go through with this. It is over. We can end this strange experiment right here and go back to the way things were. Marriages aren't all roses and sunshine. We know that. This was silly. "Forget this," I say. "You're not going anywhere, sweetheart. You don't have to go anywhere."

He is quiet for some time longer, and then he shakes his head. "No," he says, drying his tears. "I need to leave." I stare at him, frozen with my arms still around him. He pushes his point further. "You should go," he says, wiping his own tears away. He is back to business.

That's when I fall apart. I don't melt like butter or deflate like a tire. I shatter like glass, into thousands of pieces.

My heart is truly broken. And I know that even if it mends, it will look different, feel different, beat differently.

I stand up and grab my bag. Thumper follows me to the front door. I look down at him with my hand on the knob, ready to turn it. He looks up at me, naive and full of wondering. For all he knows, he is about to go for a walk. I am not sure whom I feel worse for: Ryan, Thumper, or myself. I can't bear it a second longer. I can't pet him good-bye. I turn the knob and walk out the front door, shutting it behind me. I don't stop to take a breath or get my bearings. I just get into the car, wipe my eyes, and set out for Rachel's house. I am not strong enough to stand on my own two feet.

I need my sister.

part two

NOVEMBER RAIN

I just need you to hear what I'm about to say and not try to talk me out of it. Don't judge me. Or say I'm making a mistake, even if you think I am. Making a mistake, I mean. Because I probably am. But I just need you to listen and then tell me everything is going to be OK. That's what I need, basically. I need you to tell me everything is going to be OK, even if it probably isn't."

"OK." Rachel agrees immediately. She doesn't really have a choice, does she? I mean, I've shown up on her doorstep unannounced at nine A.M. on a Saturday, screaming, "Don't judge me!" So she just has to go with it. "Do you want to come in? Or—" she starts to ask me, but I don't wait for her to finish.

"Ryan and I are splitting up."

"Oh, my God," she says, stunned. She stares at me for a moment and then unfreezes, opening the door wide for me to step in. I do. She's still in her pajamas, which seems reasonable. She probably just woke up. Chances are, she was having a perfectly nice dream when I rang her doorbell.

Once I walk past her and she shuts the door behind me, she can see I've packed a bag. It's all coming together for her.

She takes the bag from my shoulder and puts it down on the couch. "What did you—I mean, how did this—how did the two of you—are you OK? That's what's important. How are you feeling?"

I shrug. Most of the time when I shrug, it's because I'm indifferent. And yet now, even though my shrug means a million things at once, none of them is indifference.

"Do you want to talk about why you're splitting up?" Rachel says calmly. "Or should I just make you some . . . I don't know. What do people eat when they are divorcing?"

"We're not divorcing," I say, moving past her and taking a seat on her couch.

"Oh," she says, taking a seat beside me. "You said you were splitting up, so I just assumed . . ." She curls her feet in, sitting cross-legged and facing me. Her pajama pants are white with blue and salmon-colored stripes. Her tank top is the same salmon as the stripes on the bottom. She must have bought them as a set. My sister is exactly the person who wears the set together. I am exactly the person who cannot find a single matching pair.

"We're breaking up," I say. "Like, we are not going to be seeing each other for a while, but then, you know, we're going to give it another shot."

"So you're separating, then? It's a trial separation?"

"No."

"So . . . Lauren, what am I missing here?"

"You aren't supposed to judge."

"I'm not judging," she says, taking my hand. "I'm trying to understand."

"We're going on a break. We can't live in the same place anymore. We can't stand each other." The look on her face confirms that she's known this for a while, but I don't acknowledge it.

"But you're not getting a divorce because . . . ?" she asks me. Her voice is gentle. I think that's maybe the thing I need most right now. I'm functioning pretty similarly to a dog, in that, really, the words themselves don't matter. I'm just listening for high-pitched tones, sounds that are smooth and soothing. "I mean, if you guys have been having problems for a while, if it's bad enough that you don't want to live together, then what is stopping you from just breaking up altogether?"

I take a moment and think about how to answer. I mean, the word *divorce* never came up.

Obviously, it was in my head. I thought about saying it. But I never wrote it down on that sheet of options. And while I can't imagine that Ryan didn't think of it, didn't consider it, didn't *almost* say it, something stopped him, too.

I think that's important. Neither of us suggested it. Neither of us said that this thing we have together, this thing that we have broken and is no longer working, neither of us said that we should throw it away.

"I don't know why," I say when I finally answer her. "Because I made a promise, I guess. Or, I don't know, I'm hoping there's a third option for us besides living unhappily or giving up entirely."

Rachel considers this. "So how long is this break?" She says "break" as if it's a new word that I made up. "So how long is this flarffensnarler?" That's how she says it.

I breathe in. I breathe out. "One year." My resolve starts to melt away. My composure starts to crack. The true pain of what I'm doing starts to slowly seep in, not unlike the way the sun shines brightly enough to break up a cloudy day.

Rachel can see I'm starting to cry before the tears actually form in my eyes, and it further softens her into exactly the Rachel I need. She does not need to know the details. She wants only to hold me and tell me everything will be OK, even if it won't be. So that's what she does; she holds me, and she runs her hands through my hair. And she says what I've been waiting all morning to hear.

"It really will be OK," she says, her voice almost cooing to me. "I know you told me to say it. But it's actually true. This will all be OK."

"How do you know?" I shouldn't ask her things like this. I told her to say something. She said it. I can't press her on it. I can't try to get her to say things I haven't scripted for her. But she seems so confident right now, so sure that I will be OK, that I want to know more about this version of me she sees. How is the Lauren in her head going to be OK? And how can I be more like that Lauren?

"I know it will be OK because everything is OK in the end. And if it's not OK, it's not the end."

I pull back and look at her. "Isn't that from one of your mugs?"

Rachel shrugs. "Just because it's on a mug doesn't mean it's not true."

"No," I say, lying down, my head in her lap. "I guess you're right."

"You know what else I know?" she says.

"What?"

"I know you have a really great year ahead of you."

"I find that hard to believe. I'm turning thirty, and I'm on the verge of divorce."

"I thought you weren't getting divorced?" Rachel says.

I roll my eyes at her. "It's hyperbole, Rachel. A rhetorical device." I am at my most condescending when I'm at my least secure. I guess the problem is that I don't know how much of a hyperbole it is. I'll insist to everyone, my sister included, that it's not going to happen. But what if it does? I mean, what if it does?

"No, I'm serious," she says. "This part is hard. But I know you, and you don't do things that you shouldn't do. You don't take this stuff lightly. Neither does Ryan. He's a good man. And you're a good woman. If the two of you decided this was a good idea, that's because it's a good idea. And good ideas are never a bad idea."

It's quiet for a minute before we both start laughing.

"OK, that last part didn't make a whole lot of sense, but you know what I meant."

I look up at her, and she looks down at me. I always know what she means. We've always had a way of understanding each other. Maybe more to the point, we've always had a way of believing in each other. I need to be believed in right now.

"I'm glad you're here," Rachel says to me. "Not under these circumstances, obviously. But I'm glad you're here."

"Yeah?"

"Yeah, it's nice to see you, just you."

"With no Ryan?"

"Yeah," she says. "I love Ryan, but I love you more. It will be nice to have a year of just you."

She's better with words than she thinks she is, because for the first time, I can see something to look forward to this year. It will be nice to have a year of just me.

• • •

"So, delicate question, I guess," Rachel says to me. We are at her kitchen table. She has made Cinnamon Toast Crunch–encrusted French toast with fresh whipped cream. I want to take a picture, it looks so gorgeous and decadent. She puts the plate in front of me as she speaks, and I immediately stop listening to whatever she is saying. I know this will taste even better than it looks. Which is saying a lot. But this is Rachel's forte. She makes Oreo pancakes. She makes red velvet crepes with cream cheese filling. She cannot make a casserole or an egg dish to save her life, but anything that requires a bag of sugar and heavy cream, and she's your woman.

"This looks incredible," I say to her, grabbing my fork. I press the end of it against the corner of the bread and grind it against the plate until I've set my piece free. It tastes exactly like I imagined. It takes like everything is fine. "Oh, my God," I say.

"I know, right?" Rachel has absolutely no qualms about admitting that what she has made tastes great. She does it in a way that implies she had nothing to do with it. You can tell her that her pumpkin spice cake is the most delicious thing you've ever tasted, and she will say something like, "Oh, tell me about it. It's sinful," and you get the impression that she is complimenting the recipe instead of herself.

"Anyway," I say, after I have finished chewing, "what is your delicate question?"

"Well," she says, licking the whipped cream off her fork. "Who gets . . ." She pauses and then sort of gives up. She doesn't know how to say it.

"Thumper," I say, so that she doesn't have to. "Who gets Thumper?"

"Right, who gets Thumper?"

I take a deep breath. "I get him for the first two months just so everything doesn't change at once for him." I feel stupid when I say this. Ryan and I act as if Thumper is a child, and it comes out in the smallest and most embarrassing ways. But Rachel doesn't bat an eyelash.

"And then Ryan gets him?"

"Yeah, for two months after that. That brings us to January, and we will renegotiate."

"Got it."

"It sounds stupid, right?" I say. The truth is, I was eager to agree to the idea when Ryan came up with it. It meant that no matter what, we would see each other in two months, and that gave me a sense of security. It felt like training wheels on a bike.

"No," Rachel says, not even looking at me. She continues to eat her breakfast. "Not at all. Everyone has their own way of doing things."

"Well, what, then?" I ask.

Rachel looks . . . I don't know. There is something going on with her face. She seems to be holding something back. "What do you mean?" she asks.

"What are you thinking that you're not saying?"

"I thought I was supposed to be supportive!" Rachel says, half laughing and completely defensive. "I can't tell you every little thought in my head and tell you everything you want to hear at the same time."

I laugh. "Yeah, OK," I say.

We are quiet for a minute. I have scarfed down all of my food. There is nothing left to do but stare at my white plate. I try to move the crumbs around with my fork.

"But what is it, though?" I say. I want to know. I'm not sure why. Maybe I need the truth more than I need to hear what I want to hear. Maybe there is almost never a time when you don't need the truth. Or maybe it's just that you need the truth the most at the times you think you don't want to hear it. "Just tell me. I can handle it."

Rachel sighs. "I just . . ." she starts. She looks up at me. "I feel bad for Ryan."

I'm not sure what I thought she was going to say, but it wasn't that. I expected something about how I'm taking the Thumper thing too seriously. I expected something about how maybe Ryan and I should give it another try. I expected that maybe she was going to say the one thing that I fear is actually true: that I'm being a whiny-ass baby and that every marriage is hard, and I should just shut up and go home and quit this bullshit, because not being happy is not a real problem.

But she doesn't say that. She actually tears up and says, "I just . . . he lost his wife, his house, and his dog on the same day."

I don't say anything to her. I just kind of look at her. I let it sink in.

She's right. I used to love that man so much. I used to be the person who made sure he had everything he wanted. When did I become the person who took it all away?

I start to cry. I put my head down on the table, and Rachel rushes to my side.

"I'm sorry," she says. "I'm sorry! See? I'm not good at this. I suck at it. I'm the shittiest person at this. You are a good person, and you're doing the right thing."

"Thumper is just for two months," I say. "The whole thing is only for a year."

"I know!" Rachel says, holding me, squeezing my shoulders. "Ryan is fine. I know he's fine. He's one of those guys, you know, who's always fine."

"You think he's fine?" I ask her, lifting my head off the table. It is somehow awful to think that he is fine. It is almost as awful as thinking about him being miserable. I cannot stand the thought that he is OK or not OK.

"No," Rachel says. I can sense her desperation to get out of this conversation. She can't say the right thing, and she knows it, and maybe she's a little annoyed at the situation I've put her in. "Ryan is fine, as in 'He will be fine.' Not like 'He's totally fine.'"

"Right," I say, composing myself. "We will both be fine."

"Right," she says, grasping for the calm tone in my voice. "Fine."

So that's what I aim for. I aim for fine.

I am fine.

Ryan is fine.

We will be fine.

One day, this will all be fine.

There is a big difference between something that is fine and something that *will be* fine, but I decide to pretend, for now, that they are the same.

"You know you have to tell Mom soon, right?" Rachel says to me.

"I know," I say.

"And Charlie," she says. "But who knows with Charlie? That could go either way."

I nod, already lost to my imagination. I think about telling them. I think about how Charlie will crack some joke. I think about whether my mom will be disappointed in me. If she'll feel the same way I do, that I've failed. After a minute, I recognize that this line of thinking is going nowhere fast. "You know what?" I say.

"What?"

"They'll be fine."

Rachel smiles at me. "Yes, they will. They will be fine."

I go home on Sunday night at seven o'clock, the time that Ryan and I agreed on. I knew he would be gone. That was the whole point. But as I open the door to my empty house, the fact that he is gone really hits me. I am alone.

My house looks as if I was robbed. Ryan didn't take anything that we hadn't discussed ahead of time, and yet it feels as if he has taken everything we owned. Sure, the major furniture is there, but where are the DVDs? Where is the bookshelf? Where is the map of Los Angeles that we had mounted and framed? It is all gone.

Thumper runs toward me, his floppy tan ears bouncing on his head, and I fall down when his paws hit me right on my hips, knocking me off balance. I hit the hardwood with a thud, but I barely feel it. All I can feel is this dog loving me, licking my face, jumping all over me. He nudges my ears with his nose. He looks so happy to see me. I am home. It doesn't look the way it used to. But it is my home.

I walk to the back of the house and feed Thumper. He stands there, looking up at me for a moment, and then chows down.

I turn on the light in the dining room, and I see a note that Ryan has left. I wasn't anticipating that he would leave anything. But seeing the note there, I want to run to it and tear it open. What is there left to say? I want to know what there is left to say. My hands rip apart the envelope before my brain has even told them to.

His handwriting is so childish. Men's handwriting is rarely

identifiable by any sense of masculinity. It's only identifiable by the lack of sophistication. They must decide in sixth grade to start worrying about other things.

Dear Lauren,

Make no mistake: I do love you. Just because I don't feel the love in my heart doesn't mean I don't know it's there. I know it's there. I'm leaving because I'm going to find it. I promise you that.

Please do not call or text me. I need to be alone. So do you. I am serious about this time away. Even if it's hard, we have to do it. It's the only way we can get to a better place. If you call me, I will not answer. I don't want to back down from this. I will not go back to what we had.

In that spirit, I wanted to wish you a Happy Birthday now, even though I'm a few weeks in advance. I know thirty is going to be a hard year, but it will be a good year, and since I won't be talking to you on the day, I wanted to let you know I'll be thinking of you.

Be good to my boy, Thumper. I'll call you in two months to discuss the handoff. Maybe we can meet at a rest stop like a pair of divorced parents—even though we are neither.

Love,
Ryan

P.S. I fed the beast dinner before I left.

I look down at Thumper, who is now standing at my feet, looking up at me.

"You little trickster," I say to him. "You already ate."

I read the letter again and again. I break apart the words. They hurt me and fill me with hope. They make me cry, and they make me angry. Eventually, I fold the letter back up and throw it in the trash. I stare at it in there on the top of the pile. It feels wrong to throw it away. As if I should keep it. As if it should be kept in a scrapbook of our relationship.

I go into the bedroom and look for the shoebox I keep on the very top shelf. I can't reach it on my own. I go into the hallway closet and get the step stool. I go back into the bedroom closet and strain my fingers to reach the edge of the box. It falls down onto the closet floor, busting open. Papers fan across the carpet. Ticket stubs. Old Post-it notes. Faded photos. And then I see what I'm looking for.

The first letter Ryan ever wrote me. It was a few weeks after we met in the college dining hall. He wrote it on note-book paper. The page has been folded over so many times it now strains to stay flat enough to read.

Things I Like About You:

1. *When I say something funny, you laugh so loud that you start to cackle.*
2. *How, the other day, you actually used the phrase "Shiver Me Timbers."*
3. *Your butt. (Sorry, these are the facts.)*
4. *That you thought chili con carne meant chili with corn.*
5. *That you're smarter, and funnier, and prettier, and greater than any girl I know.*

A few weeks after I got the letter, he noticed that I had kept it. He found it in my desk in my dorm room. And when I wasn't looking, he crossed out *Like* and replaced it with *Love. Things I Love About You.*

He added a sixth reason underneath in a different-colored pen.

6. *That you believe in me. And that you feel so good. And that you see the world as a beautiful place.*

It was the reason I started a shoebox. But . . . I can't put the letter he left for me tonight in this shoebox. I just can't. It has to stay in the trash.

I put everything back in the box. I put the box away. I brush my teeth. I put on pajamas. I get into bed.

I call for Thumper. He comes running and lies right down next to me. I turn off the light and lie there in the darkness with my eyes wide open. I'm awake so long my eyes adjust to the night. The darkness seems to fade; what was opaque blackness turns to a translucent gray, and I can see that while I have a warm body next to me, I am alone in this house.

I'm not sad. I'm not even melancholy. I'm actually scared. For the first time in my life, I am alone. I am the single woman home alone in the middle of the night. If someone tries to break in, it's up to a friendly Labrador and me. If I hear a strange noise, I'm the one who has to investigate. I feel the same way I felt as a kid at campfires hearing ghost stories.

I know I'm OK. But it sure doesn't feel like it.

I go back to work on Monday morning, and I'm surprised at how much I don't have to talk about all of this. People know I'm married, but really, it rarely comes up. Questions like "How was your weekend?" or "Do anything fun?" are easily answered honestly while keeping the important facts to myself. "It was good. How about yours?" and "Oh, I got to spend a lot of time with my sister. What about you?" seem to get the job done. By noon, I've already learned that you can stop almost all questions about your personal life by being the person who asks the most questions.

But Mila knows me. Actually knows me. She's been my sounding board for months. She knows it all. So as we get into the car to go get lunch, her voice drops low, and she gets real.

"So," she says as she puts the car into drive, "how are you doing?"

"I am . . . fine," I say. "I really am. This weekend sucked, and I cried a lot. I spent all of Saturday night in my sister's bed, crying, while she watched some show about zombies. But then I got home last night, and . . . I'm OK."

"Uh-huh," Mila says. "Did you stretch out in bed? Pour some wine and take a bath without anyone bothering you?"

Mila's been with her partner, Christina, for five years. They have three-year-old twin boys. Something tells me these are her fantasies.

"Not exactly," I say. "I just . . . got home and went to bed, mostly."

She pulls into a spot close to the entrance, and we head in.

"If it was me," she says, "I would be relishing this. A year seems like a long time, but it's going to go so fast. You have your freedom now! You have a life to live. You can make everything smell good. You can have a floral bedspread."

"Christina won't let you have a floral bedspread?"

"She hates floral anything. Loves flowers. Hates florals."

It seems silly, but the floral bedspread feels, suddenly, like something I have to have. I have never lived alone as an adult. I have always shared a bedroom with this man. But now I can buy a blanket with huge flowers across it. Or a bow. Or, I don't know, what's girlie that men don't like? I want it. I want to relish my girliness. I want to buy something pale pink just because I can. I don't have to justify the expense to anyone. I don't have to advocate for why I need a new duvet. I can just go buy one.

"What the hell have I been doing?" I say to Mila, as we stand in line to order. "Why on earth didn't I redecorate the minute he left?"

"I know!" Mila says. "You have to go shopping straight after work. Buy all the crap you always wanted that he thought was stupid."

"I'm gonna do it!" I say.

Mila high-fives me. We eat our sandwiches, and we manage to talk about other things. We don't bring Ryan up again until Mila is parking the car back on campus.

"I am so jealous," she says. "If Christina was gone, I would light a vanilla candle in every room in the house. I would walk into each room and go"—she sniffs and releases—"ahhhh." And then, as if it had just occurred to her, "You don't have to wear sexy uncomfortable panties anymore. You can live in big, comfy underwear."

I laugh. "You don't wear comfortable underwear?"

"I wear a lace bra and panty set every day," Mila says. "I

keep my woman *happy*." She then backpedals. "I didn't mean that you didn't keep . . . Sorry. I was just making a joke."

I laugh again. "It's fine. I'm still reeling from the surprise that you wear sexy underwear every day."

Mila shrugs. "She likes it. I like that she likes it. But man, I am so jealous that you can wear granny panties now."

"I don't even know if I own granny panties," I tell her. "I mean, I just wear normal-people underwear every day. Oh, wait," I say, remembering. "I do have this one pair that I never wear anymore because Ryan used to always make fun of them. He used to call them my parachute panties."

"Super huge? Full coverage? Feels like wearing a cloud?"

"I loved them!"

"Well, go home and put them on, girl! This is your time."

My time. Yeah, this is my time.

After work, I go shopping and buy a big, fluffy white pillow, two striped throws, and a rose-colored bedspread with the outline of an oversized poppy flower on it. I look at the bed, and I think it looks as if it's straight out of a magazine. It looks so pretty.

I take a shower, using all the hot water, singing my heart out because no one can hear me. After I get out, I dry myself off with a towel and head into the bedroom. I dig into the back of my top drawer, past the bikini briefs and the occasionally necessary thongs, and I find them. My parachute panties.

I put them on and stand there in the middle of my bedroom. They aren't quite as magical as I remember them. They feel like normal underwear. Then I catch a glimpse of myself in the mirror. I can see what Ryan was talking about. They sag in the butt and the crotch. Between that and the thick waistband just below my navel, I might as well be wearing a diaper.

I look at the bed with fresh eyes. I don't even like floral patterns. What am I doing? I like blue. I like yellow. I like green. I don't like pink. I have never, in my life, liked pink. This "freedom" quickly starts to feel like such a small thing. This is what I was excited about? Buying a floral blanket? Wearing saggy underwear?

Mila can't light a candle in the house because Christina doesn't like candles and keeping Christina happy is more important than lighting the goddamn candles. That's the truth of it. She's not handcuffed to her. She wants to be with her. She'd rather be with her than light the candles. She'd be heartbroken without her, and the candles would be nothing more than a silver lining. That's all this is. It's a silver lining.

It's just a small, good thing in a situation that totally fucking sucks.

Charlie calls late one night. It's just late enough that it seems unusual for someone to call. I jump for the phone, my heart racing. My mind is convinced that it's Ryan. I am in a T-shirt and my underwear. There's a coffee stain on my shirt. It's been there for days. When you don't have anyone to witness how dirty you are, you find out how truly dirty you are willing to be.

When I look at the phone and realize it's Charlie and not Ryan, I am surprised at how sad it makes me. It makes me really sad. And then I instantly get worried. Because Charlie never calls. He's not even in our time zone.

Charlie left L.A. the minute he had a chance. He went north to Washington for school. He went east to Colorado after that. Somehow in the past year, he's found himself in Chicago. I'm sure soon he'll tell us he's moving to the farthest tip of Maine.

"Charlie?" I answer.

"Hey," he says. Charlie's voice is gruff and gravelly. He spent his teenage years hiding cigarettes from us. When Rachel and I figured it out, sometime around when he was seventeen, we couldn't believe it. Not only that he was smoking but that he didn't tell us. We understood not telling Mom, but us? He wouldn't even tell us? He stopped a few years ago. "Did I wake you?"

"No," I say. "I'm awake. What's going on? How are you?"

"I'm good," he says. "I'm good. How about you?"

"Oh," I say, breathing in deeply as I decide what I want to

say and how I want to say it. "I'm fine," I say. I guess I don't want to say it at all.

"Fine?"

"Yeah, fine."

"Well, that's not what I heard. I heard you're getting a D-I-V-O-R-C-E."

Fucking Rachel.

"Rachel told you?"

"No," Charlie says, starting to explain.

"Rachel had to have told you. No one else knows."

"Chill out, Lo. Ryan told me."

"You talked to Ryan?"

"He *is* my brother-in-law. I assumed it was OK to talk to him."

"No, I just—"

"I called him, and he told me that you guys are getting D-I-V-O-R-C-E-D."

"Why do you keep spelling it? And we're not getting divorced. Did Ryan say that? Did he say we were getting a divorce?" I can hear that my voice sounds panicked and frantic.

"He said that you are taking a break. And when I asked if it was a trial separation, he said, 'Sure.'"

"Well, it's a bit more nuanced than that, you know? It's not, like, a formal separation."

"Lauren, do you know a single couple that has been separated and then got back together? They all get divorced."

"What do you want, Charlie? Or are you just calling to make me want to die?"

"Well, two things. I wanted to call and see if you were OK. If there was anything I could do."

"I'm fine. Thank you," I say. "What was the second thing?"

"Well, this is where things get more complicated."

"That sounds promising," I say. I am now back in bed.

"Part of the reason I called Ryan in the first place was be-cause Mom has decided to throw you a surprise party."

This is just a weird joke he's playing. "Hilarious," I say.

"No, dude. I'm serious."

"Why would she do that?" I'm now up and out of bed again. I pace the floor when I'm nervous.

"She feels like we don't do enough traditional stuff, I guess. And she wanted to host a party."

"At her house?"

"At her house."

"And where do you come into all of this?"

"Well, she's flying me in."

"You're flying in from Chicago just to go to my thirtieth birthday party?"

"Trust me, I wouldn't do it if I was paying for the ticket."

"You're so sweet."

"No, I mean, you hate birthdays. I know that. I tried to tell Mom. She won't listen. And you're lucky I caught her before she called Ryan herself. She told me she was going to call him tomorrow, so I told her I'd do it since I had been meaning to call him anyway. Which, it turns out, was a good thing, but I'm pretty sure you don't want Mom to find out about this the way I just did."

"Does Rachel know yet?"

"About the party?"

"Yeah."

"I doubt it. Mom just told me a few hours ago. She said it all hinged on whether I could fly in and Ryan could get you to her place without you finding out, hence why I brought it up with him."

"That must have been such an awkward conversation," I say, something in me finally calming down. "With Ryan, I mean."

"It wasn't the best, no. He did ask about you, though."

"He did?"

"Yeah, he asked how you were doing. And I had to be, like, 'Bro, I didn't even know you two broke up. How would I know?'"

We laugh for a bit, and then I feel the need to clarify. "We didn't break up," I say.

"Yeah, all right," Charlie says. "Just listen. You gotta tell Mom before the party. She's gonna wonder where Ryan is, and it's gonna be all weird, and anyway, I wanted to give you the heads-up. I mean, you've got three weeks to do it. So that gives you some time."

"Right," I say. "Well, hey, that's exciting that you're coming home."

"Yeah," he says. "It will be nice to see you guys." It's quiet for a moment before he adds, "Also, Lauren, I get that you have Rachel and everything, but . . . you have me, too. I'm here for you, too. I love you, you know."

The fact that my brother can be such a dick is part of the reason he's able to make you feel so much better. When he says he loves you, he means it. When he says he'll always be there for you, he means it.

"Thanks," I say to him. "Thank you. I'll be OK."

"Are you kidding me? You're gonna be fine," he says, and it feels better than all the other times I've heard it.

We get off the phone, and I get back into bed. I turn off the light and grab a hold of Thumper and start to doze off, but my phone rings again. I know who it is before I even look at the screen.

"Hey, Rach," I say.

"Mom is throwing you a surprise party," she says. Her voice is not just laced with schadenfreude, it is made of it. Schadenfreude is all there is.

"I know," I say. "I just talked to Charlie."

"She's flying Charlie home so he can be there."

"I know," I say. "I just talked to him."

"She's flying Grandma Lois out, too. And Uncle Fletcher."

"Now, that I didn't know."

"Apparently, she wants everyone to meet her new boyfriend."

"She has a new boyfriend?"

"Do you even call Mom anymore?"

Admittedly, I have not spoken to my mom in weeks. She lives thirty minutes away, but it's very easy to avoid talking to someone if you never answer the phone.

"His name is Bill. He's apparently a mechanic."

"Is he her mechanic?"

"I don't know," Rachel says. "Why does that matter?"

"I don't know," I say. "I just can't see Mom, like, picking up her mechanic."

"She says he's hot."

"Hot?"

"Yeah, she says he's hot."

"This is all very weird."

"Oh, it's totally, amazingly, delightfully weird."

"I'm going to bed," I say. "I need to let my dreams sort out all of this."

"OK," Rachel says. "But you gotta tell Mom you're separated, right? I mean, you have to before the party. Otherwise, this is going to be a disaster."

"When was the last time Mom threw a party?" I ask Rachel.

"I have no idea. It was definitely the early nineties, though."

"Precisely. So this is going to be a disaster no matter what I do."

"Do you think she'll have a punch bowl?"

"What?"

"Isn't it just like Mom to have a punch bowl?"

And for some reason, this is the funniest thing I've heard all day. My mother will totally have a punch bowl.

"OK, I'm really going to sleep this time."

"Streamers. I bet you there will be streamers."

"I'm going to bed."

"You want over/under on streamers?"

"I don't think that makes sense. You have to have numbers in order for the over/under thing to work."

"Oh, right. OK, five bucks says there are streamers."

"I'm going to bed," I remind her one last time.

"Yeah, fine. I'm just saying . . . five bucks says there are streamers. Are you in or out?"

"What is the matter with you?"

"In or out?"

"In," I say. "I'm in. Good night."

"Good night!" Rachel finally says, and gets off the phone. I lay my head down and smell Thumper. He smells awful. Dogs smell so awful, and yet smelling Thumper is wonderful. He smells heavenly to me. I close my eyes, and I drift off to sleep, where my brain tries to make sense of all this news. I dream that I get to my birthday party and everyone yells, "Surprise!" I see Mom making out with a guy dressed as a race-car driver. Rachel and Charlie are there. And then, just as the yelling dies down, I look through the crowd, and I see Ryan. He makes his way to me. He kisses me. He says, "I could never miss your birthday."

When I wake up, I know it's a dream. But I can't help but hope, maybe, just maybe, it's a premonition.

So, honey, what are your plans for your birthday? The big three-oh is coming up!" my mother says when I finally pick up the phone. Her voice is cheerful. My mother is always cheerful. My mother is the type of woman who rarely admits she's unhappy, who thinks you can fool the whole world with a smile.

"Uh," I say. Do I have a chance to prevent this calamity? I could tell her that I have plans, and then she might give up on this whole thing. But she's already bought Charlie's ticket. Uncle Fletcher is coming. "No, nothing. I'm free," I say, somewhat resigned.

"Great! Why don't you and Ryan come over, and I'll make you dinner?" She says it as if the world's problems have just been solved. My mom didn't really make dinner when we were younger. There simply wasn't time. Between working a full-time job as a real estate agent and doing her best to get the three of us to and from school and finished with our homework every night, we ordered a lot of pizzas. We had a lot of babysitters. We watched a lot of TV. It wasn't because she didn't love us. It was because you can't be two places at once. If my mother could have solved that physical impossibility, she would have. But she couldn't. So even though I know she's not actually going to be making dinner, that this is all a ruse, the idea of a home-cooked meal by my mother sounds sort of nice. Not in a nostalgic way but rather in a novel way. Like if you saw a duck wearing pants.

"OK, sounds good," I say. I know that this is my moment. I

should mention that it will be just me. Here is my opportunity to start the conversation.

"Oh, I wanted to ask you," my mom jumps in. "Would it be OK if I invited my boyfriend, Bill?"

Hearing my fifty-nine-year-old mother use the word *boyfriend* is jarring. We need a new word for two older people who are dating. Shouldn't our vocabulary grow with the times? Who is taking care of this problem?

"Uh, no, that's fine. I was going to say, actually, that Ryan won't be joining us."

"What?" My mother's voice has become sharp where it was once carefree.

"Well, Ryan is—"

"You know what? Whatever works for you two works for me. I know I sometimes get greedy with wanting to see the two of you all the time."

"Yeah," I say. "And I know that Ryan—"

"I'm really eager for him to meet Bill, too," my mom says. "When he gets the chance. I know you two are busy. But one of Bill's boys is married to just this shrew of a woman, and I've been telling Bill about how I really hit the jackpot with Ryan. I guess it's different, sons-in-law versus daughters-in-law, but Ryan is such a good addition to the family. It does make me worry, though. Who will Rachel choose? Or worse! Charlie. I swear, the boy's probably got ten kids in six states, and we'd never know it. But you, my baby girl, you chose so well."

This is one of the things my mother says to me most often. It is her way of complimenting both Ryan and me at the same time. When Ryan and I first got married, he used to tease me about it. "You chose so well!" he would say to me on the way home from her house. "So well, Lauren!"

"Yep," I say. "Yeah."

And in those two affirmative words, I dig myself deeper into the hole. I can't tell her now. I can't tell her ever.

"So what does Ryan have to do that is more important than his wife's birthday?" my mom asks, it suddenly dawning on her that this situation I'm presenting is a bit odd.

"Huh?" I say, trying to buy myself time.

"I mean, how could he miss your birthday?"

"Right, no. He has to work. It's a big project. Super important."

"So you two are celebrating on another night?"

"Yep. Yeah."

"Well, that's great news for me!" she says, becoming delighted. "I get you all to myself. And you'll get to meet Bill!"

"Yeah, I'm excited about that. I didn't know you were dating anyone."

"Oh," my mom says. "You just wait. You will just die. He is so charming." I can practically hear her blushing.

I laugh. "That's great."

"So me, you, and Bill, then?" my mom confirms.

"Well, how about Rachel?" I say. I don't know why I'm playing this game. I know everyone on God's green earth is going to be there.

"Sure," my mom says. "That sounds lovely. My girls and my man."

Ugh. My mom has no idea how she sounds when she says stuff like that. I mean, maybe she does know how she sounds, but she doesn't know how she sounds to me. So gross.

"Let's tone down the 'my man' stuff there," I say, laughing.

She laughs, too. "Oh, Lauren," she says. "Let loose a little!"

"I'm loose, Mom."

"Well, get looser," she says to me. "And let me sound ridiculous. I'm in love."

"That's awesome, Mom. I'm really happy for you."

"Tell Ryan he has to meet Bill soon!"

"Will do, Mom. I love you."

I put down the phone and drop my head into my hands.
I'm a liar, liar, liar. Pants on fire.

The next couple of weeks are hard. I don't go out anywhere. I stay in bed, mostly. Thumper and I go on a lot of walks. Rachel calls me every night around six to ask me if I want to get dinner. Sometimes I say yes. Sometimes I say no. I don't make plans with friends.

I watch a lot of television, especially at night. I find that leaving the TV on as I fall asleep makes it easier to forget that I'm alone in this house. It makes it easier to drift off. And then, when I wake up, it doesn't feel quite so stark and dead in the morning if I'm accompanied by the sounds of morning television.

I wonder, constantly, about what Ryan is doing. Is he thinking of me? Does he miss me? What is he doing with his time? I wonder where he is living. Numerous times, I pick up the phone to text him. I think to myself that nothing bad can come from just letting him know I'm thinking about him. But I never send the text. He asked me not to. I'm not sure if never hitting send is a hopeful or cynical thing to do. I don't know if I'm not talking to him because I believe in this time apart or if I think that a simple text won't matter anyway. I don't know.

I imagined that by the time a few weeks had passed, by the time Thumper and I had gotten into a rhythm with our new life, I would have made a few, some, any observations or realizations. But I don't feel as if I know anything more now than I did before he left.

To be honest, I think I was hoping that Ryan would leave and I'd instantly realize that I couldn't live without him, and he'd realize he couldn't live without me, and we'd come running back to each other, each of us aching to be put back together. I imagined, in my wildest dreams, kissing in the rain. I imagined feeling how it felt when we were nineteen.

But I can see that it's not going to be that easy. Change, at least in my life, is more often than not a slow and steady stream. It's not an avalanche. It's more of a snowball effect. I probably shouldn't pontificate about my life using winter metaphors. I've only seen real snow three times.

All of this is to say that I have to be patient, I guess. And I can be patient. I can wait this out. Four and a half weeks done. Forty-seven and a half to go. Then maybe I will get my moment in the rain. Maybe then my husband will come running back to me, loving me the way he did when we were nineteen years old.

The night of my birthday, Rachel rings my doorbell promptly at six thirty.

"Well," she says, stepping into the house. "Uncle Fletcher is staying on Mom's couch. Grandma Lois apparently refused to crash at Mom's and instead decided she's staying at the Standard."

"The Standard? The one in West Hollywood?" I ask. Rachel nods. The Standard is a very hip hotel on the Sunset Strip. It has clear plastic pods hanging from the ceiling instead of chairs. The pool is packed year-round with twenty-year-olds in expensive bathing suits and more expensive sunglasses. Behind the check-in desk is a large glass case built into the wall where they pay young models to lie there by themselves and have people stare at them. You heard me.

"What on earth is Grandma doing at the Standard?" I ask Rachel.

She can't stop laughing. "Are you going to be ready to go soon?"

"Yeah," I say, heading off to look for my shoes. I call to her from the bedroom. "But seriously, how did she end up there?"

"Apparently, a friend of Grandma's just told her about Priceline," Rachel says.

"Uh-huh," I call to her as I look under my bed for the other sandal I'm missing.

"And she went to the Web site and clicked on an area of the map that looked like it was halfway between us and Mom's." Rachel lives close to me in Miracle Mile, and my mother, once we all moved out of the house and she could downsize, found a place in the hills. Grandma could have easily stayed with any of us. We're always within a twenty-five-minute car ride if you take back roads. And we always take back roads. I'd go so far as to say that finding the most esoteric way to get from one place to another is our family's biggest competition. As in "Oh, you took Laurel Canyon the whole way? It's faster to cut through Mount Olympus."

"OK," I say. I found the sandal! I walk out to the living room.

"And then she said what she was willing to spend."

"Right."

"And she agreed to stay at whatever hotel would be that cheap."

"OK, but the Standard is kind of expensive."

"Well, she must have been willing to pay a lot. Because that's where they put her."

"She was expecting, like, a Hilton or something, right?"

"That is my guess."

I start laughing hard. My grandmother is a fairly hip lady. She knows what's what. But she has the most delightfully curmudgeonly attitude toward things she calls "farcical." The last time I saw her, I told her about how Ryan and I order pizza using an app on our phones, and she said to me, "Sweetheart, that's farcical. Pick up the darn phone."

"She's not gonna like the lady in the glass wall."

"No, she is not," Rachel says, laughing.

"OK, I'm ready. Let's get this over with." I open the front door for Rachel, and then I wave to Thumper as I go.

"Happy Birthday, by the way," Rachel says to me as we head to her car.

"Thank you."

"Did you get my birthday voice mail?" she asks me.

"Yep," I say. "Voice mail, text, e-mail, and Facebook post."

"I'm nothing if not thorough."

"Thank you," I say to her as we get into the car.

It felt good to be bombarded with her happy thoughts all day. I had e-mails from friends. Mila took me out for Thai food. Mom called. Charlie called. It was a good day. But my brain was focused almost exclusively on how Ryan did not call. It shouldn't have been a surprise. It shouldn't still be a surprise. He told me he wasn't going to call. But it's all I can think about. Each time my phone beeps or I get a new e-mail, I hope. Maybe he won't be able to resist. Maybe he'll have to call. Maybe he'll want to hear my voice.

It doesn't feel like a birthday without him. He was supposed to wake me up by saying, "Happy Birthday, Birthday Girl!" like he does every year. He was supposed to take me out to breakfast. He was supposed to send flowers to work. He was supposed to come to my office and take me out to lunch. He used to put so much effort into my birthday. Specifically because he knew I hated birthdays. I don't like the pressure to have fun. I don't like to get older. And so he would distract me all day with special presents and thoughtful ideas. One year, he sent me to work with eight birthday cards so I could read one for every hour I was there.

Ryan should be making me dinner tonight. He is supposed to make me Ryan's Magic Shrimp Pasta, which is, from what I can tell, just shrimp scampi. But it always tastes great. And we only ever have it on my birthday. And he always makes it so that I will look forward to my birthday. Because I get to eat Ryan's Magic Shrimp Pasta.

He was able to take me out of my own head. He was able to make me happier, to change me into a happier person. And where is he now?

It occurs to me, however, briefly, that maybe he's there.

Maybe he's at the party. Maybe everyone knows but me. Maybe he's waiting for me.

Rachel turns on the radio, in effect blaring my own thoughts out of my head. I'm thankful. When we get off the main road, Rachel turns the music down.

"This isn't going to be that bad," she says, when she pulls into my mother's neighborhood.

"No, I know," I say. "It will be sort of like watching bad improv comedy. It's unbearable but entirely nonthreatening."

"Right, and if it's any consolation, everyone is here because they love you."

"Right."

Rachel pulls up in front of my mother's house. She turns the wheels in and yanks the emergency brake. The streets are steep and full of potholes. You have to watch where you park and where you step. I look out my window at my mom's place. My mother couldn't throw a surprise party to save her life. I can already see the shape of Uncle Fletcher's bald head through the living-room curtains.

"All right," I say. "Here goes!"

Rachel and I walk to my mom's front door and ring the doorbell. I guess that's the code. Everyone quiets inside. I don't know how many people are in her house, but it's enough to make a big difference when they quiet down.

I hear my mom come to the door. She opens it and smiles at me. I don't know why I was getting so sentimental in the car. Ryan hasn't made me Ryan's Magic Shrimp Pasta the past two birthdays. We got into a fight about whether the shrimp was fully cooked, and he hasn't made it since.

Rachel and my mother look at me expectantly, and then it happens, louder and more aggressive than I could have ever imagined.

"SURPRISE!"

I was expecting it, and yet it shocks me. There are so many people. It's overwhelming. There are so many eyes on me, so many people staring. And none of them, not one of them, is Ryan.

I start to cry. And somehow, maybe because I know I can't cry, because it will just ruin everything if I cry, I stick my head up, and I smile, and the tears recede. And I say, "Oh, my God! I can't believe this! I feel like the luckiest girl in the whole world!"

• • •

When the fanfare dies down, it gets easier to process. People stop looking at me. They turn toward each other and talk. I go over to the kitchen to get myself a drink. I am expecting perhaps wine and beer, but right in front of me, on the kitchen counter, is a punch bowl.

Charlie comes up behind me. "I spiked it," he says. I turn around to look at him. He looks much the same as when I saw him a few months ago. He's filled out since he was a teenager, grown out instead of up. He appears to have become lax about shaving, and his greasy hair implies he may have become lax about shampooing, too, but his ice-blue eyes shine brightly. It feels so nice to see my brother's face in front of mine. I hug him.

"I'm so glad to see you," I say. "If this weird party had to happen, I'm glad it at least brought you home."

"Yeah," Charlie says. "How are you doing?"

"I'm OK," I say, nodding my head the way I do. It's still uncomfortable to be the one in crisis. Charlie is normally in some sort of dramatic trouble. I'm supposed to listen to his problems. Not the other way around.

"OK," he says. He seems content to let that be it. He may feel just as awkward being supportive as I do feeling supported.

"So how was the flight?" I ask.

Charlie opens the fridge and grabs another beer for himself. He doesn't really look at me directly. "Fine," he says, as he twists off the cap and snaps it directly into the trash. Sometimes I worry that he is too good at flinging bottle caps where he wants them to go. It's something that requires practice, and I worry about how often he practices.

"You're hiding something," I say. I pull the ladle out of the punch bowl and put some punch in a clear plastic cup. I'm pretty sure my mom shopped for this party at Party City.

"No, nothing. The flight was good. Did you see the streamers in the dining room?"

"Are you kidding me?" I say, defeated. "Now I owe Rachel five bucks." I take a sip of the punch. It's strong. It's absolutely dreadful. "Oh, my God, you actually spiked this."

"Of course I did. That's what I told you." Charlie pushes his way through the doors of the kitchen and heads back into the living room. I take another sip, and it burns going down. But for some reason, I keep the drink in my hand, as a line of defense against the litany of questions I'm in for. And then I barge through the doors myself.

It begins.

• • •

"So where is Ryan?" asks my mom's best friend, Tina. I make up something about work.

Then my second cousin Martin chimes in with "How are things with you and Ryan?" I tell him they are fine.

There don't seem to be many of my friends here. No one invited Mila, for instance. It's just my mom's friends and almost our entire family. I spend a half hour deflecting birthday wishes and questions about Ryan's whereabouts as if they are bullets. But I know that Grandma Lois is the real person to fear. She has the most frightening question to ask me. If all of these well-wishers are evil mushrooms and turtles I must jump over and stomp on, Grandma is King Koopa, waiting for me at the end. What I find comforting about this analogy is that Rachel and Charlie are my Luigis. They will have to go through all of this on their own sometime in the future. Maybe they'll do it differently from how I have, but most likely, the end will be the same.

Regardless, I figure I'd better get it all over with, so I go looking for Grandma. When I find her, she is sitting on the sofa by herself. I take an extra big gulp of punch before I sit down next to her. It stings on the way down.

"Hi, Grandma," I say, hugging her. She can barely lift herself off the couch, so I do most of the work. It seems to me, when you get older, your body goes one of two ways: pleasantly plump or spritely skinny. My grandmother went pleasantly plump. Her face is round and gentle. Her eyes still twinkle. If it sounds like I'm describing Santa Claus, that's because there is a bit of a resemblance. Her hair is wild and bright white. Her belly, however, does not shake when she laughs like a bowl full of jelly. And I think that's an important distinction.

I sit down a bit too close to her, and the couch starts to sink in the middle. We're both gravitating toward the center. But it seems rude to move over.

"Honey, move over," Grandma says to me. "You're dragging me down off the couch."

"Oh, sorry, Grandma," I say, as I slide to the middle. "How are you?"

"Well, the cancer's coming back, but other than that, I'm fine." My grandmother always has cancer. I don't actually know what this means. She's never really clear on it. She just says she has cancer, and then, when you ask her about it, she won't pin down what type of cancer or whether she's actually been diagnosed. It started after my grandfather died six years ago. At first, we would get up in arms every time she said it, but now we just let it go. It's a weird family quirk that I don't even notice until there's another witness to it. A few Thanksgivings ago, we invited Ryan's friend Shawn to join us, and as we all got into the car on the way home, Shawn said, "Your grandmother has cancer? Is she OK?" And I realized that it probably seemed absurd to him that she had announced she had cancer again and no one batted an eyelash. I get the distinct feeling she is hoping for cancer so that she can be with my grandfather.

"And things are good at home? With Uncle Fletcher?" I ask.

"Things are fine. I'm boring, Lauren. Stop asking about me. What I want to know is—" Here it comes. The moment I have been dreading. Here it comes. "When are you and that handsome grandson-in-law of mine going to give me a great-grandkid?"

"Well, you know how it is, Gram," I say, sipping the punch to buy myself some time.

"No, honey, I don't know how it is. You're thirty years old. You don't have all day."

"I know," I say.

"I'm not trying to be a pain. I just think, you know, I'm not going to be around forever, and I'd like to meet the bundle of joy before I go."

Whether she has cancer or not, my grandmother is eighty-seven. She may not be around for many more years. It suddenly occurs to me that I am the only way she will ever meet a great-grandchild. Uncle Fletcher doesn't have any kids. Rachel isn't going to have one anytime soon. Charlie? Please. And because my marriage is a colossal failure, because I'm so disconnected from my own husband that I don't even know where he lives, she may never get that chance. Me. I'm the reason she won't meet the next generation. I could give that to her, if only I'd been good at being married, if only I'd succeeded.

"Well," I say, drinking the last of the punch in my cup, "I'll talk to Ryan."

"You know, your grandfather said he wasn't ready for kids."

"Yeah?" I say, relieved that she is talking about anything other than me. "And how did that go?"

"What could he do?" my grandmother says. "It was time to have kids."

"Just that simple, huh?"

"Yep." Grandma pats my knee. "Things are a lot simpler than you kids make them out to be. Even your mother. Sometimes, I swear."

"Mom seems to be doing OK," I say. I look across the room and see her talking to an older gentleman. He's tall and handsome in a silver fox sort of way. He's looking at her as if she has a secret and he wants to know what it is. "That isn't Bill, is it?"

Grandma squints. "I don't have my glasses," she says. "Is it a handsome man?"

"Yeah," I say. "In an older sort of way."

"You mean a younger sort of way," she jokes.

"Yeah," I say. "That's what I meant."

"If he's looking at her like she's a hamburger and he's on a diet, then yes. That's Bill. I met him earlier today, and he kept staring at your mother like they were teenagers."

"Oh," I say. "That's cute!"

Grandma waves me off. "Your mother is almost sixty years old. She's no teenager."

"Do you believe in love, Gram?" Why am I doing this? I'm feeling a bit buzzed, to be honest—that's probably why I'm doing this.

"Of course I do!" she says. "What do you take me for? Some sort of coldhearted monster?"

"No, I just mean . . ." I look at my mother again. She looks really happy. "Isn't that great? How in love they seem?"

"It's farcical," my grandmother says. "She's almost eligible for social security benefits."

"Did you love Grandpa the whole time?" Maybe she didn't. Maybe I'm just like her. Maybe she's just like me. Ending up like my Grandma would not be so bad.

"The whole time," she says. "Every day." OK, so maybe not.

"How?" I ask her.

"What do you mean, how? I had no choice. That's how."

I look up at my mom, a woman I respect and admire. A woman with three kids and no husband but, at fifty-nine, a new boyfriend. My mother is going to have sex tonight. She's going to have the kind of sex that makes you feel like you invented sex. And my grandmother is going to lie in her hotel room, convinced she has cancer, so that she can one day soon be with the man she had no choice but to love, the man who took care of her and stood beside her until the day he died, the man who gave her children and came home every day and kissed her on the cheek.

I don't know where I fit in. I don't know which one of these women I am. Maybe I'm neither. But it would be nice to feel as if I was one of them. That way, I'd have a road map. I'd be able to know what happens next. I'd be able to ask someone what I should do, and they could answer me, truly answer me.

If I'm not one of them, if I'm my own person, my own version of a woman, in my own marriage, then I have to figure it out for myself.

Which I really don't want to do.

• • •

I'm just coming out of the bathroom when I finally see Rachel again.

"You owe me five dollars for the streamers," she says.

"I'm good for it," I say.

"How are you holding up?"

"You mean with the charade?"

"Yeah," she says. "And the rest of it."

I breathe in deeply. "I'm good," I say. I don't know what the actual answer is. I don't think it's that I'm good, though.

"Have you met Bill yet?"

"No." I shake my head "But he seems nice from afar."

"Oh, he's totally nice. And he treats Mom like she's a princess. It's kind of weird. I mean, it's great. But then also you're, like, 'Ew, Mom.' And Mom just eats. It. Up. Ugh, you know how she is, you know? It's like, she just loves the attention."

"Well, you know Mom," I say. "I'm going to get another drink."

Rachel and I head into the kitchen. When we burst through the double doors, we catch my mom and Bill kissing. Bill pulls away, and Mom blushes. I'm nearly positive that his hand was up her shirt. Rachel and I just stand there for a moment as Charlie comes bounding in from the living room and crashes into the back of us. Mom starts fixing her hair. Bill is trying to act normal. It's easy for Charlie to put together what he's just missed. It's entirely PG-13. But it's a mother and her boyfriend being walked in on by three adult children, so it's uncomfortable.

"Hi, kids," my mom says, as if she had been doing the dishes.

Bill puts his hand out to introduce himself to me. "Bill," he says, grabbing my hand and shaking it hard. His eyes are green. His hair is salt-and-pepper gray, although more salt than pepper. He's got one of those megawatt smiles.

"Lauren," I say, making eye contact and smiling, like I've been taught to do.

"I know!" Bill says. "I've heard a lot about you."

"Ditto."

"Rachel, will you help me bring this cheese platter out into the living room?" my mom says.

"Yeah, OK," Rachel says, smiling and taking so much delight in the awkwardness of this that you'd think she'd have brought popcorn. She picks up a tray and heads out with my mother.

"I just came in for a beer," Charlie says, grabbing another one out of the fridge and heading back out. He doesn't even take the time to snap the cap in the trash. He's out of here in two seconds flat. Now it's just Bill and me.

"Happy Birthday," Bill says.

"Oh, thank you very much," I say. Why is this so awkward? I guess I don't usually meet any of my mother's boyfriends. I mean, I know she's had them, but they don't often last long enough to get invited to a birthday party. "So you're a mechanic?" I ask. I don't know what else to ask.

"Oh, no," Bill says. "We met at the mechanic. That's probably where the wires got crossed. No, I'm a financial adviser."

"Oh," I say. "I'm sorry, I didn't realize. That's funny. What a random thing to think you were."

"No problem," Bill says. "I'd love to think of myself as a mechanic. I can't fix a goddamn thing."

"Not a leaky-faucet-fixing kind of guy?"

"I can help with your taxes," he says. "That's the kind of guy I am."

Bill puts his arms behind him on the counter and rests against it. The way he relaxes makes me relax but also makes me realize that he wants to talk to me for a while. He's getting comfortable. This is . . . I think he's trying to get to know me.

"And you work in alumni relations, right? That's what your mom told me."

"Yeah," I say. "I like it a lot."

"What do you like about it?"

"Oh, well, I like interacting with the former students. You meet a lot of people who graduated recently and are looking for guidance from older alumni, and then you also get people who graduated years and years ago and are looking to mentor someone. So that's fun."

"You're inspiring me to call my own alma mater," he says, laughing. "Sounds like you're doing some good work."

I'm going to go out on a limb here and say Bill was married for a long time and my mom is his first, or one of his first, girl-friends since his wife passed away. This is all very new to him.

"So you have kids of your own?" I ask him.

He nods, and his face brightens. "Four boys," he says. "Men, really. Thatcher, Sterling, Campbell, and Baker."

Oh. My. God. Those are some of the worst names I have ever heard. "Oh, great names," I say.

"No," he says. "Their names suck. But they are family names. My wife's family. My late wife, rather. Anyway, they are good kids. My youngest just graduated from Berkeley."

"Oh, that's great," I say. We talk about Rachel and Charlie, and then, predictably, we get to the topic of my mother.

"She's really something," Bill says.

"That she is," I say.

"No, I'm serious. I'm not . . . I'm not well versed in the dat-ing pool. But your mom really gives me hope. She makes me excited again. Is that OK to say? Is that weird that I said that?"

"No," I say, shaking my head. "It's nice to hear. She deserves somebody who feels that way about her."

"Well," he says, "you know what that is, right? From what your mom tells me, you and Ryan are quite the pair."

It's all too much. My mother in love. This man baring his soul to me for no good reason. Ryan not being here. It's all too much. I walk over to the punch bowl and pour myself a cup.

It's almost full, the punch bowl. My mom must keep refilling this thing. Get a grip, Mom. No one likes the punch. I take a sip, instantly remembering how strong and foul it is. I chug the whole thing, forcing it down and putting the cup back on the counter.

Bill looks at me. "You OK?" he says.

"I'm fine, Bill." Everyone needs to stop asking me that question. My answer isn't going to change.

• • •

I've had two more cups of punch by the time the cake comes out. My breath, at this point, seems flammable. As my mother and the rest of my family join around the cake, the candles sending shadows flickering high above, I look around and have this moment where I feel as if I can see very clearly what a shit show my life has become.

I am turning thirty. I am thirty. And I'm celebrating, not with the man I have loved since I was nineteen, but with Uncle Fletcher, who is staring at me from across the table. He just wants the cake. This isn't what thirty is supposed to look like. It's not what thirty is supposed to feel like. By thirty, you're supposed to have things figured out, aren't you? You're not supposed to be questioning everything you've built your life on.

I blow out the candles, and things start to get a bit hazy. My mom starts passing out cake. Uncle Fletcher takes the biggest piece. I accidentally drop mine on the floor, and since no one seems to notice, I just leave it there. It's a terrible thing to do, but I get the feeling that if I bend down, my mind will go all woozy.

Eventually, Rachel comes and finds me. "You don't look so great," she says.

"That's not a pleasant thing to hear," I say.

"No, I'm serious," she says. "You look kinda pale."

"I'm drunk, girl," I say. "This is what drunk looks like."

"What were you drinking?"

"The punch! That deliciously horrendous punch."

"You drank that?"

"Wasn't everyone drinking it?"

"No," Rachel says. "I couldn't get even a sip down. It was nasty. I don't think anyone here was drinking that."

I look around the room and notice for the first time that no one is holding anything other than glasses of water or beer bottles.

"It did seem weird that it was always full," I say.

Rachel calls for Charlie. He strolls over as if it's a favor.

"What did you spike the punch with?" she asks him.

"Why?"

"Because Lauren has been drinking it all night."

"Uh-oh," he says playfully.

"Charlie, what did you put in it?" Rachel's voice is serious now, and at the very least, I can tell she doesn't think this is funny.

"In my defense, I was just trying to liven up what we all knew would be a rather lame party."

"Charlie," Rachel says sternly.

"Everclear," he says. The word hangs there for a little while, and then Charlie asks me, "How much did you drink?"

"Four glasses-ish." It would be a hard word to say if I felt entirely in control of my faculties. As it is, it comes out with a lot more "sh" sounds than I mean for it to.

Both Charlie and Rachel join together, albeit by accident, to say, "Shit."

Charlie follows up. "I honestly thought some people might have a glass or two, tops."

"Dudes, what is Everclear? Why is this a dig beal?" I'm

not entirely sure I said that correctly just now, but also, I'm starting to feel like if I did mess it up, it's funny, and I should keep doing it.

"It's not even legal in every state. That's how strong it is," Rachel says to me. Then, to Charlie, she adds, "Maybe we should take her home."

For once, Charlie doesn't disagree. "Yep." He nods. "Lauren, when was the last time you puked from drinking?"

"From huh?"

"From drinking."

"I have no idea."

"I'm going to tell Mom you aren't feeling well," Rachel says. "Charlie, will you get her into the car?"

"You guys are being such dillyholes." Whoa. Not a word. But should be. "Someone write that down! D-I-L-L-Y—"

Rachel leaves as Charlie takes my arm and directs me toward the door. "I'm really sorry. I swear, I thought people would realize that it was strong and not drink that much. I thought maybe Uncle Fletcher would have a glass or two and start dancing on the table or something. Something fun."

"Dudes, this was totally fun."

"Why do you keep calling me dudes?" Charlie asks.

I look at him and really think about it. And then I shrug. When we get to the front door, my mother and Rachel cut us off.

"Mom, I'm just gonna take her," Rachel says.

But my mother is already feeling my forehead. "You look clammy, sweetheart. You should get some rest." She looks at me a moment longer. "Are you drunk?"

"Yep!" I say. This is hilarious, isn't it? I mean, I'm thirty years old. I can be drunk!

"I spiked the punch," Charlie says. You can tell he feels bad.

"With what?" my mom asks him.

Rachel cuts in. "It was strong, is the point. And Lauren didn't know. And now she's had a bit too much, and I think we should bring her home."

"Charlie, what the fuck?" my mom says. When my mom swears, you know she means business. It's sort of like how you know to be scared of other moms when they use your full name.

"I thought it would be funny," he says. "No one was drinking it."

"Clearly, someone was drinking it."

"I can see that, Mom. I said I was sorry. Can we drop it?"

"Just get her home," my mom says. My mom doesn't really yell. She just gets really disappointed in you. And it's heartbreaking sometimes. I feel bad for Charlie. He tends to get it more than the rest of us. "When will Ryan be home to take care of you?" my mom asks.

Rachel cuts in. "I'll stay with her, Mom. She's just drunk. It's not a big deal."

"But Ryan will be there, right? He can make sure you're on your side, you know? So you don't choke on your own vomit." My mom doesn't really drink that often, and because of that, she thinks everyone who does is Jimi Hendrix.

"Yeah, Mom, he'll be there," Rachel says. "I won't leave until he gets there."

"Well, then, you are going to be there for a loooooooooooong time," I say.

"What?" my mom asks.

Rachel and Charlie try to stop me with "Come on, Lauren," and "Let's go, Lauren."

"No, it's cool, guys. Mom can know."

"Mom can know what?" my mom asks. "Lauren, what is going on?"

"Ryan left. Vamoosed. He lives somewhere else now. Not

sure where. He said not to call him. I got Thumper, though! Woo-hoo!"

"What?" My mother's shoulders slump. Rachel and Charlie shut the front door, dejected. We were almost out of here scot-free.

"He left. We don't live together anymore."

"Why?"

"Mostly because the love died," I say, laughing. I look around, expecting to see everyone else laughing, but no one is laughing.

"Lauren, please tell me you're joking."

"Nopes."

"How long ago was this?"

"A few weeks or so. Coupla weeks. But did you hear the part about how I got Thumper?"

"I think we should take Lauren home," Rachel says, and my mom looks as if she's about to argue with her but then doesn't.

She kisses me on the cheek. "One of you will stay with her?"

Both Charlie and Rachel volunteer. So cute. Cutest little siblings.

"All right," my mom says. "Good night."

They both say good night, and as I'm just out the door, I call to my mom, "I accidentally dropped some cake into the corner over there."

But I don't think she hears me.

Charlie and Rachel put me in the backseat, and I can feel just how tired I've been this whole time. We hit a red light, and I hear Charlie tell Rachel to take Highland to Beverly Boulevard, and then he turns toward me and suggests I get some sleep. I nod and close my eyes for a minute, and then . . .

I wake up to the sound of my doorbell ringing. The world seems cloudy and heavy, as if I can feel the air around me and it's weighing me down. I start to stand up and realize that Rachel is lying in bed next to me. Thumper is in the corner coiled into a ball.

The doorbell rings again, and I hear someone go to open the door. My head feels like a bowling ball balancing on a wet noodle. I wade through my house until I see my brother and my mother standing on either side of my front door. Charlie must have slept on the couch.

"Hey," I say to them. I can feel the sound of my voice pulsating through my head. It vibrates in my eyes and jaw. They both look at me. My mother has a cardboard drink tray of four coffees in her hand. Rachel comes up right behind me.

"Oh, good," my mom says, stepping into the house. Thumper hears her and comes running, too. "You're all up," she says.

She hands Charlie one of the cups. "Americano," she says, and she hands it to him.

He takes it and smiles at her. "Thanks, Mom."

Mom then holds out a cup for Rachel, and Rachel walks up to her. "Skim latte," my mom says.

With two more cups in the tray, my mom takes hers out and rests it on the table by the door and then takes the last one and gestures toward me.

"Double espresso," she says. "I figured you'd need to wake up."

I gently take it from her hands. "Thanks, Mom."

She shuts the door behind her, and the chill in the air ceases a bit. I know that by this afternoon, it will be sweltering and hot, but the September mornings tend to be overcast and a bit chilly. My hands are cold, and the hot cup feels great in my palms.

"No coffee for Thumper, huh?" I say, making a joke, and my mother, what a mother, puts her hand into her purse and pulls out a sandwich bag with bacon in it.

"I had some extra bacon from breakfast," she says. Thumper comes running toward her. My mom crouches down and feeds it to him, rubbing his head and letting him lick her face.

I am overwhelmed with love for my mom right now. She always knows just what to do. When do you learn that in life? When do you learn what to do?

My mom stands back up and looks at Rachel and Charlie. "Why don't you guys go for a walk?" she says.

Charlie starts to decline, but Rachel intercedes. "Yeah," she says. "We'll take Thumper." By the time Rachel grabs the leash, Thumper is so excited that to deny him would be cruel.

Charlie rolls his eyes and then resigns himself to it. "Yeah, all right."

Within moments, they are out the door, the opening and closing of which send a chill back into the house. My mom looks at me the way you'd look at a dying bunny. "I think we need to talk," she says.

"Yeah, OK," I say, and I walk back to my bedroom and get into bed. It's warm there, underneath the blankets. I can see my mother looking at my place and noticing all the things that are gone. She doesn't mention it.

"So," she says, sitting down next to me, pulling the tab of her coffee lid back, and blowing on the steam as it rises. "Tell me what happened."

At first, I try to tell her the facts. When he left. Where

everything went. I tell her about the fight at Dodger Stadium. I tell her about not feeling like I love him anymore. I tell her about the conversation about what to do. I tell her as much as I remember, as much as I can bear to think about.

But she wants more. She wants to know not just the when and the where but the how and the why. I spend so much time not thinking about these things that it's hard to start thinking about them again.

"Why didn't you tell me?" she asks.

"I don't know," I say, directing my gaze to my bedside lamp.

"Yeah, you do," she says. "You know why."

"Why?" I say. She sounds as if she knows the answer.

"No, *I* don't know," she says. "But I know you know."

"It just didn't come up naturally, I guess," I say.

"That would never come up naturally. Were you waiting for me to ask you if you and Ryan were still together? And then you could say, 'Actually, Mom . . .'?"

"I didn't want to disappoint you. I didn't want you to think that I . . . screwed it up, you know? I can fix this. I can fix it. It's not broken. I can still do this."

"Do what?"

"Be married. I can still do it."

"Who says you aren't doing it?"

"Well, I'm not currently doing it. But I can do it."

"I know you can do it, sweetheart," she says. "You, of anyone I know, can do anything you set your mind to."

"No, but, like, I don't want you to think I failed. Yet."

"If your marriage does not work out—" she says, and she stops me from interrupting before I even decide to. "Which it will, I know it will. But if it doesn't, it doesn't mean you failed."

"Mom," I say, my voice starting to crack. "That is exactly what it means."

"There is no failing or winning or losing," she says. "This is life, Lauren. This is love and marriage. If you stay married for a number of years and you have a happy time together and then you decide you don't want to be married anymore and you choose to go be happy with someone else or doing something else, that's not a failure. That's just life. That's just how love is. How is that a failure?"

"Because marriage is about a commitment to something else. It's a commitment to stay together. If you can't stay together, you fail at it."

"Good Lord, you sound like Grandma."

"Well, isn't that the truth of it, though?"

"I don't know," my mom says. "I don't know anything about marriage, obviously. I was only married for a few years, and where is he now?"

Where *is* my father now? Honestly, that's a question I rarely think about. He could have a family in North Dakota, or maybe he's living on a beach in Central America. Or he could be in the phone book. I have no idea. I've never checked. I haven't ever searched for him, because I've never felt as if anything was missing. You only seek answers when you have questions. My family has always felt complete. My mother has been all I've needed. I forget that sometimes. I take for granted her ability to guide me, to guide our family, as its one true leader.

"But the way I see it," she continues, "your love life should bring you love. If it doesn't, no matter how hard you try, if you are honest and fair and good, and you decide it's over and you need to go find love somewhere else, then . . . what more can the world ask of you?"

I think about what she's said. I don't really know what I think, I guess. "I just don't want you to dislike Ryan," I say.

"Honey, I love that boy as if he was my own child. I'm serious about that. I love him. I believe in him. I want him to be happy, just as much as I want you to be happy. And I could never fault anyone for doing anything in the name of their own truth." Sometimes my mom speaks as if she's a guest on *Oprah*. I think it's because she spent twenty years watching guests on *Oprah*. "When you first started dating Ryan, I liked him because I could tell he was a good person. I learned to love him because he always put you first, and he treated you well, and I trusted him to do right by you. I still believe he does what he believes is the right thing for both of you. That doesn't change because you two say you're not in love anymore. That's always been who he is."

"So this isn't the sort of thing where when we get back together, you won't like Ryan anymore?"

My mom laughs and sighs at the same time. "No," she says. "This isn't one of those things. All I care about is that the two of you are happy. If only one of you can be happy, I have to go with blood on this one and choose you. But I want you both to be happy. And I believe you're doing what it takes to be happy. Whether I understand it or would do the same thing in your shoes, or any of that, that doesn't matter. I believe in the two of you."

It's weird how words from the right mouth at the right time can bolster you up and make you strong. They can change your mind. They can cheer you up. I'm glad Charlie spiked the punch. I'm glad I told my mom.

I can hear Charlie and Rachel come back in through the front door, and I assume that means that this conversation is over, but my mom calls out, "Give us another minute, OK?"

I hear Rachel call out, "Yup," from the living room and then start talking to Charlie. Charlie's voice carries louder than any of ours. Our voices might bounce off the walls, but his penetrates through them. I can hear his muffled laughing as I listen to the rest of what my mother has to say.

"Now, the one thing I am going to tell you, Lauren, is that

you cannot hide this, OK? You need to be strong and be you and stop caring what people think and tell the goddamn truth. Be confident and proud of what you and Ryan are trying to do."

"What are we trying to do?" I say. "I don't understand what there is to be proud of."

"You're trying to stay married," she says. "And be happy doing it. I've never accomplished it. So to me, that's brave. To me, you are brave."

It feels weird to hear, because this whole time, I've just been waiting for someone to call me a coward.

"OK," my mom calls out. "You can come in now."

Rachel comes to the door. Charlie is there behind her, and Thumper is at her feet. As I look at them in my house, I realize that it's been a long time since we were all a family, just us. Ryan has been such a part of me that he became a part of this. But maybe it's OK that he's not a part of this right now. It's nice to look at the faces around the room and see . . . my family.

My mom waves her hand to let them know that they are welcome. They all come sit on the bed, Thumper pushing his way into the middle, trying to get the attention of all of us.

"Everything OK?" Rachel says.

"Everything is good," I say, and that seems to work as enough of a segue to get the conversation away from my marital troubles and toward other things, like what Charlie is going to do with his life. (He has no idea.) If Rachel is dating anyone (Whom would she be dating?) and whether Thumper may need another dose of flea medication. (Yes.) Charlie's flight leaves tonight, and I think it's making my mother sentimental.

"Can we do dinner at my house tonight?" she asks. "As a family?"

"My flight leaves at ten," Charlie says.

"We can take you," I tell him, referring to Rachel and myself. "We will just leave Mom's around eight."

"I could serve dinner around six?" she offers.

"Serve dinner?" Rachel asks. "Like, you're gonna make our dinner?"

My mom frowns at her. "Why do you kids act like I've never made a meal?"

The three of us look at one another and start laughing. As much as we are all a family, we are also three siblings with a mother. Sometimes it is three against one.

"I have made dinner before, you know," my mother continues, ignoring our laughter. "You'll see. I'll make something great."

I appear to be the one feeling the most charitable. "OK, Mom. You got it. We'll be there at six. Ready to eat a home-cooked meal."

"Oh, you kids have made me so happy! I can't even tell you. All three of you at my house for Sunday dinner." She gets up off the bed. "Grandma and Fletcher are leaving in a few hours, so I should go have lunch with them. Then I'll go grocery shopping. Not sure what I'm going to make," she says. "But this is going to be great." She nods to herself. "Just great."

She gathers her things and says good-bye to all of us. I walk her out to her car to thank her for talking to me earlier.

"Honey, you do not need to thank me," she says, getting into the front seat of her SUV. "I have three grown children. To be honest, it's a relief to be needed."

I laugh and hug her through the car window. I didn't even realize I needed her until she just said it. How stupid is that? "We'll see you tonight," I say.

"Six o'clock!" she calls out as she pulls out of the driveway.

I nod and wave. I watch her drive away. I watch as her car, so big and fast, is eventually so far away that it looks small and slow.

Dinner is burnt, but I don't think my mom actually realizes it. Despite the charred chicken and lumpy potatoes, all of the elements seem to click. No one really mentions Ryan. We make fun of Rachel. We ask about Bill. Charlie seems happy to be there. No one acknowledges how terrible the cooking is. To be honest, I don't think any of us really care.

Mom made too much food. Or maybe we just couldn't stand to eat very much of it. Either way, there are plenty of leftovers. By the time we have taken in all the dishes and put all the extras into Tupperware containers, it is time to head out.

"Well, who wants to take the chicken? Charlie? Will you eat it on the plane?"

"You want me to bring half a roasted bird carcass on a plane?"

Mom frowns at him and hands the chicken to Rachel. "You'll eat it, right?"

"Sure," she says. "Thanks, Mom." Then she looks at Charlie and shakes her head. My mom pawns the green beans and carrots off on me and then thrusts the container of sweet potatoes at Charlie.

"You can take the potatoes, at least," my mom says, but Charlie isn't having it. He won't relent. That's part of what I've never understood about him, or what he's never understood about life. Sometimes you should just take the potatoes and say thank you and then throw them in the trash when Mom's not looking.

We say our good-byes and then head out on the road. Rachel has agreed to drive, because I'm still hungover from last night. I feel as if it will be days until I'm OK to operate heavy machinery. Charlie grabs the front seat, so I sit in the back.

I hate driving to the airport. LAX is a nightmare, but it's more than that. The route is such an unattractive view of Los Angeles. You don't see beaches and sunsets. You don't see palm trees and bright lights. You see strip malls and parking garages.

So I don't bother looking out the window and instead close my eyes and listen as Charlie and Rachel debate whether to take the freeway or La Cienega Boulevard. Rachel wins because she's driving and because she's right. The freeway will be clear at this time of night.

When we get to the terminal, Rachel turns left into the parking garage.

"Why are you parking the car? Just drop me off," Charlie says. It doesn't make a lot of sense, but our family doesn't really drop people off. We pay the money to park the car. We walk across the lanes of traffic. We see you off at the security checkpoint. I'm not sure why.

"Stop, Charlie," Rachel says. "We're walking you in."

Charlie rolls his eyes and starts to bitch about it and then stops himself. "OK," he says. "All right." So maybe he has learned to take the potatoes sometimes.

We park and walk out. Truth be told, we don't have much to talk about. But when Charlie checks in and walks to the gate, when it's time to say good-bye, I'm suddenly sad to see my little brother go. He's ornery, and he's kind of a jerk. He doesn't say the things you should say to people. He spikes punch with Everclear. But he's a good guy, with a kind heart. And he's my little brother.

"I'm going to miss you," I say to him as I hug him.

"Me, too," he says. "And I'm proud of you, or whatever. You know, for what it's worth."

I don't press him on it, the way I want to. I don't sit him down and say, *What makes you say that? What do you really think of what I'm doing? Do you think I can fix this? Do you think Ryan will come back to me? Is my life over?* I just say, "Thanks."

Rachel hugs him, too, and then he takes off, up the escalator and back home to Chicago, where people have seasons and cold air. I've never understood it. People come from all over the country to experience our sunny winters and mild summers. Charlie got out as soon as he could, looking for snow and rain.

As Rachel and I are walking back to the car, we get lost and end up on the floor below at Arrivals. It occurs to me that Arrivals is a much nicer place to be than Departures. Departures is good-bye. Arrivals is hello.

I happen to look toward the revolving doors. I see dads coming home to their families. I see men and women in business suits finding their drivers. I see a young woman, probably a college student, run toward the young man waiting for her. I see her wrap her arms around him. I see him kiss her on the lips. I see, on their faces, that feeling I once knew so well. I see relief. I see joy. I see that look people get when the thing they have been dreaming of is finally in front of them, able to be touched with the tips of their fingers and the length of their arms. I think I stare for a second too long, because she turns to look at me. I smile shyly and look away. I think of when it was me, when I was the one waiting at Arrivals for that one person I ached for. Now I'm the lady looking.

For a moment, I think that if I saw him right now, if Ryan were here, I'd have the same look on my face as this couple has. I want him in my arms that badly. But how long would it last? How long before he said something that pissed me off?

When Rachel and I finally get headed in the right direction, we walk out onto the street level and wade our way through people hailing cabs and hopping into their friends' cars. We are standing at the crosswalk, waiting to cross the street, when I see two people waiting for a shuttle. As quickly as I would recognize my own face in the mirror, I know what I am looking at. There is absolutely no doubt in my mind that I am looking at the back of Ryan's head.

It doesn't even register as weird at first; my brain simply processes it as a normal, everyday occurrence. Oh, here is that person who's always around. Here he is. Except this time, he is holding the hand of a slim, tall brunette. And now he's bending down to kiss her.

My heart drops. My jaw drops. Rachel starts crossing the street, but I just stand there, frozen. Rachel turns around to see me there, and her eyes catch mine. She follows my gaze, and she sees it, too. Ryan. Ryan at Arrivals. Ryan. At Arrivals. Kissing a woman. My heart starts beating so fast that I almost feel I can hear it. Is it possible to hear blood pulsing through you? Does it sound like a quiet, violent gong?

Rachel grabs my hand and doesn't say anything. She is determined to get me out of this situation. She wants me to cross the street. She wants me to get into the car. But we have missed the walk signal, and we can't just run through this steady stream of cars, as much as, right now, that feels like the only thing to do.

It's good that she's holding me. I fear that I lack the self-control not to go over there and knock him down. I want to pummel him to the ground and ask him why he would do this. Ask him how he looks at himself in the mirror. I swear to

God, it's as if I can physically feel the pain. It's a physical pain. And it's searing through me. And then the light turns, and the white walk sign is on, and I put one foot in front of the other, and I move forward, and I think of nothing but how much this hurts and which foot goes where. When we get to the other side of the street, when the walk sign turns into a red hand, I turn around and look at him. We are now separated by a sea of speeding cars.

When my eyes find him again, when they fixate on the front of his face, I can plainly see that I was wrong. It's not him. It's not Ryan.

I can spot Ryan in a crowd. I can recognize his scent from another room. Just a few months ago, we were separated at the grocery store, and I found him by recognizing his sneeze from a few aisles away. But at this airport, this time, I got it wrong. It's not Ryan. All of that fear and jealousy and hurt and pain so sharp I thought it could cut me—it wasn't real. It was entirely imaginary. It's stunning, really, what I can do to myself with only a misunderstanding.

"It wasn't him," I say to Rachel.

She slows down and looks. "Wait, are you serious?" she says, squinting. "Oh, my God, you're right."

"It wasn't him," I say, stunned. My pulse slows, my heart relaxes. And yet I am still overstimulated and jumpy. I slow down my breathing.

Rachel puts her hand on her chest. "Oh, thank God," she says. "I did not want to have to talk you down from that."

We get into the car. I put on my seat belt. I roll down the window. *It's OK*, I tell myself. *It didn't happen.*

But it will someday.

He's going to kiss someone else, if he hasn't already. He's going to touch her. He's going to want her in a way that he no longer wants me. He's going to tell her things he never told me. He's going to lie there next to her, feeling satisfied and happy. She's going to remind him of how good it can feel to be with a woman. And while all of this is happening, he's not going to be thinking about me at all. And there's not a thing I can do to stop it.

Over the course of the next few days, it is all I can think about. I am seething with jealously over something that I have no evidence of. It consumes me to the point where I can't sleep night after night. By Friday, I can't keep all this angst to myself. I ask Mila's advice.

"Do you think he's already slept with someone?" I ask her when we're getting tea from the office kitchen.

"How should I know?"

"I just mean, do you think that he has?"

"Why don't we talk about this at lunch?" Mila says, looking around the kitchen in the hopes that no one is listening.

"Yeah, OK," I say.

Mila and I go out for Chinese food, and she brings it up. It takes her about four minutes. Which is four minutes longer than I wanted to wait, but I didn't want to seem like a crazy person.

"Do you want the truth?" she says.

I'm not clear on how to answer, because it's entirely possible that I want to be lied to.

"Yes," she says. "I think he probably has."

It's a knife in my chest. I've never been the jealous type with Ryan. It was always so clear that he wanted no one but me. For so much of our relationship, it was obvious that he loved me and desired me. I never felt threatened by any woman. He was mine. And now I've set him free.

"Why?" I say. "Why do you think that?"

"Well, first of all, he's a man. That's the biggest piece of evidence. Second of all, you said yourself you two were not having all that much sex. So it's probably been pent up inside of him. He probably slept with the first woman who looked at him the right way."

I take a long sip of my soda. It becomes a gulp and then sort of a chug. I put my cup down. "Do you think it's with someone prettier than me?"

"How on earth would I know that?" Mila says. "You have to stop torturing yourself. Accept that it has probably happened. The stress of questioning whether it has or has not happened is too much. You have to just assume that it has happened and start to deal with it. He slept with someone else. What are you going to do?"

"Die, mostly," I say. Why does this feel so awful? Why does it feel so much more awful than when he left? Deciding to separate was hard. Actually separating was hard. But this? This is something entirely different. This is devastating. This is . . . I don't know. It feels as if I will never feel better in my entire life.

Mila grabs my hand. "You're not going to die. You are going to live! That is the point here. C'mon! You were not happy with him. Let's not sugarcoat the past. You were deeply unhappy. You said yourself that you didn't love him. You two are going your separate ways. If anything, this should just show you that it's time for you to find your own way."

"What does that mean, though?" I say. Isn't that what I've been doing?

Mila puts down her fork and clasps her hands, getting down to business. "What are you doing this weekend?" she asks me pointedly. "Do you have plans for tonight?"

"Well, I got a new book from the library," I say. Mila makes a face but doesn't interrupt me. "And then I heard LACMA is free tomorrow, so I thought maybe I'd check that out. Haven't been in a while." I made that last part up. I have absolutely no plans to go to LACMA. I haven't gone to an art museum since college. Probably not going to start now. I just didn't want to admit that I have no plans at all.

"Uh-huh." Mila is not impressed.

"What?" I say.

"That sounds pretty close to what I'm going to do, except instead of LACMA, I'm going to take Brendan and Jackson to get their hair cut."

"OK . . . ?" I say.

"I'm in a committed relationship with twins, and you're single."

Single? No. I am not single. "I am not single," I say. "I'm . . . married but . . ."

"Estranged?"

"Oh, that's an awful word." I don't know why it's such an awful word. There's just something about how all the vowels and consonants come together that I don't care for.

"You're single, Lauren. You live alone. You have no one who expects you to be anywhere at any given time."

"Well, Rachel sometimes . . ." I don't even finish the sentence. "Fine, I'm single," I say. "What is the point?"

"Get out of the house! Go get drunk and screw someone you don't know."

"Oh, my God!" I don't know why I find it so shocking. I guess it's that she's talking about me. Me! I mean, I know that is what people do. They go out to bars, and they meet strangers, and they have casual sex with them after a few dates or no dates or however many dates they feel they need to justify what they want to do. I get that. But I have never done that. I never really had the opportunity. And now, I guess, I do have the opportunity, but it feels as if I've missed the starting line for that sort of thing; that race took off without me. I gather myself and look at Mila, but her face doesn't change.

"I'm serious," she says. "You need to get out there. You need a love affair or something. You need to get laid. By someone who isn't Ryan. You need to see what it's like with someone else. Have you even ever slept with someone besides Ryan?"

"Yeah," I say, somewhat defensively. "I had a boyfriend in high school."

"That's it?"

"Yes!" I say, now definitely defensive. "What is the big deal?"

"It just isn't enough people."

"It is!" I say.

Mila shakes her head and puts down her fork. She tries another approach. "Do you remember what it was like the first time you kissed Ryan?"

"Yeah," I say, and within a second, I feel as if I'm back there. I'm leaning across the table, over my burger and fries. I'm kissing him. And then I remember how it felt when he kissed me back. When he kissed me on the way home. When he kissed me good-bye. Even after kissing became a thing we did like breathing, without thinking, without care, I held on to those first kisses. I relished the way my heart stopped for a second whenever our lips met.

"Remember how good it felt to be kissed for the first time? How it felt electric? Like you could power a whole house off your fingertips?"

"You've really thought about this."

"I just love the beginnings of relationships," Mila says wistfully. "The first time Christina kissed me . . . nothing compares to that. Now I kiss her, and it's like, 'Hey, how are you? What smells? Is it the trash?'"

We both start laughing.

"Anyway, I can't help but be excited for you, knowing that you have the chance to have that feeling again. You can meet someone and feel those butterflies again, if you want to."

"No, I can't," I say. "I have a husband to go back to."

"Yeah, in ten and a half months. Some marriages don't even *last* ten and a half months. You can have a love affair, Lauren. One that makes you feel like you did when you were nineteen. If it were me, that's what I would be doing."

I let this settle for a minute as I think about it. It does sound nice, in a lot of ways, and it also sounds terrifying and messy. How can I have a love affair when I'm married? How can I juggle those two huge relationships? An active romance and an inactive marriage?

"Do you think Ryan is having a love affair?" I ask Mila.

Mila loses her patience. "That's what you're taking from this?"

"No," I say. "I get your point. I do. I'm just . . . if he was . . . what would that mean?"

"It would mean absolutely nothing."

"Nothing?"

"Nothing. Did you love your high school boyfriend?"

I shrug. "Yeah, I did."

"Do you give a shit about him now?"

"No," I say, shaking my head.

"Well, that's a love affair for you."

• • •

Despite Mila's advice, I continue to obsess. I think about it on the drive home. I think about it as I'm feeding Thumper. I think about it while I'm watching TV, while I'm reading a book, while I'm brushing my teeth. It drives me mad. My brain replays the same imagined images over and over. It falls down a rabbit hole of *what if*s. I just want to know what is going on in his life. I just want to hear his voice. I just want to know that he's OK and he's still mine. I can't have lost him yet. He can't be someone else's yet. I can't do this. I can't live like this. I can't live without him. I can't. I have to know what he's thinking. I have to know how he is.

I want to call him. I have to call him. I have to. I pick up the phone. I push the icon next to his name, and then I immediately hang up. It didn't even get a chance to ring. I can't call him. He doesn't want me to call him. He said not to call him. I can't call him.

My laptop is right in front of me. It's easy to grab. When I open it up, I'm not sure what I'm looking for. I'm not sure what I'm doing. And then, opening the browser, I know exactly what I'm doing. I know exactly what I'm looking for. I don't bother trying to hide it from myself. I have gone into the deep end. I have lost control.

I sign into Ryan's e-mail.

His in-box loads, and it's empty. I stop myself. This is wrong. It's incredibly, very, super, really, totally, completely, and absolutely wrong. I move my cursor to the menu, and I hover over where it says "Sign out." This is where I should click. This is what I should do. I can turn around. I can pretend I never did this. I don't have to be this person. For a second, it feels so easy. It seems so clear. *Just log out, Lauren. Just log out.*

But before I click it occurs to me that he never changed his password. He could have, right? It would make sense if he had. But he hasn't. Does that mean something?

I notice the number seven by his drafts folder. He has seven unsent e-mails. I don't even think, really, it's just an impulse. I drag the cursor down and click the folder open. There I see seven e-mail drafts, all addressed to me. All with the subject "Dear Lauren."

They are addressed to me. They are for me. I can click on these. Right?

· · ·

August 31

Dear Lauren,

Leaving the house today sucked. I don't know why we did
this. When I wrote you that letter, it took everything I had not
to rip it up and sit down and just stay there until you came
home and we could sort this all out.

But then I thought about the last time you were happy to see
me when I got home, and I couldn't remember when that
was. And thinking about that made me so mad that I picked
up the last of my things and I walked out the door.

I didn't say good-bye to Thumper. I couldn't do it. It makes
me sick to think about sleeping in this stupid apartment
tonight. I don't have a bed yet. I don't have much of anything
yet except our TV. My friends have helped me put everything
where it sort of belongs, and they left about an hour ago.

I'm miserable. I'm fucking miserable about this. I was
glad when my friends left, because I didn't have it in me to
pretend to be OK anymore. I'm not OK. I feel sick. I've lost my
wife and my dog. I've lost my home.

I don't know. I don't know why I'm writing this. I don't even
know if I'm going to send it. Part of me thinks that you and
I have been so dishonest with each other lately that a little
honesty, a little discourse, might improve things. I have spent
so long saying, "Sure, I'll go to the mall with you to pick out
new lipstick," when I didn't want to. Saying, "Yeah, Greek
food sounds great," when it doesn't, that I hate you for it now.
I hate Greek food, OK? I hate it. I hate how we can never just

get a hamburger anymore. Why does every dinner have to
be a tour of the world? And if so, why can't we just stick with
Italian and Chinese?

Ah. See? This is why I know that it's good that I left. I hate you
for liking falafel. I don't think that's healthy.

But also, I don't know that it's so unhealthy that it means I
have to sleep alone tonight on this shitty carpet.

But then I think about going home. I think about walking
through the door and you not even getting up off the couch.
I think about how you'll just look at me and say, "Pho for
dinner?" and I want to punch the wall.

So, fine. I'm here. I'm alone. I'm miserable. And I know
it makes me a terrible person, but I really hope you're
miserable, too. That's the truth. That's how I feel right now. I
really, really hope that you're miserable, too.

Love,
Ryan

• • •

September 5

Dear Lauren,

I know I told you not to call me, but sometimes I can't believe
you aren't calling me. I can't believe you're able to just live
your life like I was never there. How can you do that? It
makes me furious to think about sometimes. You're probably
just going to work and acting like everything is fine.

I told my parents about us today. It wasn't easy. They were not happy. They got really mad at you, which I thought was weird. I tried to explain to them that this isn't about one or the other of us. I tried to tell them that it was a joint decision. But they weren't listening. I think, you know how they are, they have such a narrow view of marriage. And they are disappointed in me. They made that clear. They kept saying, "This is not how you should be handling your problems, Ryan." And they kept saying they were upset at you for taking my house and my dog. They can't see clearly, I don't think. They think we should split it up so that one of us gets Thumper and the other one gets the house. Neither of us should get both. I don't know. I don't agree with them. I don't see it that way. It doesn't feel right to take the house from you, and it doesn't feel right to take Thumper away from his home so abruptly.

I know I said that I wanted to date other people, but now that I'm out in the real world, it feels really strange to think about. Very unnatural. How is that even supposed to work? It doesn't make sense. To think about kissing someone other than you? I almost feel like I don't remember how to do it. There is a new girl at work who keeps flirting with me, and sometimes I think that I'm supposed to jump on it, go for it or whatever. I don't know. I don't even want to talk about it.

I'm still not sure if I'm going to send these to you. Sometimes I think I will. There is a part of me that feels like years ago I stopped fighting with you. It just became easier to agree with you or ignore you. I feel like I just said whatever you wanted to hear. And I stopped being honest. I stopped telling you what I really thought. What I really wanted. And so maybe if I tell you all of this now, maybe we can clear the air, maybe we can start again. The other part of me thinks that if we do tell each other everything, if I send you this stuff, we might not survive it. So I don't know what I'm going to do.

I'm not sure you'd care, anyway. I mean, sometimes I think you don't really see me anymore. I know you see me, see me. But I'm talking about the fact that sometimes I don't think you listen when I say things. Sometimes I think you just assume you know what I'm going to say next, or what I'm going to do next, or what I'm going to feel next, and your eyes glaze over as if I'm the most boring person you've ever met.

You didn't use to think that, though. I remember in college, one of the reasons it was so nice to be around you was that you made me feel like I was the most interesting person in the room. You made me feel like I made the funniest jokes and told the best stories. And I don't know, I don't think that was fake. I think you really thought that.

And now I don't think you think that at all. I think I'm like looking at the back of a cereal box for you. I'm just something you sit and stare at because I'm there.

This is getting sad. I hope you are doing OK. Sometimes I think I should send you these just so you might write back and I can hear how you are. I wonder how you are all the time.

Love,
Ryan

• • •

September 9

Dear Lauren,

Do you remember when we moved in with each other for the first time? Right after we graduated from college? And it was such a hot day, and we moved into the shithole apartment in Hollywood, and it was way too small, and the kitchen smelled like some sort of weird chemical? And you almost started crying because you didn't want to live in such a crappy apartment? But it was all we could afford. I was living off of the last of my parents' graduation gift money, and you were starting your job in the alumni department. And I remember thinking, as we crammed into that small bed that first night, that I was going to take care of you. I was going to work hard and get you a better apartment. And I was going to be the man who gave you the life you wanted. And I mean, things don't really work out exactly how you think. You were the one who made enough money so that we could afford to move out of that place and into Hancock Park. But I mean, I negotiated with the landlord. I did everything I could to convince her, because I wanted you to have everything you wanted. I really did think I did a good job of taking care of you. I always wanted you to feel safe with me, to feel loved by me, supported by me.

I learned how to stop trying to solve your problems and just let you vent about them. I learned that you need a few minutes in the morning before you can talk to somebody. I learned that you never leave yourself enough time to get somewhere and then you freak out about being late. And I loved it about you.

Why wasn't that enough?

Doesn't it seem like it should have been enough?

Back then, moving in together, lying in that tiny bed, I just
thought that my job was clear. All I had to do was support you
and love you and listen to you and take care of you. And it all
seemed so easy back then.

Now it seems like the hardest thing in the world.

What am I doing sitting here writing to you? I'm wasting my
time.

Ryan

• • •

September 28

Dear Lauren,

The last time we had sex was in April. Just in case you were
wondering. Which you're not. But you never seemed to care
very much, and I do care. So if I ever do send these to you,
I think you should know that the last time we had sex was
almost five months before I moved out. That's four months
before you told me you didn't love me anymore. Four months
of us living in the same house, pretending to be good to
each other, pretending to be happy, and not laying a hand on
each other. I figured I'd wait until you noticed. And you never
noticed. So, you know, in case you ever notice and you want
to know. It was April. And it sucked.

• • •

September 29

Dear Lauren,

Happy Birthday! I know that you're at a surprise party.
Charlie called me a few weeks ago before he knew we were
whatever we are. Anyway, I know your family is with you. I
know you're probably having a blast. It's nine o'clock right
now, so you're probably living it up as I type this. I'm hanging
out here at my apartment. There is only so much you can do
to distract yourself from the fact that it's your wife's thirtieth
birthday and you're not with her. You know?

I gave up on that about a half hour ago, and now I've just
been nursing a beer and thinking about you.

I almost got up off the couch and drove over to your mom's
place to be there.

But I figured that was a bad idea.

Because what happens? We see each other and we admit
how hard this is and we end this crazy experiment, and then
what? In two months, we're back where we were. We haven't
changed. So nothing would change. You know?

So instead, I'm sitting here, doing nothing.

I just want you to know that I thought about it. I thought
about showing up at the house with two grocery bags, ready
to make you Ryan's Magic Shrimp Pasta.

I didn't do it, but yeah, I guess I just want you to know that I thought about it.

Happy Birthday,
Ryan

• • •

October 1

Is Thumper doing OK? It's killing me being away from him. It's so stupid, but I was in the grocery store the other day getting dinner for myself, and I remembered that I needed laundry detergent, so I went into the aisle to get it, and it was also where they kept the pet food, and I thought, "Oh, do we need food for Thumper?" and, you know, it just flashed into my mind for a split second before I remembered that I don't live with him anymore.

Love,
Ryan

• • •

October 9

Dear Lauren,

I'm not going to take Thumper. This pain of living without both of you, it's too hard. It's too lonely. It's too sad. I can't do that to you.

Love,
Ryan

• • •

I can't see through my tears anymore. Looking at these is sort of like standing in a burning-hot shower and seeing how long I can bear it. I'm way past the point of worrying about whether this is wrong. I know it's wrong. I know he isn't sure whether he wants me to see these. But I also know that I have to read them. They matter too much. I care too much. It's too much.

These letters are the evidence of how ugly our marriage has become and yet proof that we are tied to each other. We can hate and love, miss and loathe each other all within the same breath. We can never want to see each other again while never wanting to let go.

He hates me as much as he loves me. I hate these letters as much as I love them. The pain and the joy are locked together, tightly bound. I read the letters over and over again, hoping to separate one from the other, hoping to discern whether love or hate wins out in the end. But it's like pulling on the ends of a finger trap. The more I try, the tighter they cling to each other.

When I finally get hold of myself, eyes dry, nose running, light-headed, I go into the kitchen and pull a piece of bacon out of the fridge. I put it in a pan. I wait for it to sizzle and pop. When it does, I put it in Thumper's bowl. He comes running as he hears the sound of the bacon hitting the stainless steel. He eats it within half a second. I pull out another piece and put it in the pan as he waits. That's when I really put the pieces together. If Ryan sends me that e-mail about me keeping Thumper, then I won't see him in a few weeks. I really will be on my own for the foreseeable future.

On a scale of one to ten, how bad is it to log into someone's e-mail without them knowing?" I ask Rachel over the phone. I'm sitting at my desk at work. I've read the e-mails tens of times. Some parts I even know by heart.

"I guess I'd need to know the particulars," she says.

"The particulars are that I logged into Ryan's e-mail and read some of his e-mails."

"Ten. That is a ten out of ten. You should not have done that."

"In my defense, they were addressed to me."

"Did he send them to you?"

"They were in his drafts folder."

"Still ten. That's really bad."

"Wow, you're not even going to try to see my side of it?"

"Lauren, it's really bad. It's dishonest. It's rude. It's disrespectful. It completely undermines—"

"OK, OK," I say. "I get it."

I know what I've done is wrong. I guess I'm not really wondering if it's wrong. I know it's wrong. What I'm looking for is for Rachel to say something like, *Oh, yeah, that's wrong, but I would have done the same thing, and you should keep doing it.*

"So I should not keep doing it?" I ask her. Maybe if I go about this directly, I can get the answer I'm looking for.

"No, you absolutely should not."

"Oh, for fuck's sake!" I say. I should not have done it. But what can I do? I already did it. And does it really matter if I keep doing it? I mean, it's already done. If he asks, *Have you logged into my e-mail account and read my personal e-mails that were addressed to you?* I will have to answer yes whether I did it once or one hundred times.

"Let's say he addresses another one to me, though," I say. "Then it's OK to look."

"It's not OK to be checking in the first place," Rachel says. "I have to get back to work," she adds. "But you better cut it out."

"Ugh, fine." It's quiet for a moment before I ask my final question. "You're not judging me, right? You still think I'm a good person?"

"I think you're the best person," she says. "But I'm not going to tell you what you're doing isn't wrong. It's just not my style."

"Yeah, fine," I say, and I hang up the phone.

I walk over to Mila's desk.

"On a scale of one to ten, how bad is it to log into someone's e-mail without them knowing?"

She looks up from her computer and frowns at me. She picks up her coffee cup and crosses her arms.

"Is the person you? And the other person Ryan?"

"If it was . . ." I say.

She considers it. "I can see where you'd think I was the person to help you justify this, because really, I would probably read them if I were in your position," she says, swiveling back and forth in her chair. A victory! "But that doesn't mean it's OK." Short-lived.

"He's writing to *me*, Mila. He's writing *to* me."

"Did he send them to you?"

"WHY IS EVERYONE SO PREOCCUPIED WITH THAT?"

Everyone turns and looks in my direction. I switch to a whisper.

"The letters are *for* me, Mila," I say. "He didn't even change his password. That's basically like he's admitting he wants me to read them." I'm now too close to her face, and my whisper is breathy. I'm pretty sure she can tell I had an onion bagel for breakfast.

Mila politely backs away a bit. "You don't have to whisper. Just don't shout. A normal tone of voice is fine," she says in an exemplary normal tone of voice.

"Fine," I say, a bit too loudly, and then I find my rhythm again. "Fine. All I'm asking is that if you were me and you knew that he was writing to you, baring his soul to you, saying the things that he never said when you were married, saying things that broke your heart and made you cry and made you feel loved all at the same time—if that was happening, are you telling me you wouldn't read them?"

Mila considers it. Her face turns from stoic to reluctant understanding. "It would be tempting," she says. I already feel better just hearing that. "It would be hard not to read them. And you have a halfway decent point about the password."

I pump my fists in the air. "Yes!" I say.

"But just because something is understandable doesn't mean it's the right thing to do."

"I miss him," I say to Mila. It just comes out of my mouth.

Mila's resolve fades. "If it was you writing the letters, would you want him to read them even if you didn't send them?"

My gut answer is yes. But I take my time and really think about it. I stand and look at Mila and consider her question. I put myself in Ryan's shoes. The answer that keeps coming back is yes.

"Yes," I say. "I know that answer seems self-serving, but I really mean it. He said in his letters that he feels like he often didn't tell me how he really felt. That he kept a lot of stuff inside just to make things easier, and then he started to resent me. I did that, too! I would sometimes choose to just go along with what he wanted or what he said so that I didn't cause a fight. And somewhere along the way, I started to feel like I couldn't be honest. Does that make sense? Things became so tense, and I started to resent him so much that I was suddenly furious about everything, and I didn't know where to start. I think he feels the same way. This could be an opportunity for us. This could be what we need. If it were me writing to him, trying to bare my soul, trying to show the real me, I would want him to read it." I shrug. "I would want him to see the real me."

Mila listens, and when I'm done, she smiles at me. "Well, then, maybe it is the right thing for the two of you," she says. "But you're taking a huge risk. You need to know that. This *could* be exactly what he wants. He may be happy to know that you can understand him better and that you know the deepest parts of his soul and you accept him for that. That might be what he's hoping for." From her tone, I can tell that she's not done, but I wish that was the end of the sentence. "But he also might be furious." Here we go. "He might be livid that you betrayed his trust. He might not trust you again. It could be a terrible way to start off this new chapter in your lives together. When the year is over and he comes back, how can you tell him all that you know? Are you going to admit what you did? And do you really, truly, in your heart, feel like he is going to say, 'OK, sounds good'?"

"No," I say. "But I do think that more good will come from it than bad."

Mila looks unconvinced.

"I feel like I have an opportunity to learn who my husband is in a whole new way. I have an opportunity to get to know him without a filter. I can learn what I did wrong. I can start to understand what he needs from me. What I can do better the next time around. I'm going to learn how to love him again. I'm going to learn how to be a better wife to him, how to give him what he needs, how to tell him what I need. This is good. I have good intentions. This is coming from a good place."

I set out to convince Mila. I just wanted someone to tell me that it was OK to do something I knew wasn't OK. But in doing so, I've convinced myself somehow.

"Well, I wash my hands of it, then," she says. "It sounds like you know what you're doing."

I nod and head back to my office. I have no idea what I'm doing.

Mila calls to me just as I'm almost out of earshot. "Mexican?" she says.

I look at the clock. It's twelve forty-seven. "Give me five minutes."

When we get into the elevator to head downstairs, I ask Mila if she likes Persian food.

"Yeah, it's all right."

"Greek food?"

She shrugs. "It's OK."

"Vietnamese?"

"Don't think I've ever had it. Is it like Thai?"

"Sort of," I say. "It's like pho, which is a soup. Or banh mi. Sometimes stuff is served with a fish sauce."

"Fish sauce? A sauce made of fish or a sauce for fish?"

"No, it's made of fermented fish. It's delicious."

"I don't know. I really want Mexican," she says as we get off the elevator.

I nod my head. It's that simple. Why didn't Ryan ever just say, *I really want Mexican.* Why sit through all of those foods he didn't like? I would have gone out for a burrito instead. I wouldn't have even minded. Why didn't he know that?

"You know," Mila says. She's walking a bit ahead of me

and trying to find her keys in her purse. "If you think Ryan will be happy with you reading his e-mails and spying on his most vulnerable moments, then it's only fair that you subject yourself to the same."

"What do you mean?"

"What scares you? What do you want?"

"I don't know. I guess I—"

"Don't tell me," she says. "Put it in an e-mail."

That night, I check his e-mail drafts one more time before going to bed.

• • •

October 15

Dear Lauren,

It's sex. Honestly, it's sex. It's the one thing that, I think, I couldn't tolerate being broken and the one thing that just completely broke down. That's what this is all about for me. I think I could have had more patience with you in other areas if you'd just been a little bit more interested in actually having sex. I think I could have been more thoughtful toward you. I think I could have been happier to spend time with you. I think I could have been better at listening to you. If I hadn't been so pissed at you for never, ever, EVER WANTING TO HAVE SEX.

What the fuck? It's not even that difficult, Lauren. I wasn't asking you to become some sort of sex queen. It just would have been nice to have sex twice a week. Twice a month? It would have been nice to have you initiate it maybe once a year.

It always felt like you were doing me a favor. As if I was asking you to do the dishes.

And I don't know why I never screamed at you about it.
Because I screamed at you in my head. Sometimes I'd get so
pissed off after you said "Not tonight" for the twentieth night
in a row that I would go and take a cold shower and scream
at you in my mind. I would actually have a full-on fight with
you in my head, anticipating the things you would say and
screaming my responses to myself. And then I'd towel off
and get into bed next to you and never say any of it out loud.
You would just sit there with your fucking book in your hand,
acting like everything was fine.

Why didn't I just tell you that nothing was fine?

I can't be a husband to you if you treat me like a friend.

I need to HAVE SEX, LAUREN. I NEED TO HAVE SEX WITH MY
WIFE FROM TIME TO TIME. I NEED TO FEEL LIKE SHE LIKES
HAVING SEX WITH ME.

I can't spend months of the year masturbating quietly in the
bathroom because you "aren't up to it tonight."

Ryan

• • •

I want to scream at him. I want to tell him that if he wanted
me to like having sex with him, then he probably should
have tried a bit harder to make it good for me. I want to tell
him that it's a two-way street. That he wasn't the only one
who was going to bed unsatisfied. I want to tell him that the
only difference between him and me was that at least I gave
him an orgasm every couple of months. But then there's
another, huge, big, aching part of me that wants to say, *Come*

home, come home. We can fix everything now that I know this.

I get into bed and try to get some sleep. I toss and turn. I stare are the ceiling, but sometime in the night, my brain finally shuts down, and I fall asleep.

When I wake up, I have so much I am dying to say.

• • •

October 16

Dear Ryan,

Here are some things I think you should know:

The couch no longer smells faintly of sweat, because no one goes running and then doesn't take a shower before they lie on it.

I have really been enjoying the act of throwing away my receipts. I no longer have to account for every single penny that goes in and out of the bank account. Sometimes I go to the store, realize I forgot my coupon, and then just buy the thing anyway. Why? Because fuck you. That's why.

I tip twenty percent every time. Every. Time. I no longer care that you think eighteen is standard.

I am really looking forward to an entire Dodgers season going by without a single trip to the clusterfuck that is Dodger Stadium.

Do you understand how a broom works?

I have always hated eating at that stupid Chinese restaurant

on Beverly Boulevard that you love so much. It's not that
good.

That joke you tell about the nuns washing their hands at the
Pearly Gates is totally gross, not funny at all, and fucking
embarrassing.

Men who have beards are supposed to trim them. You can't
just let it grow and think it looks nice. It takes upkeep.

And speaking of hair, you need to learn to trim your pubic
hair. I don't know how much clearer I could possibly make
this. Apparently, buying you a beard trimmer and saying,
"Ha ha ha, I think this also works on pubes," was not clear
enough.

If you're looking for reasons why our sex life was an
unmitigated disaster, maybe you should consider the fact
that you haven't put in a modicum of effort since, I don't
know, senior year of college. Do you even understand how
women experience pleasure? Because it's not through
relentless, rhythm-less pounding.

I stop typing and look at what I've written. I want so badly
to delete those last parts. It's all so embarrassing and uncomfortable. What if he really read this? What if he really
saw it?

I delete it. I have to delete it. I can't say that stuff.

But then I remember that I told Mila that I want to be honest. I told her that the reason I thought I should read Ryan's
e-mails was that I needed to hear his honesty. I needed him to
be unfiltered. How can I justify reading his honest thoughts if
I delete my own?

So I press control-Z. It reappears on the screen.

It has to stay there. I have to do this right. He's probably not ever going to read this. So really, I'm typing to myself. Maybe that's the problem; maybe I'm nervous to admit some of this stuff, even to myself.

That's why I have to do it.

I hit save and get redirected to my in-box. Where I now see I have one new e-mail.

From Ryan. He actually sent me an e-mail. He pressed send on one of them.

• • •

October 16

Dear Lauren,

I'm not going to take Thumper. I think it's best he stay there.

Take care,
Ryan

Before I can take a breath, hit the reply button, and type "Fine," I think better of it. I type "OK." I hit send.

So that's it, then. The training wheels are off. I have no firm plans to see my husband again. I probably won't see him for almost a year.

I stand up. I get into the shower. I get dressed. I feed Thumper. I go to work. I go through the motions of my day. When I get home, before I feed Thumper or take my shoes off, I sign in to his e-mail again.

There's a new draft I haven't read before.

• • •

October 16

Dear Lauren,

I've met someone.

Ryan

The sound that comes out of my mouth, it's not a cry or a sob.

It's not a scream, either.

It's a whimper.

I print it out. I go into the hallway closet. I get the step stool. I go to the bedroom closet. I grab the shoebox. I open it and put the letter in.

I let the paper sit there in the box of memories. It sits on top of the ticket stub from when we took the train to San Diego and spent the weekend lying on the beach. It sits on top of the photo of us at the Crab Shack in Long Beach, where we went with my family for his twenty-third birthday. It sits on top of Thumper's first collar, the bright pink one we bought him on the way home because Ryan said he refused to "cater to gender norms for dogs, and this one is on sale." It sits on top of the dried flower petals from my wedding bouquet.

It sits on top of all of that. Because I can't pretend this isn't happening anymore. I can't pretend this isn't part of our story.

I take off my wedding ring and put it in the box. It is, for now, better kept with the other mementos.

After that, Ryan stops writing to me altogether.

For a week or two, I check his drafts folder every day, hoping to see something. But he never writes.

Halloween comes, and I buy a big variety pack of candy for trick-or-treaters, but when I get home, I find myself wondering if Ryan and his mystery girl are dressing up together, doing a couple's costume. I distract myself by turning my front light out and eating the candy myself. I give the nonchocolate ones to Thumper.

After a few weeks of sulking, I resolve to just check his e-mail every once in a while. I take up hobbies to distract me. Thumper and I start going for hikes in Runyon Canyon. We walk up the mountain until we can barely move, until we think we can't go one more step, and then we keep going. We never let the mountain win.

After a while, Rachel starts coming with us. She also encourages me to start running. So I do. I run every other day. As the weeks go by, the temperature starts to get cold in Los Angeles, so I buy a tight-fitting fleece. My shins start to hurt, so I buy proper shoes. I push myself farther and farther down the street. I run longer. I run faster. I run until one day, my face looks thinner and my stomach feels tighter. And then I keep running. It quiets the voices in my head. It calms my nerves. It forces me to think of no one, nothing, but the sound of my breath, the banging of my heart inside my chest, and the fact that I must keep going.

Eventually, I don't check Ryan's e-mail at all.

part three

THAT'S THE WAY LOVE GOES

It's a Sunday morning in late November, and even though it was only sixty degrees yesterday, it is eighty-five today.

"This weather makes no sense to me," Mila says. "Not that I'm complaining. I'm just saying that it makes no sense to me."

Christina is watching the kids. Mila's only request for the morning was, "I don't care where we go. Just get me away from children and moms." So I figured the Rose Bowl flea market would be fun. She seemed to be in a pretty bad mood when I picked her up, but she perked up once we got on the road. Now that we're here, she seems much more like herself. The only issue is that neither of us is really shopping for anything in particular, so we are just aimlessly wandering through the aisles.

A booth of dream catchers draws Mila in, and she starts looking. "What do dream catchers even do?" she asks.

"I'm going to avoid the obvious answer of 'catch dreams,'" I say.

"Yeah, but what does that actually mean? Catch dreams?"

"No idea," I say. I don't want to talk loudly enough that the booth owner hears us and insists on giving us a ten-minute lesson. I made this mistake once with a guy selling antique chamber pots. As I see the owner coming over, I aim to change the subject by saying, "Let's change the subject."

Mila walks away from the dream catchers and heads further in. "OK," she says. "How about we discuss me setting you up on a blind date?" She turns to me and makes an overly excited face, as if her abundance of excitement about this idea might sway me at all.

"That's a no. That's actually an 'absolutely not,'" I say.

"Oh, stop," she says. "You need to meet somebody! Have a good time!"

Do I think it would be nice to meet somebody? Sure, yeah. Sometimes I do. But a blind date? No. "It's just not my style."

"What *is* your style? Meeting people in study hall?"

I open my mouth wide to indicate that I am insulted. "It was the *dining* hall, for your information."

"Look, you haven't been in the dating world for a long time, so I think it's important that you understand that people don't meet people standing in line at the pharmacy or when they go to reach for the same magazine at the bookstore."

"Then how do they meet them?"

"Blind dates!" she says. "Well, also online, but you're not ready for that. It's all about blind dates."

That's absurd. Obviously, people meet people other ways. Although the truth is, I don't really know how anybody meets anybody outside of college. And I don't know that I want to find out just yet. "I'm just not sure if I'm ready," I say. I head toward a booth selling silver jewelry and start trying on rings.

"Suit yourself," she says. "Christina says he's cute, though."

"You have someone in mind already? What, do the two of you sit at home snuggled up in your matching pajamas talking about my sad life?"

Mila joins me at the ring booth. "First of all, we have never worn matching pajamas. We're lesbians, not twins," she says. "And second of all, no, we do not snuggle and talk about your sad life. We do, however, sometimes get bored and try to meddle where we don't belong. I see it as a public service."

"A public service?"

"You think you're the first person I set up on a blind date?

My sister and her husband? Me. Christina's boss and her boy-friend? Me."

"Didn't you also set up Samuel in admissions with Saman-tha in the housing office?"

Mila waves it off. "That one was a mistake. I thought the Sam/Sam thing was adorable, and it clouded my vision. But Christina says this guy is really cute. He's recently divorced. Mid-thirties. Eighth-grade social studies teacher, so you know he's probably a sweetheart."

"I don't know," I say. "It sounds complicated. I'm not look-ing for anything serious. I don't know. I just . . . I don't think so."

"OK," she says, falsely resigned. "I'll just have Christina tell him it's a no go."

I put down the ring I was looking at. "She already talked to him?"

"Yeah," Mila says, shrugging. "It's a shame, too, because he was excited about it. She showed him your picture, and he said you were beautiful."

I look up at her, skeptical. "You're not making this up?"

She puts her hand up as if swearing an oath. "Hand to God."

I smile at her, despite myself.

Mila smiles back at me. She got further than she thought she would.

I walk past her to the booth next to us. It's a man selling hats. Half of them are Dodgers caps. It's enough to make me wonder where my husband is at this very moment. He stopped writing me long ago. I have no idea what his life is like. He could be in bed with a blond woman. He could be making her breakfast. He could be in love. He could be hav-ing sex with her this very minute. That man who stood on the steps of Vernal Fall and told me he couldn't live without me . . . I wonder what he's doing right now, living without me.

"You OK?" Mila asks me, when she finally gets my attention. "You look distracted."

"Yeah," I say. "I'm fine." It's not the full truth, exactly. But it's much less of a lie than it used to be.

After work on Monday, I'm at the Farmers Market at the Grove when my phone starts to ring. I put down the gourmet jam I'm looking at and dig into my purse to try to find my phone.

It's Charlie.

"Hey," I say.

"Hey, do you have a minute?"

I walk away from the stand and find a place to sit. "I've got nothing but time," I say. I say this to be kind, but also, I actually have nothing but time. Being single leaves you a lot of time to spare. "What's up?"

"I'm going to come home for Christmas," he says.

"That's great! We are all going to Mom's, and I think there is talk of Bill joining us. And Grandma is coming. Not sure about Uncle Fletcher, but I would assume so. So it will be nice to have it with—"

Charlie cuts me off. "Listen, I need your help with something."

"OK . . ."

"I have some news to tell everyone, and I'm not sure how to do it. And so I was wondering what you thought first."

"OK," I say. This is a novel feeling, Charlie caring what I think. But I'm also cautiously terrified. If Charlie is seeking out my advice, if he doesn't think he can handle it himself, then this has got to be big, right? It's got to be bad.

"You're sitting down? Or I mean, you have time to talk?"

"Oh, my God, Charlie, what is it?"

He breathes in, and then he says it. "I'm going to be a dad."

"You're going to see Dad?" How does he even know where Dad is? Did Dad call him?

"No, Lauren. I'm having a baby. I'm going to *be* a dad."

There are people walking past me, shoppers haggling over tomatoes and avocados, kids calling for their mothers. There are cars whizzing by in the distance. Butchers selling various cuts of meat to women on their way home from work. But I can't hear any of that. I just hear my own breathing. All I can hear is my own deafening silence. What do I say? I decide to go with, "OK, and how do you feel about that?"

Charlie's voice starts to brighten. "I think it's great, honestly. I think it's the best news I've gotten in my entire life."

"You do?"

"Yeah. I'm twenty-five years old. I have a job I don't care about. I live across the country from my family. My friends are . . . whatever. But what am I doing? What have I done that's so great? I keep moving from place to place, thinking I'm going on these adventures, and nothing ever comes of it. And then I happen to meet Natalie, and two months later, I get a call saying that I'm . . . This is good. I really think this is good. I can be a father to someone."

This is surreal. "And how is it going to work with this Natalie person?" I'm sticking to logistical questions, because I'm out of my league, emotionally.

"Well, that's part of what makes this complicated but possibly really fortuitous."

"OK," I say.

"Natalie lives in L.A., so . . . I'm moving home."

Whoa. My mom is going to have a grandchild to play with. My grandmother will have a great-grandchild. Charlie solved the problem. He took the pressure off of me. It's not up to me anymore. That's good, right? "Wow, this is a lot to take in!" I say.

"I know. But here is the thing. She's an amazing woman. And I really think she is someone I can try to make it work with. She's smart, and she's funny. We have a great time together."

"How did you two meet?

"We met on an airplane," he says. "And we . . . hooked up. And I didn't think anything of it. So, you know, that part is a hard sell."

"An airplane?" I say, but I'm putting the pieces together faster than I can talk. My brother slept with a woman he met on the plane when he came home for my birthday. That's what we're talking about. "Ew, Charlie!" I say, laughing. "Was it, like, *on* the airplane?"

"In an attempt to protect the dignity of myself and my child's mother, I decline to answer." So yes, it was.

"Holy crap," I say, marveling at just how sudden and insane this all is. "So you are moving in with someone named Natalie. And you two are having a baby."

"Yep. We've been talking every night after work, calling each other, e-mailing. I really like her. We get along very well. We have the same ideas so far about how we want to handle this."

"That's great," I say. "When is she due?"

"End of June."

"Well, Charlie," I say, "congratulations!" Admittedly, there is a part of me that feels leapfrogged, passed over, rendered irrelevant.

Charlie sounds relieved. "Thank you. I'm pretty scared to tell Mom."

"No," I say. I can feel myself shaking my head. "Don't be. You sound happy. And Natalie sounds great. And this is, like, the best news Mom could hope for. You're moving home, and she gets a grandchild. I'm telling you, she's gonna be so happy."

"You think so? I feel like most moms probably don't want to hear their sons say, 'So I knocked up this girl.'"

"Right, it will be a shock, for sure. But that's also not what you're saying. You have a plan. You feel good about it. If you feel good about it, she's going to feel good about it. Have you told Rachel?"

"No," he says. "I just wanted to get your take on whether I should call now or do it in person at Christmas. I feel like Rachel can be a bit judgmental about these things. She's kind of defensive about being single. It's been so long since she even dated anyone, you know? I want to be sensitive to that."

"So you figured you'd call your almost-divorced sister," I say, teasing him.

He laughs. "Oh, come on, you and Ryan will be fine. You said so yourself. I'm not worried about you," Charlie says. "If anything, I called you because you're the one who always knows what to do."

In a time when I feel as if my whole life is in shambles, when I feel as if the last thing I know is *what to do*, it swells my heart to think that my little brother might look up to me. But if I tell him any of that, if I let on how much it means to me, I'll lose it right here in the Farmers Market. So instead, I keep a lid on it. "I think your instincts are right to do it in person," I say. "If you're coming home for Christmas, maybe just give Mom the heads-up and tell her that you're going to bring a friend or something? I'm assuming you'll be staying with Natalie?"

"Yeah," Charlie says. "So I guess I should maybe let Mom know I won't be staying with her, that I'll be staying with someone else. That will trigger her suspicions that something is up, but I'll just keep it under wraps until I see her. Better to tell her in person, you're right."

"Yes, exactly," I say. "And don't worry. She really will be happy."

"Thank you," Charlie says, and for the first time, I feel the usual edge to his voice is gone.

"I'm so curious," I say. "So you meet her, and you, you know, wherever you, you know. And how does she track you down? When she finds out she's pregnant and she knows it's yours, how does she find you all the way in Chicago?"

"I gave her my number," Charlie says, as if the answer is perfectly obvious.

"You gave your number to a woman you barely know, who you had sex with once on an airplane?"

"I always give my number to one-night stands," Charlie says. "Condoms are only ninety-eight-percent effective."

And that, right there, is my little brother. He somehow manages to be just as thoughtful as he is cynical. And now he's going to be someone's dad.

And I'm going to be someone's aunt.

"Hey, Charlie?" I say.

"Yeah?"

"You're gonna be a great dad."

Charlie laughs. "You think so?"

I don't actually have any idea. I have no evidence whatsoever. I just choose to believe in him. And for a second, I understand why everyone thinks my marriage will be OK. They don't have any evidence. They just choose to believe in me.

Mila comes into the office the next morning with blood-shot eyes and a deep-seated frown.

"Whoa, are you OK?" I ask her.

"I'm fine," she says, putting her keys down on her desk and taking her purse off her shoulder. It drops with a thud.

"You're sure you're good?"

She looks up at me. "Do you want to go grab coffee?" she asks. Ours isn't the sort of office where people often just leave to go get coffee the minute they come in, but I doubt anyone will really notice.

"Sure," I say. "Let me get my wallet."

Mila puts her purse back on her shoulder as I run to my desk and grab my bag. We are quiet until we hit the elevator bank. I press the down button, the elevator *ding*s, and luckily, there is no one on it.

"I didn't sleep last night," she says, as the doors close.

"At all?"

"Nope. And I got about four hours the night before but only about two the night before that." Her posture is that of a defeated woman. She's got her arm propped on her hip, as if it's supporting her.

"Why?"

We unexpectedly stop on the fourth floor. A woman in a black skirt suit steps in and presses the button for the second floor. It's clear we were talking. It's also clear that we are now not going to talk because she's in here. It's an uncomfortable fifteen-second flight for all of us. When the elevator finally stops again, the woman steps out, the doors slowly close, and in perfect synchronicity, our conversation continues.

"Because Christina and I have been fighting all hours of the night lately," she says.

"Fighting about what?"

Ding.

We are on the first floor, making our way through the lobby, heading toward the coffee stand. Mila and I never come here, because we don't like weak coffee and stale bagels. But sometimes you need to go get coffee more than you actually need coffee. And this is one of those times.

"We fight about everything. You name it! The kids, who should feed the dog, if we should be looking for a bigger place, when the right time to buy a house is, whether or not we should have sex."

"Do you guys have sex a lot?" I ask. I think, on some level, I'm looking for empirical evidence that I am normal. That all couples have trouble with sex. Maybe they don't have sex that often, either. "Is it sort of a problem with you two?"

"No, we have plenty of sex," she says. "That's rarely the issue. It's more like should we when the kids are awake?"

So there goes that theory. The cheese stands alone.

She steps up to the coffee stand. "Hazelnut latte, please," Mila says to the man running the place.

"Ma'am, I'm sorry, we are out of milk," he says to her. He said he was sorry, but he doesn't seem the slightest bit concerned.

"You're out of milk?"

"Yes, ma'am."

"So you just have black coffee?"

"And sugar," he adds.

This is what happens when people will buy your coffee regardless of the quality. If your location is good enough, you don't even have to have anything to sell.

"OK," she says. "Regular coffee, black. You want anything?" she asks, gesturing to me.

I wave my hand to say no. The man hands Mila a cup of coffee and charges her two bucks.

"So you guys are just fighting about a lot of stuff?" I ask, getting us back on track. Mila sits down on a bench in the lobby, and I sit down next to her.

"Yeah, and then, when we're done fighting, one of the twins gets up, and I can't go back to sleep."

"Jesus," I say. "What do you think is going on?"

"With the fighting?"

"Yeah."

Mila looks despondent. "I don't know. I honestly don't know. We didn't used to fight that often. A squabble here or there, you know? None of this scream-until-you-see-the-sunrise crap."

"Has anything happened that might have put you two on edge?"

She shrugs, sipping her coffee cautiously. "Raising kids is hard. Taking care of a family is hard. And I think sometimes it gets to one or the other of us. Right now, it's getting to both of us at the same time. Which is not good."

Her purse beeps, and she fishes through it to find her cell phone. I'm assuming it's a text from Christina, because her face grows furious.

"I swear to God," she says, shaking her head, "I'm going to kill her. I am going to *kill* her."

"What did she do?"

She shows me the text message. It just says, "Can't pick up Brendan and Jackson from day care. You do it?" It seems relatively harmless, and yet I know there is a context that turns that text into an infuriating betrayal. I can imagine when you add up the sleepless nights and the unkind words, the history, and the resentments, that simple text might be enough to break the camel's back.

"What are you gonna do?" I ask.

Mila breathes in deeply, takes a sip of coffee, and stands up. "I'm going to get over it," she says. "That's what I'm going to do. I'm going to drink about five of these," she says, gesturing to the coffee, "to get me to five o'clock, then I'm gonna pick up my kids, I'm going to find a way to be nice to my partner, and I'm going to go to bed. That's what I'm going to do."

I nod. "Sounds like a plan."

We head back toward the elevators, and as we do, I wonder why I couldn't do that. Why couldn't I find the answer in five cups of coffee and being nice when I got home? I don't know. I don't know that I'll ever know. Maybe part of it is that I'm not Mila. Maybe part of it is that Ryan's not Christina. Maybe part of it is that we don't have kids. Maybe if we had kids, we would have fought through this all differently. I don't know why Ryan and I are different. I just know that it's OK that we are.

Because I don't want to go home tonight and work hard at being nice to somebody. I just don't feel like it right now. I like that I get to go home and do whatever I want. I get to watch what I want on TV. I get to take a really long shower. I get to order Venezuelan food. Thumper and I will get into bed around midnight, and we will sleep soundly, a luxurious amount of room between us in our bed.

And I think if you like your evening plans, you're not allowed to regret what led you to them. I think that should be a rule.

When Mila and I get into the elevator, she thanks me for listening. "I feel better. Much better. I just needed to vent, I think. How are you? Let's talk about you."

I laugh. "Nothing much to report," I say. "Things are fine."

"That's good," she says.

It's quiet, and I try to fill the silence. "You can do it," I say. "You can set me up on that date."

I don't know why I say it. I guess I'm trying to make her feel better.

Mila pushes the stop button on the elevator, and it halts, forcing me to push off of the wall for balance.

"Are you just doing this to make me feel better?" she asks me.

"No," I say. "I just . . . I think it's time I had some fun." I guess that's true. I do think it might be kind of fun. Sort of.

She smiles wide. "Oh, this is going to be great!"

Mila hits the button again, and we start to ascend.

"I'm proud of you," she says.

"You are?" I ask her, as the doors open and we start walking.

"Yeah," she says. "This is a big step for you."

It is? Ah. I guess it is. I think I should have thought about this more.

A few hours later, she comes into my office with a smile on her face and more coffee in her hand. "Can you do Saturday night?"

"This Saturday night?" I thought this was some far-off idea. I did not think we were talking Saturday night.

"Yeah."

"Um . . ." I say. "Sure. Yeah. I guess I can do Saturday."

"I'll give him your number," Mila says, and then she comes over to my desk and takes over my computer. "Do you want to see a picture of him?"

"Oh, yeah, totally," I say, remembering that I'm supposed to be attracted to this person.

She pulls up a photo.

He's handsome. Light brown hair, square jaw, glasses. In

the photo, he's planting a tree with some kids. He has on a T-shirt and jeans, with gardening gloves and a huge shovel in his hand.

I look at the picture. I really consider it. I could kiss him, I think. You know, maybe. Maybe he is a person I could kiss.

I spend my Saturday morning cuddled in bed with Thumper. We watch a lot of reality television, and then I read magazines until noon.

I start to call Rachel to tell her that I've agreed to a blind date tonight, but as I dial her, my phone starts ringing at the same time. The dialing and ringing all at once knock me for a loop, and I manage to hang up on everyone after somehow leaving a voice mail of myself going, "Uh, what? Wait, Ah!" for Rachel.

Just as I go to check my missed calls to see who called, it rings again, and I answer. "Hello?"

"Lauren?"

"Yeah."

"Hi, it's David."

I'm nervous. The good kind. I remember this kind. It doesn't feel exactly like butterflies in your stomach. It's more like hummingbirds in your chest. Either image, though, taken literally, is entirely frightening. "Oh, hey, David," I say, "How are you?"

His voice is friendly and calming. It's a nice voice. "I'm good, you?"

"Yeah, I'm good."

It's quiet for a moment, and my mind races through options of things to say, but ultimately, I come up empty. *Someone say something.*

"I was thinking maybe seven o'clock? There's a great Greek place on Larchmont if you like Greek. I mean . . ." He starts to stumble. He sounds kind of nervous. "I mean, some people don't like Greek. Which is fine."

This might be easier than I thought.

"Greek sounds great. Were you thinking of Le Petit Greek?" When it comes to Greek food, I know what's where.

"Yes!" he says, excited. "Have you been there?"

I used to make Ryan take me there when I wanted moussaka. I should have noticed he only ever ordered the steak. He doesn't even really like steak.

"I have, yeah," I say. "I love it. Great choice."

"OK, so seven o'clock," David says. "You'll know it's me because I'll be wearing a red rose on my lapel."

"Nice," I say. I'm not sure if he's joking, so I don't want to laugh at him.

"That was a joke," he says. His tone is eager to clarify. "Maybe I should do something like that, though. I'll wear a black shirt. Or . . . yeah, a black shirt." He might be more nervous about it than I am.

"Cool," I say. "You have yourself a date." I immediately find myself embarrassed for hitting the nail too closely on the head. It's embarrassing, right? To call a date a date?

"OK," David says. "Looking forward to it."

I hang up and put the phone on the table. I look at Thumper, who is now sitting under the table at my feet. I have to duck underneath the table to see him, to really look him in the eye.

"It's not weird that he didn't offer to pick me up, is it?" I ask Thumper. He cocks his head slightly. "It's just, like, the way people do things, right?"

I take his yawn as a yes.

My phone rings again and startles me. Rachel.

"What the hell did you leave on my voice mail?" she asks me, laughing.

"I got confused."

"Clearly."

"I have a date tonight," I tell her.

"A date?" she says. "Like, with a man?"

"No, it's with a panda bear. I'm really excited."

"You think you're ready for that? With a man, I mean? I understand you're not actually dating a panda bear."

I sigh. "I don't know. I mean, Ryan's dating someone."

"If Ryan jumped off a cliff, would you?"

Is it bad that there was a time in my life when I might have considered saying yes to that? I'm inclined to think it's beautiful that I once believed in someone that much, that completely, and without reservation.

David has parsley in his teeth, and I'm not sure how to tell him.

"Anyway, so I took a job teaching social studies to eighth-graders in East L.A., and I thought it would be for a year or two, but I just really like it," he says. He laughs at himself a bit, and it's really charming. It is. But he has parsley on his front tooth. And it's a big piece. It's not so much that I mind. I mean, parsley is not the measure of a person. It's just that I know he's going to go to the bathroom at some point, and he's going to look in the mirror, and he's going to see it. And he's going to come back out and say, "Why didn't you tell me there was a huge piece of parsley in my teeth?" And I'm going to have to sit here and shrug like an idiot.

"You have a—" I start, but he accidentally speaks over me.

"I mean, in college, I was convinced I would graduate with my political science degree and next stop, the Senate! But, you know, life had other plans," he says. "What about you?"

"Kind of the same thing," I say. "I work in the alumni department at Occidental."

"That sounds like it could be fun."

"Yeah," I say. "It's a good job. Same as what you're talking about. It's not what I set out to do. I was a psych major. I just assumed I'd be a psychologist, but I found this, and I don't know, I really like it. I find myself getting really excited when we are putting together the newsletters, planning reunions, that sort of thing."

David takes a sip of his white wine, and when he does, the parsley manages to wash away.

"Isn't it nice," he says, "once you've outgrown the ideas of what life should be and you just enjoy what it is?"

Of all the things people have said to me about my marriage, none has resonated like this does. And he's not even talking about my marriage.

I lift my glass to toast.

"Here's to that," I say. David *clink*s his wineglass to mine and smiles at me. You know what? Without the parsley there to distract you, it's quite a smile. It's bright white and streamlined. His face is handsome in a conventional way, all cheekbones and angles. He's not so attractive that you'd stop traffic to look at him. But neither am I. He's just a humbly good-looking guy. Like, if he were the new doctor in a small town in the Midwest, all the local women would schedule an appointment. He's that kind of attractive. His glasses sit comfortably on his nose, as if they have earned the right to be there.

"So what kind of stuff are you into?" David asks me. "I mean, when you're not at work, what are you doing?"

"Uh . . ." I say, unsure of how to answer the question. I read books. I watch television. I play with my dog. Is that the stuff he means? It doesn't seem very interesting. "Well, I just recently started hiking and running. I like taking my dog out in the sun. I always feel good about myself when he gets tired before I do. It's rare, but it does happen. I guess, other than that, I hang out with my family, and I read a lot."

"What do you read?" He takes a bite of his salmon as he listens to me.

"Fiction, mostly. I'm getting into thrillers lately. Detective stories," I say. The truth is, I've stopped reading anything with a love story in it. It's much less depressing to read about murder. "What about you?"

"Oh, nonfiction, mostly," he says. "I stick to the facts."

It's quiet for a moment. Admittedly, it is hard to keep up a conversation with a stranger and pretend he is not as much of a stranger as he is. I try to come up with something to say. I talked to him about his job already. What do I ask?

"Sorry," he says. "This is my first date in a very long time. I'm sorry if it's awkward."

"Oh!" I say. "Me, too. First time on a date in a while. I have no idea what I'm doing."

"I haven't dated anyone since Ashley," he says, and then confirms what I already have deduced. "My ex-wife. Christina keeps trying to set me up with people. But I never . . . this is the first time I've agreed to it."

I laugh. "Mila was really pushing it."

"So I take it you are also a victim of the institution?" he says, smiling. "Divorced?"

"Well," I say, "I'm separated. My husband and I. We're separated."

"Well, I'm sorry to hear that," David says.

"No, me, too," I say. "About yours."

David laughs to himself. "Well, we never separated. I found her sleeping with one of her coworkers. I filed for divorce as fast as I could."

"That's awful," I say, putting my hand to my chest. I've known David for, like, an hour. But I can't believe someone would do that to him.

"You don't even know the half of it," he says. "But I won't get into that. I told myself, 'Don't talk about Ashley at dinner.'"

I laugh knowingly. "Oh, trust me. Same here. I'm relearning how to talk to people since Ryan left. Honestly, this is my first date since I was nineteen. I have a whole list of things I've told myself not to do."

"Let me guess. Don't talk about your ex. Don't talk about

how lost you feel being alone again. Don't talk about how weird and awkward it is to sit across the table from someone *other* than your ex."

I add a few myself. "Don't eat off his plate, just because you're used to being able to do that. Don't admit you haven't been on a date in eleven years."

David laughs. "We're doing better with some than with others." He tips his wineglass toward me, and I reciprocate. Our glasses *clink*, and we drink.

We laugh our way through dinner. We order more wine than we should. As buzzed becomes tipsy, the filter of what to say and not say starts to wash away. We tell each other the things we don't tell other people.

He tells me he wakes up sometimes thinking he should just take her back. I tell him Ryan is dating someone else and that when I think about it, I think my heart might implode. I tell him I'm not sure I ever had much of a life outside of Ryan. He nods knowingly and tells me that in his darkest hours, he wishes he never caught her. That he just never found out. That he could live his whole life being the guy who didn't know that his wife was cheating. He tells me he liked life better then. I tell him I'm starting to wonder who I even am without Ryan. I tell him I'm not sure I ever knew.

It's the first time I've told someone the uglier truths about how much it hurts. It's the first time someone has been able to tell me they hurt, too. It is comforting when you share your pain with someone, and they say, "I can't even begin to understand how difficult that must be." But it is better when they can say, "I understand completely."

When dinner ends, he walks me to my car. We walk down Larchmont Boulevard past the closed shops and cafés, all decorated with wreaths and lights in preparation for Christmas next week. It would be a romantic moment if we hadn't spilled our guts to each other, exposing our wounds and washing away all mystery. When we get to my car, David kisses me on the cheek and smiles at me.

"Something tells me we've friend-zoned each other," he says.

I laugh. "I think so," I say. "But a friend is a good thing to have."

"It's too bad we're so clearly not ready," he says, laughing. "You're a beautiful woman."

I blush, and yet I am relieved. I'm not ready to go on a date that ends with passion. I'm just not ready. I grab David's hand. "Thank you," I say, opening my car door and getting into the front seat. "Keep my number, will you? Feel free to call me when no one else gets it."

He smiles that nice smile. "Ditto," he says.

Charlie calls me the night before he's supposed to get into town.

"It's all set, I guess. Mom knows I'm staying with someone else. That went over like a lead balloon."

"She'll be fine, trust me."

"Yeah, and Natalie is a little nervous."

"Oh, yeah, I would be, too. It's a scary thing." Am I nervous? To meet her? I think I kind of am.

"I told her, though, everyone loves pregnant ladies. Especially ones carrying my kid."

My kid. My little brother just said "my kid." It still doesn't entirely make sense to me. But it is happening. I need to remember that. Just because it's been a secret and I haven't had anyone to talk to about it doesn't mean that it's not real. It's real, and it's about to become realer.

"OK, so you'll just meet us at Mom's, then?"

"Yeah," he says. "What time is dinner again?"

"Dinner is at five, but I think we are opening presents around one or two."

"That means two."

"Huh?"

"Mom told you one or two so that you get there at one and she has more time with you, but really, she's planning on two."

"Why are you saying it like it's some diabolical plan?"

"I'm not."

"Well, there's nothing wrong with your family wanting to spend more time with you."

"I know," Charlie says. "But we'll be there at two instead of one. That's all I'm saying." He's being precious with his time because he has someone he wants to spend time with. He wants to be alone with Natalie. He doesn't want to spend his entire day with his family. Me? I'll happily spend the entire day with my family. What else would I be doing?

"OK, then, I'll tell Mom you'll be there at two."

"Cool."

"And Charlie?"

"Yeah?"

"You got Mom a gift, right?"

"We're still doing that?"

"Yes, Charlie, we're still doing that. I gotta go. Rachel is calling on the other line."

"Cool. OK, 'bye. And don't tell her yet!"

"I won't. I got it." I hit the button to change calls, and I drop Rachel. What the hell? How hard is it to navigate two phone calls on the same phone at the same goddamn time? I call her back.

"Learn how to use your phone," she says.

"Yeah, thanks."

"So we have a problem."

"We do?"

"Well, I do. And I'm inclined to make you help me, so it's sort of your problem, too."

"OK," I say. "Let's hear it."

"Grandma read an article that says white sugar is linked to cancer."

"OK," I say. "So I'm going to guess that Mom is insisting that all of the desserts you make be sugar-free."

"Have you even heard of such a ridiculous thing?" Rachel is the one being ridiculous here. We live in Los Angeles. It would take me five minutes to go out and find a gluten-free, sugar-free, dairy-free, vegan cupcake if I wanted.

"You can do it," I say. "Dessert is like breathing to you. You have got this."

"She doesn't even have cancer," Rachel says. "You know that, right? I mean, we never talk about it, but I think it's clear the woman is cancer-free."

I start to laugh. "You seem to have forgotten that that's good news," I say.

Rachel laughs. "No!" she says. "I love that she's cancer-free, I'm just not sure why that means I have to make sugar-free pumpkin pie."

"All right, how about this?" I ask. "You look at recipes now and find some you think will be good. Send me the list of ingredients that you don't already have. I'll go to the grocery store tomorrow and get them all. And then I'll come over and help you cook every last one of them."

"You would really do that?"

"Are you kidding? Absolutely. Mom didn't ask me to bring anything this year. I should pull my own weight."

"Wow," Rachel says, her voice lighter. "OK, thank you." Then she adds, "You have to get to the store before five or six, I bet. Just letting you know. The stores are gonna close early for Christmas Eve."

"I will. I promise."

"And will you also get some of that fake snow stuff?"

"What stuff?"

"They have it at the grocery store sometimes in the Christmas aisle. The stuff that you spray on the windows and it looks like snow?"

I know what she's talking about. Mom used to spray it

on all the windows around the house when we were little. She'd light a candle that smelled like firewood and sing "Let It Snow." My mother has always put a big emphasis on showing us a proper Christmas. One year, Charlie started crying because he'd never seen snow, so my mom put ice in a blender and then tried to sprinkle it on top of him. I wonder if Charlie remembers that. I wonder if he's going to put ice in a blender for his own snow-deprived child.

"You got it. You just give me a list, and I'll get it all," I say.

I hang up and put the phone down.

I look around the house. I don't have anything to do.

I decide to text David. I don't know why. I guess because it is something to do. Someone to talk to.

Ever think that the real problem with living without your spouse is that you're sometimes just really bored?

I figure he may not answer. Or he may not see it until later. But he texts me back right away: *Soooooo bored. I underestimated how much time being married takes up in a day.*

I text him back: *It's like I resent the lack of distraction now. And I hated how much he distracted me before.*

He responds: *The worst is at work! I used to IM with her when the kids were taking tests or watching a movie. Now I just read CNN.*

Me: *It's Dullsville.*

Him: *Ha ha ha. Exactly.*

And that's it. That's all we say to each other. But . . . I don't know. I feel better.

C"an you hand me that?" Rachel calls to me. She has on a polka-dot apron, her hair in a high bun. She has flour on her face. The pumpkin pie is in the oven.

Now she's started on sugar-free sugar cookies. I made a joke earlier: "I guess they are just called *cookies*, then, huh?" She laughed, but I could tell her heart wasn't in it. We've been at this since eight thirty this morning, when I showed up with everything on the list she sent me. I expected that list to include weird chemicals, but it was really just honey and Stevia.

"Hand you what?"

"That." Rachel isn't even looking at me. She's not even pointing. "The . . ." She makes an empty gesture with her hand. "The . . ."

Somehow, with her waving hand and the large lump of dough she has in front of her, I figure out what she needs. "The rolling pin?" I pick it up and hand it to her. Its weight causes it to land with a *thump* in her hand.

She stops and pauses for a second. "Thank you," she says. "Sorry, I'm doing too many things at once."

She puts flour on the rolling pin and starts to roll. "Have you heard this thing about Charlie bringing a date to Christmas?"

"Hm?" I say. God, I'm bad at lying to my sister. We don't keep secrets from each other. It's not what this family does. So I don't really know how to do it. What should I say, exactly? Should I be noncommittal? Like never really say anything either way? Plausible deniability? Or do I just out-right lie to her face, say something entirely untrue with such conviction that I almost believe it myself? This stuff is just not my strong suit.

"Charlie is bringing a date to Christmas," she says. The dough is flat, and now Rachel is searching around her kitchen for something. Not in there, I guess. Or there. There she goes. She's got it. "Check these out!" she says proudly. She pulls out cookie molds in the shapes of finely intricate snowflakes.

"Those are so cool!" I say. "But they look really difficult to use."

Rachel shrugs. "I practiced last week. We're good."

I go to her refrigerator and grab a bottle of seltzer water. The cap won't turn, I can't get it to open, and so I hand it to her. She wordlessly cracks the seal and hands it back to me. "You should quit your job," I say.

"What?" She's only half paying attention. She's starting to place the cookie molds on the dough.

"I'm serious. You are so good at this stuff. You make the most decadent desserts and awesome breakfasts. You should open a bakery."

Rachel looks up at me. "I can't do that."

"Why not?"

"With what money?"

"I don't know." I shrug. "How does anyone start a business? Business loan, right?"

Rachel puts the mold down. "It's not realistic."

"So you've thought about it?"

"I mean, sure. Everyone thinks about trying to make money doing the things they love."

"Yeah, but not everyone has such a passion and talent for something you *can* really make money from," I say. Rachel works in HR, which always struck me as an odd match. She's a right-brained person. I always imagined her doing something more traditionally creative.

"There are way more talented bakers than me," she says.

"I don't know," I say. I'm entirely serious. "You are really, really good. And look at you, you practice using snowflake cookie molds in your spare time. How many people can say that?"

"I'm not saying I don't love it."

"Think about it," I say. "Just think about it."

"It's just not realistic."

I put my hands up. "I'm just saying think about it."

After a few hours, Rachel and I gather up the cookies and the pie. We gently move the gingerbread house she made last night into the back of my car. I grab the two cans of snow and throw them into my purse. As I get into the front, Rachel has the key in the ignition, but she is looking down, almost in a daze. I expect her to start the car, but she doesn't.

"Yoo-hoo," I say, as I wave my hand in the air to get her attention.

She looks up. "Sorry," she says, turning the key. Then she looks at me. "You really think I'd be good at it, though? The bakery thing?"

I nod my head. "Better than good. Seriously."

She doesn't respond, but I can see she takes it to heart. "Merry Christmas, by the way!" she says as we hit the freeway. "I can't believe I forgot to say that this morning."

"Merry Christmas!" I say back to her. "I think it's gonna be a good one."

"Me, too," she says. Her gaze is straight ahead at the road, but her mind isn't on this freeway.

My phone buzzes, and I look down at it. I think, for a split second, that it might be Ryan. Maybe on Christmas, we can bend the rules.

But it's not Ryan. Of course it's not.
It's David.
Merry Christmas, new friend.
I text back: *Merry Christmas to you, too!*
It's not from Ryan, but I'm smiling nonetheless.

M erry Christmas!" my mother calls to us before she even opens the door. You can hear the thrill in her voice. This is always the happiest day of her year. Her children are home. She gets to give us presents. We're all on our best behavior. In general, she gets to treat us as if we are still kids.

She opens the door wide, and Rachel and I both say "Merry Christmas!" in unison. When we get inside, Grandma Lois is sitting on the couch. She goes to get up, and I tell her she doesn't have to.

"Nonsense," she says. "I'm not an invalid."

She takes a look at the desserts on the table. "Oh, Rachel, they are so gorgeous. Look at the detail on those cookies. I'm sorry to say I can't have any. I read recently that they have done studies correlating white sugar to cancer."

"No, Mom," my mom says. "Rachel made it all sugar-free." She turns to Rachel for confirmation. "Right?"

"Yep," Rachel says, suddenly proud of herself. "Even the sugar cookies!"

"So I guess they're just *cookies*, then?" my mom jokes, and she is not much of a joker, so you can see her eyes start to crinkle as she holds back a smile, waiting for other people to laugh.

"Good one, Mom!" I say, and high-five her. "I tried that one earlier today."

Everyone starts to talk about the things you talk about at Christmas. What is cooking, when it will be done, how good everything smells. Grandma usually takes over Mom's kitchen every Christmas, making everything from scratch, but this year, my mother lets us know, she pitched in.

"I made the sweet potatoes *and* the green beans," she says proudly. Something about her childlike pride reminds me of the can of snow.

"Oh!" I say, "Look, Mom! Rachel and I brought spray snow." I pull out the cans. "Awesome, right?"

She grabs them from my hands and shakes them immediately. "Oh, this is great! Do you guys want to spray, or should I?"

"Let them do it, Leslie," my grandmother says to my mother. The way she says it, the way it's a suggestion that should be heeded, the way it's laced with love and derision, makes me realize that my grandmother is sort of a bossy mom. I always think of my grandmother as *my* grandmother. I never think about the fact that she is my mother's mother. My mom isn't at the top of the totem pole, which is what it often feels like. Rather, she's just one piece of a long line of women. Women who first see themselves as daughters and then grow to be mothers and eventually grandmothers and one day great-grandmothers and ancestors. I'm still in phase one.

My grandmother sneaks a piece of sugar cookie and eats it, but it's not a very stealthy move, because we all see her.

"Oh, my!" she says. "These are fantastic. You're sure you didn't use any sugar?"

Rachel shakes her head. "Nope, none."

"Leslie, try this," she says to my mother.

My mother takes a bite. "Wow, Rachel."

"Wait, are they that good?" I say. I was with her all morning; you'd think I'd have tried one. I take a bite. "Jesus, Rachel," I say, and my grandmother slaps the back of her hand against my arm.

"Lauren! Don't take the Lord's name in vain on Christmas!"

"Sorry, Grandma."

"Where is Uncle Fletcher?" Rachel asks, and my mom starts shaking her head and waving her hands behind Grandma's back. The classic "Don't ask" signal, signaled classically too late.

"Oh." Grandma sighs. "He decided not to come after all. I think, maybe, you know, he needs some time to himself."

"Oh, that makes sense," I say, trying to ease the conversation along. This seems to have made my grandmother a little sad.

"No," she says, nodding. "I think I'm realizing that your uncle is a little . . ." She lowers her voice to a whisper. "Weird."

She says it as if being "weird" is a thing people don't speak about. Uncle Fletcher has never been in a relationship. He lives at home with his mother. He makes his living selling things on eBay and taking temp jobs. I'm pretty sure that if they release a computer game good enough, he will die playing it in his underwear.

"You just figured this out now, Grandma?" Rachel asks. I'm surprised she's feeling bold enough to say that—none of us talks about Uncle Fletcher's eccentricities—but it seems to make my grandmother laugh.

"Sweetheart, I once believed your grandfather when he told me you don't get pregnant the first time you do it. That's how we got Uncle Fletcher in the first place. So I've never been the sharpest tool in the shed."

If we don't talk about Uncle Fletcher's weirdness, we definitely don't talk about my grandparents having sex. So after the comment sits in the air a bit, waiting for us all to realize it has actually been said, it cracks us open. My mother, Rachel, and I are laughing so hard we can't breathe. My grandmother follows suit.

"Grandma!" I say.

Grandma shrugs. "Well, it's true! What do you want from me?" We all catch our breath, and Grandma keeps the conversation going. "So where is Ryan today? Surely he's not working on Christmas."

I just assumed that my mother would have done my dirty work for me and told my grandmother about what was happening. In fact, I assumed she told her months ago. I was sort of surprised that Grandma never called me to bring it up. And when I called her on Thanksgiving, I was pleasantly surprised when she didn't mention anything. But it's plain to see that she has no idea. Oh, the naiveté of wishful thinking.

I look to Rachel, but she starts paying more attention to the cookies than necessary, averting everyone's gaze, especially mine. My instinct is to make something up, to avoid this conversation and put it off for another day, but my mother is giving me a look that makes it clear she's expecting a braver version of her oldest daughter. So I try to be that daughter.

"We . . ." I start. "We split up. Temporarily. We are separated. I guess that's the term."

Grandma looks at me and cocks her head slightly, as if she can't quite believe what she's hearing. She looks at my mother, her face saying, *What do you have to say about this?* And my mother gestures back to me, her arms saying, *If you have a problem, you tell her yourself.* My grandmother looks back to me and takes a breath. "OK, what does that mean?"

"It means that we reached a point where we were no longer happy, and we decided that we wanted more out of . . . marriage than that. So we split up. And I'm really hoping that after we spend this time apart, we will find a way to . . . make it work."

"And you think being apart will do that?"

"Yes," I say. "I do. I think we sort of pushed each other to the brink, and we both need some air."

"Did he cheat on you? Is that what's happened?"

"No," I say. "Absolutely not. He wouldn't do that."

"Did he hit you?"

"Grandma! No!"

She throws her hands up in the air and back down on the counter. "Well, I don't get it."

I nod. "I thought you might not, which is why I haven't broached it with you." Rachel is so clearly avoiding being a part of this conversation, she might as well be whistling off to the side.

"So you just decided you weren't 'happy'?" She uses air quotes when she says "happy," as if it's mine alone, a word I made up, a word that doesn't belong in this conversation.

"You don't think being happy is important?"

"In a long-term marriage?"

"Yes."

"Not only is it not the most important thing, but I would argue that it's not even all that possible."

"To be happy at all?"

"To be happy the whole time."

It's so confusing, isn't it? I mean, why fill our minds with everlasting love and then berate us for believing in it?

"But don't you think that it's something to strive for? To try to be happy the whole time? To try to not just grin and bear your marriage but to thrive in it?"

"Is that what you think you're doing?"

"I believe this to be the best way to learn how to love my husband the way I want to. Yes."

"And is it working?"

Is it working? Is it working? I have absolutely no idea if it's working. That's the whole problem. "Yes," I tell her. I say it with purpose and with confidence. I say it as if there is no other answer. Maybe I say yes because I want her approval, because I want her to back off, because I want to put her in her place. But I think I say yes because I believe, on some level, that thoughts become words, and words become actions. Because if I start saying it's working, maybe in a few days or a few months, I'll look back and think, *Absolutely. This is absolutely working.* Maybe that conviction has to start right here, with a little white lie. "Yes, I do believe it's working."

"How?"

"How?"

"Yes, how?"

Now my mother and Rachel are not pretending to do anything else. They are listening intently, their ears and eyes aimed toward me.

"Well, I have missed him far more than I ever realized I would. When he left, I thought I wasn't in love with him anymore, but I didn't realize just how much I *did* still love him. I do still love him. The minute he left, I felt the hole in my life that he filled. I couldn't have done that without missing him, without losing him."

"One might argue that you can get that kind of perspective from a long weekend away. You got anything else?"

I want to prove to her that I know what I'm doing. "I mean, I don't know if it's anything to talk about here," I say.

"Oh, please, Lauren. Let's hear it."

I'm exasperated. "Fine. Fine. I can see now, now that he is gone, and I have real worries that he might be with someone else, I mean, I think he is with someone else. I know he is. And I'm jealous. At first, I got seethingly jealous. I realized that I had stopped seeing him as someone who, you know, was attractive, I guess. I was taking him for granted in that way. And now that I know that he is dating, it's very clear to me what I had when I had it."

"So what you're saying is that you forgot your husband was

desirable, and now that you can see another woman desiring him, you remember?"

"Sure," I say. "You can say that."

"Do you have cocktail parties?"

"Grandma, what are you talking about?" Rachel says, finally interjecting. I know my grandmother loves me. I know she wants what's best for me. I know she has very specific ideas of what that is. So while I do feel defensive, I don't entirely feel attacked.

"I'm asking her a serious question. Lauren, do you have cocktail parties?"

"No."

"Well, if you did, and you invited some young women, and you left your husband's arm for a minute, you'd notice that he'd end up talking to a number of very pretty young ladies, who would be glad to take him off your hands. And you'd go home to have the best sex of your life." She puts up her hand to wave us off before we ever start. "Excuse me for being vulgar. We're all ladies here."

"That's what worked for you, Grandma," I say, pushing the image of my late grandfather flirting with young women and then having sex with my grandmother out of my mind. "Don't you respect that something else might work for me?"

My grandmother considers me. My mom looks at me, impressed. Rachel is staring at us, desperate to see what happens next. My grandmother grabs my hand. "Make no mistake, I respect *you*. But this is stupid. Marriage is about commitment. It's about loyalty. It's not about happiness. Happiness is secondary. And ultimately, marriage is about children." She gives me a knowing look. "If you had a baby, no matter how unhappy you were together, you'd have stayed together. Children bind you. They connect you. That's what marriage is about."

Everyone just sort of looks at her. Not saying anything. She can see that no one is going to agree with her. So she eats a cookie and wipes the crumbs off her fingers.

"But you know, you kids these days. You do what you do. I can't live your life for you. All I can do is love you."

That's as much of a victory as anyone gets from Lois Spencer. I'll take it.

"You're sure you still love me?" I ask, teasing. I have always, always, always already known the answer to that one.

She smiles at me and kisses my cheek. "Yes, I most certainly do. And I admire your spirit. Always have."

I blush. I love my grandmother so much. She's so cranky and such a know-it-all, but she loves me, and that love may be fierce and opinionated. But it is love.

"One thing," she says. "And this goes for all of you, actually."

"You've got our attention, Mom," my mother says.

"I'm old. And maybe I'm a traditionalist. But that doesn't mean I don't know what I'm talking about."

"We know, Grandma," Rachel says.

"What I'm saying is, I can try to respect the way you do things, but don't forget that the old way works, too."

"What do you mean?" I ask her.

"I mean, if you had hosted a cocktail party, and you had left him to his own devices, and you had flirted with other men and he'd seen it, or he had flirted with other women and you'd seen it, if you had spent a few weekends apart from each other sometimes, given each other some space now and again, maybe you wouldn't need a whole year apart now. That's all I'm saying."

The doorbell rings, and it ends the conversation. In mere moments, Charlie will be walking through the door with the mysterious Natalie. But long after my grandmother and I are done talking, her words stay in my mind. She might very well be right.

• • •

Natalie is gorgeous. She's not gorgeous in a hot, sultry way. Or even a skinny, supermodel sort of way. She's gorgeous in that way where she just looks healthy and happy, with a beautiful smile, in a pretty dress. She looks like she works out, eats well, and knows what clothes look good on her. Her laugh is bright and loud. She listens to you; she really looks at you when you're speaking. And she's thoughtful and well mannered, judging from the poinsettia she gives my mother. I know she had sex with my little brother in the bathroom of an airplane, but it's hard to reconcile that with the person I see in front of me. The person in front of me brought Rocky Road fudge to Christmas.

"I made it this morning," she says.

"Is it sugar-free, sweetheart?" my grandmother says, and Natalie is understandably confused.

"Oh, no, I'm sorry," she says. "I . . . didn't know that that was . . ."

"It's fine," my mom says. "My mother is being absurd."

"It's not absurd to want to ward off any further cancer," my grandmother says. "But thank you so much, dear, for bringing it. We can give it to the dog."

Everyone stares at one another; even Charlie is at a loss for words. My mom doesn't even have a dog.

"I was joking!" Grandma says. "You all are so thick it's farcical. Natalie, thank you for bringing the fudge. Sorry that this family can't take a joke."

When Grandma turns her head, Charlie mouths "Sorry" to Natalie. It's sweet. I think he may be trying to impress her. I've never seen Charlie try to impress anyone.

"It's so nice to meet you all," Natalie says.

"Come," my mom says. "Let's put the presents down by the tree. Can I get you two anything? Charlie, I know you probably want a beer. Natalie, I have some mulled wine?"

"Oh." Natalie shakes her head casually. "Water is fine."

Eventually, we all sit down by the tree.

"So Natalie, tell us about yourself," Rachel says.

And Natalie, kind, sweet, naive Natalie, tries to answer, but Charlie steps in.

"That's such an annoying question, Rachel. What does that mean?"

"Sorry," Rachel says, shrugging defensively, as if she's been falsely accused of a heinous crime. "I'll try to be more specific next time."

The doorbell rings again, and my mother stands up to get it. She comes back in with Bill by her side.

"Merry Christmas!" Bill announces to the room. He has gifts in his hands, and he puts them down at the tree. Everyone gets up and hugs. Mom gets him a beer.

The small talk begins. People start asking one another questions. None of them is interesting. I learn that Natalie works in television casting. She's from Idaho. In her spare time, she likes to pickle things. When she asks me if I'm married, Charlie interrupts.

"Awkward topic," he says, immediately sipping his beer. The entire family hears, and each one of them laughs. Every one of the sons of bitches laughs. And then I laugh, too. Because it's funny, isn't it? And when things are funny, it means they are no longer only sad.

So Merry Christmas to me.

• • •

I've eaten far too much. Too much ham. Too much bread. Too many spoonfuls of sweet potatoes. When the sugar-free sugar cookies get passed around, I squeeze a few into the nooks and crannies of my stomach, and then I'm ready to pass out.

My mother has had enough glasses of mulled wine to stain her teeth a faint purple. She's getting a bit snuggly with Bill at the table. My grandmother is on her second piece of pie, sneaking her spoon into the sugar-laden whipped cream when she thinks we aren't looking. Charlie, meanwhile, appears stoic and sober. Natalie is smiling. Rachel is accepting compliment after compliment on her cookies, with a false modesty rivaled only by Miss Piggy. Charlie stands up.

So here we go, here it is. Oh boy oh boy oh boy.

"So . . ." he starts. "Natalie and I have some news."

That's all my mom needs. That's it. She's crying. I don't think she even knows why she's crying, what she thinks Charlie is going to say, or whether she's happy or sad.

Rachel looks up at Charlie as if he's a mental patient and she's not sure which way he's going to veer today.

Natalie is still smiling, but it's starting to buckle at the corners.

"We are going to be having a baby together."

Waterfalls. My mother's eyes are like two waterfalls. And not the kind that trickle from a little stream, either. These are the kind that gush, the kind that, were I white-water rafting, I would see up ahead and go, "Oh, shit."

Rachel's jaw has dropped. Bill isn't sure which way this is all going. And then my grandmother starts clapping.

She starts clapping! And then she stands up and she walks over to Charlie and Natalie, and she gives them huge, wet kisses on their cheeks, which has to be so very weird for Natalie, and she says, "Finally! Someone's giving me a great-grandchild!"

Charlie thanks her for being so great about it, but all attention is on Mom.

"Do you two have a plan?" she asks.

"Yep." Charlie nods. "I'm moving back here to L.A., in with

Natalie. We're raising the baby together. I feel like the luckiest man in the world, Mom. I really do."

"And what about a job?"

"I have a few interviews lined up next month."

That's all she needs to know, I guess. Because the tears that could have been from joy or sadness only a few seconds ago now only make their way to her chin if they can get past her giant smile. She runs to Charlie and hugs him. She holds on to him, clinging to him. She is sloppy in her movements, operating from gut, moving out of emotion. She hugs Natalie.

Natalie stands up, clearly overwhelmed but doing her best, and hugs my mom back, squeezing her tight. "I'm so glad you're happy," Natalie says.

"Are you kidding me? I'm going to be a grandmother!"

"It's a nice club to be in," Grandma says, and she winks at me. It's a sweet moment. I have forgotten how special a wink can make you feel.

When the commotion has died down, attention falls to Rachel. "I'M GONNA BE A FUCKING AUNT?" she yells, running toward them and hugging them so hard that she rocks them from side to side.

"Rachel!" Grandma says.

"Sorry, Grams. Sorry." She turns to Natalie, putting her hands on Natalie's upper arms. "Natalie, welcome to the Spencer family! We are so, so, so excited to have you!"

When everyone looks at me, I realize that I'm supposed to react, too. "Oh!" I say, "AHHHHHH!" and then hug them both. We all stand there, around them, suffocating them, overwhelming them, wanting to take part in their joy. It's then that I realize this is really happening. Our lives are changing. One of us is growing up. Everyone thought it would be me. And it's not. It's Charlie.

The truth is, it makes me feel like a failure, in some small way. It makes me feel as if I've veered off the path, as if I've been treading water while Charlie swam the race. But that's a tiny piece of me. The rest of me can't believe my baby brother is growing up to be a strong, solid man. The rest of me can't believe I'm going to have a little baby in my life to shower with presents. The rest of me can't believe that my grandmother is finally going to get that great-grandchild she's been asking for, that she has gotten news so great it has silenced her usual judgments.

It's a good day. And it's a wonderful Christmas. And I wish Ryan were here to see it. I wish he and I were going home to the same place. I wish we were going to get into bed tonight and gossip about the rest of them, the way we used to. It's at moments like this that I remember how much a part of all this he was.

The five of us—Rachel, Mom, Grandma, Natalie, and myself—surround Charlie, and maybe he's looking for an escape. Maybe he needs a breath of fresh air. He looks at Bill, and Bill stands up and puts out his hand. Charlie breaks away from us to shake it.

"Congratulations, young man," Bill says. "Best decision you'll ever make."

Charlie looks down at the floor, ever so briefly, and then he looks Bill in the eye and says, "Thanks." I think maybe every man wants to get a pat on the back when he shares the news that he's becoming a father. I'm just glad Bill is here to give it to him.

• • •

"So when are you getting married?" Grandma asks, as Natalie helps Mom and me with the dishes. Rachel, Charlie, and Bill are still at the table. Natalie and I are stacking plates. Grandma and Mom are loading the dishwasher.

"Oh," my mom says. "Lay off her, Mom. They don't have to get married just because they are having a baby."

"Well," Natalie says, "probably July, actually."

"July? I thought you said the baby was due in June," my mom says.

"For the wedding," Natalie says. "The baby will be born by then. It seems easier than trying to fit into a wedding dress."

"*After* the baby is born?" my grandmother asks.

But at the same time, my mother is using the exact same tone and inflection to say, "Wait, you're getting married?"

"Yeah." Natalie catches herself. "Wait, did we not say that?"

"You said nothing about a wedding," I say, as Rachel comes into the kitchen with a few empty serving bowls.

"Whose wedding?" Rachel asks.

"You said you were living together," my mom says. She says it slowly, approaching the sentence as if it's a bomb that might detonate at any second.

"We are getting married," Natalie says. "I'm sorry we didn't mention that part! Charlie!" she calls out. She's right to call in the reserves.

Charlie pops in through the door, and we all stare at him. All five of us. His sisters. His mother. His grandmother. His . . . fiancée?

"You're getting married?" I ask him.

"Yeah," says Charlie, as if I asked him if he likes chicken. "Of course. We're having a baby."

"Finally, someone makes sense in this family!" my grandmother says.

"Mom, will you go into the dining room and keep Bill company?" my mom asks her.

Grandma must be feeling charitable, because she puts down the dish in her hand and walks out.

"Having a baby doesn't mean you have to get married," Mom says.

Natalie inches toward Charlie. I think, perhaps, we are no longer doing a very good job of making her feel welcome. My mom notices the shift in her body language.

"I mean, it's great news," my mom says. "We're just surprised is all."

"How is marrying the mother of my child a surprise?" Charlie asks. Charlie really should learn to leave well enough alone.

"No, you're right," my mother says, backing off. This backing off is entirely for Natalie's benefit. Once Natalie is out of earshot, she'll say how she really feels. That's how you know that Natalie isn't really family just yet. "It shouldn't have been a surprise. You're absolutely right."

"It will be an awesome wedding," Rachel adds lamely.

But she's trying, so I try, too. "Congratulations, new sister!" I say. It comes out so forced and unnatural that I resolve to shut up.

"Thanks," Natalie says, clearly very uncomfortable. "I think I'll go see if there is anything else to bring in."

We all know there isn't a single thing to bring into this kitchen. But none of us says anything. When Natalie is finally gone, my mother starts speaking very gently.

"You don't have to do this," she says. "It's not the nineteen fifties."

"I want to do it," Charlie says.

"Yeah, but why not take your time to think about it?" Rachel says.

"Why are you assuming I haven't?"

"How long have you two even known each other?" my mom asks.

"Three months."

"And she's three months pregnant?" my mom asks.

"Yes."

"Got it," my mom says, starting to wash dishes. She's frustrated, and she's taking it out on the pots and pans.

"Don't judge me, Mom."

"Who's judging?" she says, moving the plates into the sink and running the water over them. "I'm just saying, take your time. You have your whole life to decide whom to marry."

"What are you talking about? Natalie is pregnant. We are moving in together. She is going to be my wife."

"But moving in together doesn't mean she has to be your wife. You can raise a child together and see how the relationship goes," I say.

"Lauren, you're supposed to be on my side here," Charlie says, and it makes me feel . . . included somehow. As if I am in possession of something extra that makes Charlie and me a team. Charlie isn't on a team with anyone. So the fact that he thinks I'm on his side, well, it makes me want to be on his side.

"I am on your side," I say. "I'm just saying that you have never been married before, Charlie. You don't know what it really entails."

"Neither do you!" Charlie says. His tone is uncontrolled and defensive, as if we've cornered a rat. "I just mean that everyone is figuring it out, right? Mom, you tried it your way, and that didn't work for you. Lauren, you're not sure how to do it. Who's to say mine won't work just because it doesn't look like yours?"

Rachel chimes in. "I guess I'm not needed in this conversation."

"Of course you're needed," Charlie says. "I want you all to be on board with this. I really like this woman. I think I can make this work for us."

"You can't just make a marriage work because you want it

to work, Charlie." My mom says it, but I might as well have said it myself.

"But you had no problem when I said we were raising a baby?" he asks.

"They are two totally different things," she says. "If you two don't work out, you can co-parent."

"I don't want to co-parent!" Charlie says. "I want a family."

"Co-parenting is a family. Single-parent homes are families." My mom is starting to take this as an indictment of her, and I can understand why. I think it's about to become one.

"No, Mom. That's not the kind of family I want. I don't want to live across town from my kid. I don't want to meet Natalie in the parking lot of a Wendy's on Sunday afternoons to drop him off, OK?"

This is something that Charlie learned from television. Our dad never took us for the weekend. He didn't live across town. He just left.

"OK," my mom says, trying to keep herself calm. "You have to do what you think is right for your children."

"Thank you," Charlie says.

"But I have to do what is right for my children," she says. "And so I'm going to tell you that marriage is hard work. No matter how hard I tried, I could not succeed. It was impossible for me. Can you think of another thing that I have ever told you was impossible?"

Charlie listens and then shakes his head. "No," he says quietly.

"And your sister," my mom says, as she gestures toward me, "is a very smart woman, a loving woman, who means well and almost always does the right thing." I stole a Capri Sun from the grocery store when I was eleven. I swear she's never forgiven me.

"I know," says Charlie.

"And even *she* isn't sure how to make one work."

"I know," Charlie says.

"So listen to us when we say that marriage is not to be taken lightly."

"Once again, no one cares about my opinion!" Rachel says bitterly. How quickly we all regress when we're in the same room.

"Oh, for heaven's sake, Rachel," my mom says, losing her temper. "So you don't have a boyfriend. Big deal. No one's treating you like a leper."

"When every conversation is about someone's boyfriend or husband, then I do think—" Rachel shuts herself up. "Whatever. It's not about me. Sorry."

My mom puts her arm around her and squeezes her into the crook of her body. Rachel resigns into it. My mom keeps going, looking directly at Charlie. "You don't have to marry Natalie to prove you're not your father. Do you get that? You couldn't be your father in a million years."

Charlie doesn't say anything. He looks at the floor. It must be so different being a boy without a dad instead of a girl without a dad. I should stop assuming they are the same thing.

"You have a lot of options," Mom says. "And all we want you to do is think about them."

"Fine," Charlie says.

"Are you going to think about them?" she asks him.

"Already have," he says. "I've made up my mind. I want to marry Natalie."

"Do you love her?" Rachel asks.

"I know I will," Charlie says. "I know I want to."

His tone makes it clear that we have reached the end of the conversation. A part of me feels like saying, *You can lead a horse to water, but you can't make him drink*, and the other part of me thinks that if anyone can out-stubborn marriage, it's Charlie. If anyone can trip and fall into a happy marriage, it's my baby brother. And also, in the deepest part of my heart, I think he's right. I may be married, but I don't know a damn thing about marriage. So who's to say Charlie's way is any worse than anyone else's?

"July it is, then," my mom says, smiling. She gestures for Charlie and me to come toward her and Rachel. Charlie looks at me, and I cock my head to say, "Come on, a hug won't kill you."

The four of us bear-hug. "The rest of them out there, they're fine and all. But this . . ." My mom squeezes the three of us tight. It's more of a metaphorical gesture now; we're too old to fit anymore. "This is my family. You guys are my meaning of life."

We're so squished together that now I'm having trouble breathing. I figure Charlie will be the first one to break the huddle, but he doesn't.

"I love you guys," he says.

From deep inside the belly of the pack comes Rachel's muffled voice, "We love you, too, Charlie."

When it gets late and Grandma starts complaining that she's tired, we all start packing our things. I gather my own pile of new sweaters and socks. Rachel grabs her new slow cooker. We throw all the wrapping paper away. Charlie and Natalie start saying good-bye to everyone.

"Welcome to the family," my mom says to Natalie, as they make their way to the front door. She hugs her. "We couldn't be happier to have you." She hugs Charlie for a long time, holding him tight. "So you're flying out tomorrow?" she asks. "And then when do we have you back for good?"

"I'm packing up my stuff over the next few weeks, and then I should be moved into Natalie's place by mid-January."

My mom laughs. "Oh, Natalie, I think you're going to be

my favorite kid. You're giving me a grandchild and bringing my son home!" She puts her hand on her heart and frowns the way people do when they are really, really happy.

They head to their car. I know they are going to talk about us. I know Natalie is going to ask how things went. I know Charlie is going to tell her that everyone loved her. He's not going to tell her what we said, but she's going to know the gist of it anyway. I know at some point, Natalie is going to ask Charlie if Grandma really has cancer. And Charlie is going to have to explain how all of this works.

When Rachel and I start to head out, I offer to drive. Rachel hands me the keys, and when she does, Grandma asks us for a ride. "Oh," I say. "I thought you were staying here."

"No, dear. I'm staying at the Standard."

Rachel starts laughing.

"Again?" I say.

"They have a lady who sits in a glass box behind the check-in desk. It's a riot!" Grandma says.

Rachel, Grandma, and I give Mom a kiss good-bye amid cheers of "Merry Christmas!" and "Thanks for the socks." We leave the house to her and Bill. From the look on Bill's face, I get the distinct impression he's got some weird Santa sex costume waiting for her or something. Gross.

We get into the car, and before I even turn on the ignition, Grandma starts in. "What do we think about this Bill guy?" she says.

Rachel turns her head and then her shoulders toward Grandma in the backseat. "I like him," she says. "You don't like him?"

"I'm just asking what you think," Grandma says diplomatically.

I keep my eyes on the road, but I join the conversation. "I think he seems really taken with Mom. I think that's nice."

"You two are a far cry from when you were little. You used to hate every man she dated."

"No, we didn't," Rachel says.

"We didn't even meet that many of them," I say.

"She stopped introducing you," Grandma says. "Because you used to get so upset."

I don't remember any of this.

"Are you sure? You're not thinking of Charlie or something?" Rachel asks.

"Honey, I remember it like it was yesterday. You hated every man who walked in that house. Both of you did. I remember she used to call me up and say, 'Mom, what do I do? They can't stand any of them.'"

"And what did you say?" I ask.

"I said, 'Stop introducing them, then.'"

"Huh," Rachel says, turning forward.

Huh.

"Sweetheart, don't take Sunset," my grandmother says when I get over the hill into the city.

"Grandma, you don't even live here!" Rachel says.

"Yeah, but I pay attention to the way your mother goes. Take Fountain, and then cut up Sweetzer. It's better."

I spend late Christmas night with Thumper, reading a mystery about a family murdered in a small Irish town. The detective is on the outs with the department and really has to solve this one to prove he's got what it takes. With Thumper next to me, his head resting on my stomach, I admit, this is a great way to end a holiday.

My phone rings around eleven. It's David.

"Hi," he says. His voice is soft and shy.

"Hi," I say. I can feel myself smiling wide. "How was your Christmas?"

"It was nice," he says. "I spent the day with my brother and his wife and kids."

"That sounds fun," I say.

"It was fun," he says. "His kids are four and two, so it's cute to see them open a playhouse and get all excited."

"And then you spent the rest of the day trying to put it together for them," I offer.

David laughs. "I'll tell you, those instruction booklets are torture. But it's nice to be able to do that."

"I'm going to be an aunt myself, actually," I say. "So I'm looking forward to all of that stuff."

"Oh, wow, congrats!" he says.

I thank him, and there is a long pause.

"Well, yeah," David says. "I don't know why I called, I guess. I just wanted to see how your Christmas went. I was thinking about you. And . . . you know . . . holidays can be lonely, so I just . . . wanted to see how you were . . . faring."

Sometimes you want to forget the fact that you're alone, and instead, you want to relish the feeling that someone understands you, someone is fighting the same battle that you are. Also, you know, sometimes you just want to feel wanted and desired. Sometimes you want to feel what it feels like with someone new. Sometimes you forget about whether you're *ready* to do something, and you just let yourself *do* it.

"David," I say warmly. "Would you like to come over?"

There is a brief pause. "Yes," he says. "Yes, I would."

• • •

"Oh, my God!" I am yelling. Or maybe I'm not. I don't know. "Oh, my God!" Oh, my God. Oh, my God.

God, yes.

Oh, God.

Oh. God.

Oh. God.

Oh. God. Oh God. Oh God. Yes. Yes. Yes. Yes. Yes. Yes. Yes.

YES.

And then I fall on top of him.

And he thanks me as he catches his breath. And he says, "I needed that."

And I say, "Me, too."

• • •

The next morning, I wake up to hear Thumper scratching at the door. He's not usually shut out of the bedroom.

I open the door and let him in. He jumps on David, smelling him, investigating. He's wary. David wakes up to Thumper's snout in his armpit.

"Excuse me, Thumper," David says groggily. Then he turns and looks at me. "Good morning." He smiles.

"Good morning." I smile back.

He rubs his eyes. He looks vulnerable without his glasses, as if I'm seeing the real him that not everyone gets to see. He squints at me.

"Do you need your glasses?" I laugh.

"That would be great. I just can't . . . well, I can't see them anywhere. Because I can't see without them," he says, as he feels for them.

I pick them up off the nightstand on his side. In doing so, I lean over him, my body brushing his. I can feel how warm he is to the touch.

"Sorry," I say. "Here you go."

He kisses me before he takes them out of my hand. The kiss is deep and passionate. I forget who I am, who he is, for a second.

He takes his glasses out of my hand, but he doesn't put them on. He puts them back on the nightstand. And he kisses me again, pulling me down on top of him. I guess the weirdest part about all of this is how it doesn't feel weird at all.

"Mmm," he says. "You feel good."

My hips fall onto his hips. My legs fall to the side. He moves his pelvis, pushing and pulling us tighter.

"Thumper," he says, looking right at me. "Get out of here, would you?"

Thumper ignores him. I laugh.

"Thumper," I say, "Go!"

And Thumper goes.

I melt into him.

At first, I am doing the things I know I should do. I am arching my back, I am grinding my hips, but somewhere along the way, I forget to do the things you're supposed to do.

I just move.

When I'm naked and underneath him, when I'm moaning

because he's doing all the right things, he breathes into my ear. "Tell me what you want."

"Hm?" I manage to get out. I don't know what he means, what he wants me to say.

"Tell me what to do to you. What do you like?"

I don't even know how to answer him. "I'm not sure," I say. "Give me some options."

He laughs and lifts my hips off the bed, running his hands down the length of me.

"Yes," I say. "That."

• • •

After David leaves, I go to my computer and open an e-mail draft. For the first time in a long time, I have something to say.

Dear Ryan,

How come you never asked me what I wanted? How come you never cared about what I needed in bed? You used to pay attention, you know? You used to spend hours touching me, finding things that made me tingle. When did you stop?

Why did it become easier for me to just satisfy you and then move on to something else? Why didn't you stop me and say that it was my turn? Why didn't you offer more of yourself to me? You never asked me what I liked. You never asked me my wildest fantasies.

David asked me last night what I wanted, and I didn't know how to answer him. I don't even know what I want. I don't know what I like.

But I can tell you that I'm going to figure it out. And I'm going to learn to ask for it.

If you come home, if we make this work, sex has to be about me, too. It has to. Because I remember what it's like, now, to be touched as if your pleasure is the only thing that matters. And I'm not going to let anyone make me forget again.

Love,
Lauren

My grandmother calls me from her hotel room later that day.

I pick up the phone. "Hey, Grams," I say. "What's up?"

"I had a thought."

"Oh?"

"About your problem, you and Ryan."

"OK . . ."

"Have you ever read Ask Allie?"

"What is that?" Good Lord, is she about to recommend an advice column?

"It's an advice column." Yep, she is.

"Oh, OK," I say. "Not sure about that."

"It's a really good one! This woman has the best advice. Last week, a lady wrote in about how she doesn't know how to deal with the fact that her son wants to become a Mormon."

"Uh-huh," I say.

"And Allie said that it's not about what religion he chooses but that the lady should be proud of having a son who thinks for himself and takes an active role in his spirituality. But she just said it so beautifully! Oh, it was beautiful."

"It sounds like it," I say. I don't know. I guess it sounds like it.

"Well, I think you should write to her!"

"Oh, no, no, no. Sorry, Grandma. I don't think that's for me."

"Are you kidding? I'm sure Allie would have something to say about it."

"Well, yeah, but—"

"Don't decide now. I'll send you some of her columns. You'll see."

"I can just Google it."

"No, I'll send them."

"OK, sounds good."

"You are going to be impressed with her, though. And maybe she could really shed some light on what you guys are going through. You might even be able to help people going through the same thing. I'm sure there are plenty of people your age dealing with the same challenges." She pauses for a moment. "I guess what I'm saying is that maybe she could offer some insight."

"Thanks, Grandma," I say to her. There is a small lump in my throat, but I swallow it down.

"Of course, sweetheart," she says. "Of course." She sounds as if she might be swallowing the lump in her throat, too.

I think we should throw Natalie a baby shower," Rachel says as we're hiking through Runyon Canyon the next Saturday morning. Thumper is, as always, leading the charge.

"Yeah, that would be nice," I say. "We should do everything we can to make sure she feels welcome. We sort of botched it the other day."

"Right," Rachel says. "We blew that one. But I do really like her. She seems awesome."

"I hope their baby has her coloring. Can you imagine? What a gorgeous baby that will be."

Thumper has stopped to smell something, and Rachel and I stop with him. We're standing off to the side waiting for him as we talk.

"You knew, right?" Rachel says. "He told you ahead of time?"

I can't look directly at Rachel until I decide what I'm going to say. I pretend to look at whatever Thumper is smelling, and in pretending, I actually notice that he's about to step in mud. I yank his collar, but he steps right in it anyway. Now both his front paws are covered in it. I should just come clean.

"Yeah," I say. "I did. He told me a bit before." I really feel like shit about this. Our family always spills the beans about everything, and this time, I kept the beans.

I watch as Rachel's face starts to lose resolve. She doesn't look me in the eye for a few moments. She stares at the gravel path beneath our feet.

"You OK?" I ask.

"Yeah," she says, her voice cracking and her eyes looking

forward. She starts walking ahead, and so I follow her, dragging Thumper along.

"You don't sound OK," I say.

"Why didn't he tell me?" she asks. "Did he say why he didn't want me to know ahead of time?"

What do I do? Do I tell her the truth and possibly hurt her feelings? Or do I keep yet another secret from her? I opt to split the difference. "I think he was afraid that you wouldn't take the news well."

"But why? I love Charlie! I'm always happy for Charlie. I'm always happy for everybody."

"I think sometimes we worry that you can't handle some of the love talk. We all have some sort of love life to discuss, for better or worse, in my case." I shrug. "But you know, you haven't been able to find a relationship, and I think . . . maybe . . . it's hard to . . ."

"I seem bitter," Rachel says.

"Yeah, a little."

"You know, it's funny. I swear, I don't even think about being single that much."

I look at Rachel as if she's trying to sell me the Brooklyn Bridge.

"No, I'm serious!" she says. "I really like my life. I have a perfectly fine job. I can afford to live on my own. I have the best sister in the world." She vaguely gestures to me, but it's clear she's not saying it to flatter me. She's saying it because she thinks it's true, and it's one of the things in her life that she's happy about. Ironically, that's even more flattering. "My mom is doing well. I get to spend my nights and weekends with people I love. I have plenty of friends. And the best part of my week is every Sunday morning when I wake up around seven thirty, go into the kitchen, and bake something completely new from scratch while listening to *This American Life*."

"I didn't know you did that," I say. We have stopped moving again. Our feet just sort of gave up on moving forward and instead planted themselves firmly in their places.

"Yeah," she says. "And to be honest, I don't really feel like anything is missing."

"Well, isn't that—" I start to say, but Rachel isn't done.

"But that's not how the rest of you all live," she says.

"What do you mean?"

"I mean, Mom always has someone. Even if we don't meet him and it's not as serious as she's been with Bill, she's always talking about meeting some guy."

"Right," I say.

"And Charlie is always dating someone. Or impregnating them, as the case may be."

"Right," I say, laughing.

"And you," she says. She doesn't need to extrapolate further. I know what she means.

"Right."

"That was part of why I was so excited for you to have time away from Ryan, you know?"

"Sure."

"It just seemed like maybe you could have my kind of life, too."

"Living alone?"

"Living alone and being on your own and finding your Sunday morning hobby. I was excited about the idea that I'd have someone to talk to and it wasn't always about boyfriends or husbands or girlfriends."

"Right." Even separated from my husband, I am still preoccupied with the opposite sex. Maybe not all the time. But still. On some level, my love life is a defining factor in my life. I've never been a person who had a career passion, really. I like my job at Occidental in part because it affords me a life outside of work that I really enjoy. I make enough money to have the things I need and want. I have time to spend with my family and, in the past, with Ryan. Love is a big part of who I am. Is that OK? I wonder. Is it supposed to be that way?

Rachel is quiet for a moment. "I just . . . I don't feel like I'm missing out on love, really."

"You don't?"

"No," she says. "Honestly, the problem is that I just feel like I don't fit in."

I never thought about it that way. Rachel just always seemed as if she was jealous or unhappy being single. I didn't realize that perhaps it was the way the rest of us considered her singleness that really bothered her.

"I want to meet someone," Rachel says. "Don't get me wrong."

"OK."

"But if that doesn't happen until I'm forty or fifty, I think I'm OK with that. I have other things I'm interested in."

"And if you don't have kids?"

"I don't want to have kids," Rachel says. "That's the other thing." She's never said this before. We don't talk about it that often, I guess. And I suppose I never asked her. I just assumed that she did. How hetero-normative of me. "I love kids. I'm excited for Charlie's kid. I'm excited for when you have kids. But you know? I just haven't ever felt that longing to have my own. I look at new moms sometimes, and I immediately feel stressed out for them. I saw this family the other day at the mall. It was these two parents and then these two kids. The boy was a teenager, the girl was maybe ten, and I just . . . I felt this very clear sense of 'I don't want that.'"

"Well, you might," I say. In my head, I'm thinking that she'll feel it once she meets someone, and then I realize, Jesus Christ, it's so ingrained in me that I can't get it out of my brain, even when I'm consciously trying to get it out of my brain. Marriage and kids. Marriage and kids. Marriage and kids.

"Sure," she says. "I might. But listen, you and Charlie, you want that normal family life so bad. You wanted it so bad you met someone at nineteen and never looked back. Charlie wants it so bad that he's going to marry a woman he barely knows." She shrugs. "I don't need it."

My sister and I are alike in so many ways, and it is that similarity where I have always found comfort. But the truth is, we are two distinct women, with two distinct sets of wants and needs. This basic difference between us was always there. I just never saw it, because I was never looking.

"I'm really glad this came up, actually," I say. "I'm happy you said all of this."

"Thanks," she says. "I think it's been on my mind for a while."

"I forget sometimes that you're not me," I say. "You seem so much like me that I just assume you think all the same things I do."

"We're still pretty similar," she says. "You know me better than I know myself sometimes."

"I do?"

"Yeah," she says, nodding. "I have an appointment with a bank on Tuesday."

"You do?"

"I'm looking into a small-business loan."

"For the bakery idea?"

She smiles, embarrassed. "Yeah."

I high-five her. "Oh, my God! This is such great news!"

"You don't think it's a disaster waiting to happen?"

"I really don't. I swear. I really think you would be so good at it."

"I was thinking of doing a line of sugar-free stuff, too, seeing as how the sugar cookies went over so well."

I laugh. "Finally, Grandma's cancer does us a favor."

Rachel nods and laughs. "I knew it would be good for something!"

We move on to talk about other things, but on the car ride home, one thing just keeps playing over and over in my mind. *You want that normal family life so bad. You wanted it so bad you met someone at nineteen and never looked back.*

I couldn't see it until she said it, and yet now it seems so blazingly clear that it's all I can see. It's amazing the things that have been written across your forehead for so long that even when you're looking in the mirror, you don't see them.

At home, there's an envelope waiting in my mailbox from one Mrs. Lois Spencer of San Jose, California.

Here they are, sweetheart. A few of Ask Allie's columns. Think about it. Love, Grandma.

She printed them out from the Internet and mailed them to me. I laugh to myself as I look them over and then stick them in a box of miscellaneous stuff. I tell myself that I'll sit down and read them soon. Then David calls asking if he can come over, and I say yes. I jump into the shower.

By the time I'm dressed and dry, I've already forgotten where I put the Ask Allie articles. They simply aren't on my mind. I'm not thinking about what advice I need to fix my marriage. I'm not reflecting on what my grandmother thinks of what I'm doing.

I'm not reflecting at all, really.

I'm starting to just live.

In January, I help Charlie move into his apartment with Natalie. The entire family goes out for a big Italian dinner at Buca di Beppo, the plastic checkered tablecloths and old-timey photos reminding us all of when we came here as kids, when Mom would order two extra bowls of pasta and tell us it was our lunches for the week.

In February, I help Rachel put together her business prospectus. I help her research possible bakery locations. I help her learn the ins and outs of applying for a small-business loan. She asks me if I'd be willing to cosign, and I tell her I can't think of another person I'd be ready to vouch for more than her.

In March, Charlie and Natalie decide to have the wedding at the house of one of Natalie's friends in Malibu. Their house apparently backs up onto the beach. I determine that Natalie must have obscenely rich friends. The save-the-dates go out. The caterer is hired. Charlie's only job is to choose a DJ. So that won't be done until June.

By the beginning of April, Natalie is in her third trimester. And my mom is struggling with how to handle her relationship with Bill. He thinks they should move in together. She does not.

And meanwhile, I sneak texts with David. I open my door to him late at night. We call each other when we need a friendly ear or want an understanding touch. I like David a lot, and I know he likes me. But he's still in love with the woman who cheated on him. And I . . . am in no position to be loving anyone. So we are good to each other and good for each other, and we are, essentially, that thing I've heard about from teenagers: friends with benefits. And there is something freeing about having sex with a man you don't see a future with. It's all butterflies and orgasms. There's no politics or unspoken words. And when he's going too fast, you just say, "Slower."

When Mila asks me if Ryan has been writing to me, I tell her the truth. "I have no idea," I say. "I haven't checked in months."

part four

MOST OF THE TIME

Rachel, Mom, and I have been planning Natalie's baby shower. When we asked Natalie if we could throw it for her, she seemed really overjoyed and flattered. We asked her what sort of theme she wanted or what she'd like to do, and she just said that she was sure she would love whatever we came up with. She tries so hard to be accommodating and kind, and it's really sweet, but sometimes I want to grab her by the shoulders and say, "Tell us the truth! Do you like the color yellow?" So at least we know.

Rachel, Mom, and I are sitting at this pizza place, trying to come up with a theme, but somehow the conversation evolves—or devolves, I guess, depending on how you look at it—into whether Mom should let Bill move in.

"I just don't think I'm ready for something like that," my mom says, as the waiter puts our pizzas on the table. The minute it's in front of them, both my mom and Rachel start damping their slices with napkins to soak up the grease. I just bite right into mine.

"You guys have been dating for a while now," Rachel says.

"Yes, but right now, on the nights that he doesn't stay with me, I miss him."

"Right," I say. "Which is why you would ask him to move in . . ." I'm speaking with my mouth full, which my mother normally abhors, but she's too focused on her own problem to notice me.

"No!" my mom says. "I like missing people. You know when

you call someone just to hear their voice? Or you wait all day until you can see them that night? If Bill lives with me, he stops being this person I can't wait to see, and he becomes the man who leaves his dirty dishes in the sink."

"But you can't sustain this part," I say. "The natural process is that the relationship becomes more serious as time goes on." Of course, there are exceptions to this.

"Yeah, or it fizzles out," my mom says. "I don't need a life partner. I'm not interested in a partnership. Someone to share the bills. Someone to raise children with. I did all of that, and I did it on my own. I make my own money. I pay my own bills. I want love and romance. That's all."

"But after a while, relationships become more about partnership and less about romance. That's just how it works. It's the nature of love. If you want to stay with Bill, he's eventually going to stop bringing you flowers," I say.

My mom shakes her head. "This is why I don't want to commit to Bill."

"Wait, what?" Rachel asks. "You are in love with Bill, right?"

"Right. *Right now*, I'm in love with Bill. And eventually, we will grow tired of each other."

"And when that happens?" I ask.

"We'll break up," she says, shrugging. "I want romance in my life. That's what I want. And I don't need anything else from a man. I've lived my whole life, or, I guess, my life since you guys were little, dating for fun. If the romance dies, I want to be able to leave, is what I'm saying. I want to be able to have that feeling again with someone else. It's how I've been living my life for a long time. It works."

"So you'd never get married again?" I say.

"You just chew 'em up and spit 'em out?" Rachel adds.

"You two are ridiculous. All I'm saying is that I'm not look-ing for all of the work that comes with a long-term relationship. The best part of a relationship is the falling-in-love part. And there's nothing wrong with admitting that."

"You don't think Bill's different? You don't think there is a way to have a long-term relationship that is worth the work?" Rachel says.

My mom starts to answer, but I jump in. "I guess if romance is your primary goal, then you can't let him move in. I get it. Romance fades. It just does. If you don't like the other stuff, then I get why you'd have to have an exit strategy."

"I still think romance and commitment don't have to be mutually exclusive," Rachel says, but she says it in a wistful way, as if she's pontificating on the theory of love instead of the practicality of it.

I think back to when Ryan made my stomach flip, the way he used to look at me. The way his attention was enough to lift me off the ground. The way it felt as if anything could happen.

What if I never have that feeling again? That sense where your nerve endings are so raw that you can physically feel everything that he says? That feeling where your head is light, your stomach is empty, and your legs are on fire?

Ryan is supposed to come home in three months so that we can decide if we want to spend the rest of our lives together. I mean, the goal here is to spend the rest of our lives together. If I really feel that romance doesn't last, if I really think that's true, am I ready to never feel that tingle again? Was I ever ready?

"Let's talk about something else," my mom says. "Lauren looks like she's about to cry."

"No, I'm sorry," I say. "I was trapped in my own mind for a second. But we should get back to Natalie's shower, right? What else do we have to go over?"

"Well, actually, before we get back to that, I just remembered that I need a copy of your social security card to add to my loan package as the cosigner," Rachel says.

"Oh, sure. When do you need it?"

"Thursday?"

"Yeah, that's fine. I'll find it. It's in my house somewhere."

"I am so proud of you," my mom says to Rachel. "This is such a brave thing you're doing."

"It's stupid, right?" Rachel says. She still can't fully believe in herself just yet. But I know she must believe in herself a great deal when she's alone, working out what to do. Because you don't go to the bank and discuss a small-business loan unless you're serious. You don't scout out bakery locations unless you believe in yourself at least a little bit.

"If no one ever did anything stupid, I wouldn't have you girls and Charlie," my mom says.

It's supposed to be encouraging, but Rachel says, "So you do think it's stupid."

And then she and I start laughing before my mom can defend herself.

"Oh, you two are such a pain in the ass," she says. "I swear."

My desk is full of clutter. I used to sit down and actually do work at this desk in years past. I remember when Ryan and I first moved in and we had the extra space, and I would make a big show of sitting down at my desk to do things because it felt so fancy to have an extra room for things like desks. And then slowly, I got over the desk and started using it as storage for stuff that didn't have a home.

I start searching through drawers for my social security card. It could be anywhere. I am not a person who labels files. One time, I labeled a file folder "Important Files." That's how lazy I am when it comes to organizing. I dig through the bottom drawer first, front to back. Oh, here is it. Here is my "Important Files" file. I open it, hoping to find the card, because, really, if you have an "Important Files" file, wouldn't that be a good place to have put your social security card?

I have my birth certificate. I have my diploma. I have my old student-loan contracts. The title to my car. I even have the court order for my change of name from when my mom changed our last names after our dad left. She changed them all back to Spencer, her maiden name. Until I was about six years old, we were Lauren, Rachel, and Charles Prewett. I look at the document for longer than I realize. My eyes are focused on it, but my brain is elsewhere. I'm momentarily mesmerized, thinking about the life of Lauren Prewett. Would things have turned out differently if I'd kept my father's name? Would I have met some nice young boy with the last name Proctor or Phillips in homeroom, the two of us seated next to each other thanks to the work of alphabetizing? Would my heart have held out for my dad longer if I'd kept his name? I don't know. There's nothing to know, really, because none of those things happened. But I'm thankful to my mother for changing it, for taking the time to go down to the courthouse and change our fates, for rightfully claiming us as her own.

I finish with the folder, and there's no social security card. I put it back in the drawer. I shuffle through the things on the top of my desk, and that's when I find Grandma's Ask Allie columns. I glance at them, and one or two words catch my eye. I find myself sitting back, putting my feet up, and reading.

One man's wife has been diagnosed with Parkinson's, and he's scared about how their life is going to change. He calls himself "Worried in Oklahoma."

A mother writes in to say that she and her husband know their son is gay, because he has told his two siblings. But he hasn't come out to them yet. She wants to know how to let their son know that he can be honest with them. She signs her letter "Eager to Be Supportive."

There's a woman who thinks her mother shouldn't be driving anymore and needs advice on how to broach the subject with her. She calls herself "Hoping to Be Gentle."

Allie tells "Worried in Oklahoma" that it's OK for him to be scared and to find people other than his wife to talk about his fears with. "Talk about them so much with other people," she says, "that by the time your wife is ready to talk about what scares her, you have answers. Above all else, find someone who can say to you, 'Me, too.'"

Allie tells "Eager to Be Supportive" that it sounds as if she's concerned that her son doesn't know she loves him unconditionally. "Don't be. You've spent twenty-three years unintentionally telling him this with every fiber of your being. That love has shown through everything you've said and done. Unconditional love is the freedom to follow your heart and still have a home. You have given that to your son, and now all you have to do is sit back, be patient, and wait for him to use it."

Allie tells "Hoping to Be Gentle" that she can try to be as gentle as she likes, but the underlying message is going to hurt her mother. But that hurt is necessary in love, because "if your family won't tell you the truth, who will? Be the daughter your mother needs. Be the daughter who does ugly stuff for the right reasons. That's where the deep, beautiful, mystifying love of family truly kicks in."

She's not talking to me or about me or with me or for me, and yet everything she says resonates. Allie is good. Allie is real good.

Mila comes into the office in the morning with a latte for me.

"To what do I owe this gift?" I say, happily taking it. I didn't get much sleep last night.

"They gave me the wrong one by mistake, so I took a sip, realized it was the wrong one, and they had to let me keep both," she says.

"Well, thank you," I say. "I needed this." The coffee is still hot in the cup, so hot that it's burned my tongue. I'm now going to have that annoying numbness for the rest of the morning.

"Up late?" Mila asks, her voice implying something salacious.

"Are you asking me if I was up late having sex with David?"

Mila laughs. "Wow, you really don't understand subtlety."

"I'd argue you don't understand it as much as you think you do," I say.

She hits me with the back of her hand. "So you were, then?" she asks.

"No, actually," I tell her. "I stayed up reading the backlog of posts from this advice columnist."

Mila's shoulders slump. "I'm bored now. I was interested when I thought you were getting laid."

I laugh. "You know, you never cared about my sex life when I was with Ryan. Now, with David, suddenly, you're fascinated."

"I'm not *fascinated*," she says. "I don't wanna know, like, what you guys *do* and stuff. I just like living vicariously through you. New love. The fun of sleeping with someone you're just getting to know. It's fun, isn't it?"

"Yeah," I say, nodding my head. "It is. It is fun."

"I don't have that anymore," she says wistfully. "And that's fine. I'm not complaining. I love Christina more than anything. I feel like the luckiest woman in the world to have her."

"But things slow down after a while," I say. "I get it."

"I mean, we haven't been together all that long. Five years is long, I guess. But not that long. It's the kids. Things slow down with kids. It's like she's not just this beautiful woman for me to explore and discover. She's my kids' mom. She's my partner raising them. It's . . ."

"Boring?"

"Yeah. And boring is great. I love boring. It's just . . ."

"Boring."

Mila smiles at me. "Right." She takes a sip of her coffee. "Hence why I need to get my thrills from your sex life, even if it is with a man. I can overlook that."

"You know," I say to her, my voice escalating to a wild idea, "you could write to Ask Allie."

"Who?"

"The advice columnist I've been reading. She's great. Oh, God, I was reading one last night, about this woman who can't get over the trauma of being mugged at gunpoint years ago, and Allie said the most beautiful thing—"

Mila puts her hand up. "I'm going to stop you right there."

I look at her.

"You sound like a loony."

I start laughing. I think it's because she said "loony." "I do not sound like a loony!" I say.

"Oh, yes, you do. You sound exactly like a loony." Now she's laughing, too.

"Maybe *you're* the loony," I ask her.

Mila shakes her head. "That's exactly what a loony would say."

"Stop saying the word *loony*, please."

Mila smiles and starts walking back toward her desk. "Enjoy your coffee," she says. "Loony."

Admittedly, I floated the idea to Mila in part because I'm considering doing it myself. I wasn't hoping to be called a loony, but maybe I don't care if it makes me a loony. Maybe.

April 18

Dear Ryan,

I'm considering writing to one of those advice columnists about us. That's how confused I still am.

When we started this, I thought that I just needed some time away from you. I just needed time to breathe. I needed a chance to live on my own and appreciate you again by missing you.

Those first few months were torture. I felt so lonely. I felt exactly what I wanted myself to feel, which was that I couldn't live without you. I felt it all day. I felt it when I slept in an empty bed. I felt it when I came home to an empty house. But somehow, one day, it just sort of became OK. I don't know when that happened.

I thought at one point that maybe if I learned who you truly are, then I could love you again. Then I thought maybe if I learn who I really am, what I really want, then I could love you again. I have been grasping at things for months, trying to learn a lesson big enough, important enough, all-encompassing enough that it would bring us back together. But mostly, I'm just learning lessons about how to live my

life. I'm learning how to be a better sister. I'm learning
just how strong my mother has always been. That I should
take my grandmother's advice more often. That sex can be
healing. That Charlie isn't such a little kid anymore.

I guess what I'm saying is that I've started focusing on other
things. I don't feel all that desperate to figure us out and fix
this. I feel sort of OK that it's not fixed.

That's not the direction this is supposed to go, is it?
Love,
Lauren

• • •

I read the letter over and over. I change a word here and there.
I add commas and spaces. On some level, I think maybe I'm
delaying the moment when I hit save, trying to make sure I
want my words taking up space somewhere out there in the
ether of the Internet. But I'm not willing to delete them. So
eventually, I stop preening, and I hit the button. Save.

I get up and decide to go for a run. I put on my shorts. My
sports bra. My T-shirt. My running shoes. I say good-bye to
Thumper. I hide my keys under the doormat. I take off.

As my heels round the pavement, as my heart starts to
pump faster, as my body wants to slow down and I push it
forward, all I can do is think about what I wrote. Is it true? Do
I not feel any closer to knowing how to fix my marriage? Am
I not sure I want to?

I go home and take a shower. And I think about my letter.
I make myself dinner, and I think about my letter.

If I mean what I wrote, then doesn't that mean that I have
to face the idea of the end? Could this be the beginning of
the end of *us*?

What would I do with my life?

I'm not sure what possesses me. It's almost an instinct rather than an action. I grab my computer and log into Ryan's e-mail. I don't know what I'm expecting to find. I guess I'm expecting to find that he has forgotten me. That he has moved on. That he doesn't think about me. But I look at the number next to his drafts folder. There are three more letters.

I open the folder. They are all to me. All from within the past three weeks. Ryan has started writing to me again.

• • •

March 31

Dear Lauren,

I had to get away from you. I had to stop writing to you. I had to stop telling you everything that was going on. I noticed how I was talking to you throughout the day, in my head, even when I was mad at you, even when I wanted nothing to do with you. I had to stop doing that. I had to stop seeing you as someone to talk to.

So I stopped writing.

And writing to no one, talking to no one, felt lonely. So I had to stop being lonely.

At first, there was Noelle. Noelle is a perfectly nice woman, and she was very sweet to me and very patient with my reservations about everything, but I just wasn't that into her.

And then there was Brianna, and that was fine.

And then I met Emily. And Emily is somehow different enough from you that she doesn't remind me of you but not so different that I feel like I'm dating the opposite of you on purpose. And because of that, I think I was able to stop thinking about you so much. I just started thinking about Emily. I don't mean to hurt you when I say this, but I looked forward to seeing Emily as much as possible, and I forgot about you. As much as a person can forget about his wife, I guess. I really felt like I was able to be present and engaged with her. We've even gone away together a few times, and each time, I've felt like Emily's boyfriend, as opposed to your husband.

And I just really needed that.

And then yesterday was her birthday. And I thought that maybe I should make her something, you know? So I made her Ryan's Magic Shrimp Pasta. Which didn't even feel weird. I know it was our thing, but I don't know. It seemed like a perfectly reasonable thing to do.

And I made it, and she ate it, and she said thank you, and then we went out to a bar with some of her friends. And that should have been enough. That should have been fine.

But I just kept thinking about the first time I made it for you, the way you gushed over it. The way you ate so much more than you should have and you almost made yourself sick. I kept thinking about the way your eyes lit up every year when I said I would make it. I don't think Ryan's Magic Shrimp Pasta was about you, I realized. I think it was about me. I think I thrived on your approval. It was like a battery that kept me going. I looked forward to your birthday as much as you did. And it was because I knew that on your birthday, I was the one who made the day worthwhile. It made me feel like I mattered. It made me feel like I was doing something right.

But Emily just ate the Ryan's Magic Shrimp Pasta and said thank you and wiped her mouth and asked if I was ready to go. She didn't get it. And this feels so silly to put into words, but it really felt like in not getting Ryan's Magic Shrimp Pasta, she didn't get me.

And it made me miss you. Not you, my wife. Or you, the woman who has been with me since I was nineteen years old. You. Lauren Maureen Spencer Cooper. I missed you.

And it wasn't a passing feeling. It was real. I truly felt there was a hole in my life and the only thing that could fill it was you.

I think this is working, Lauren. I think we're gonna be OK.

Love,
Ryan

• • •

April 3

Dear Lauren,

I drove by the house this evening. I didn't mean to. I had a dinner I had to go to in downtown, and I took Olympic back across town. I was listening to the radio. They were doing a piece about this serial killer in Colombia, and I was so fascinated I think I stopped paying attention to my driving.

When I got to the corner of Olympic and Rimpau, I should have gone straight, but my hand flicked on my turn signal, and I took a right, leading me to the wrong home. It was muscle memory. You make a right turn day after day after day for years, and . . . you know how it is.

I realized I had made a mistake just as I hit the stop sign on Rimpau and 9th, but it was too late. I was going to have to drive by if only to turn around.

When my car got up to our driveway, I admit, I slowed down. I saw the light was on. And then I noticed another car parked in the driveway. I heard Thumper bark. I swear I heard him. I came to a complete stop, I'm embarrassed to say, and I looked into the window a few seconds. I don't know what I was hoping to see. You and Thumper, probably. But what I saw was you and someone else. Someone, I'm assuming, you're dating.

I turned off the car. I actually turned the key and pulled it out of the ignition. I undid my seat belt, and I had my hand on the door handle. That's how close I came to walking into my own house and punching that guy in the fucking face.

But two things stopped me. The first was that I knew it was the wrong thing to do. I knew, as I sat there with my hand on the handle, that it was wrong and I shouldn't do it. That it would jeopardize everything. That it would make you feel spied on. I didn't want you to feel that way.

And the second thing was that I was supposed to be at Emily's in twenty minutes. And how could I explain to her where I was? How could I have explained to you why I had to leave?

I put my seat belt back on, I put the key back in the ignition, and I high-tailed it out of there. I ran through the stop sign. I almost slammed into someone when I hit the red light onto Wilshire. I was ten minutes late to Emily's, and when she asked, I told her I hit traffic.

So I guess what I'm saying is that I'm a hypocrite. And when I come home, we need curtains for the front window.

Love,
Ryan

• • •

April 17

Dear Lauren,

Charlie just called me and told me that he's having a baby? With some woman named Natalie? And he lives in Los Angeles now? And they are getting married?

I'm going to be an uncle, and I didn't know. I understand why you didn't tell me. I understand why you didn't call. I told you not to. I brought that on myself.

But I wish we could talk about this. I wish we could have talked about this. There's a lot to say, and you're the only one to say it to. Part of me thinks if I saw you today, I'd fall in love with you all over again. And another part of me thinks that I would feel something entirely different. Better, even. Because you're not just the girl I'm infatuated with, you're not the girl I just met. You're you. You're me.

This year has been a success, for me. I know it's not over. I
know the hard part, getting back to a good place together,
finding ways to make it work again, I know all of that is still
ahead. But I am bursting with the energy to do whatever it
takes. Does that make sense?

I'm ready to tackle this marriage. I was missing the energy
before. And I have the energy now.

Love,
Ryan

• • •

I crumble to the floor.

In all of the possible scenarios, I always assumed the question was whether or not I would end up brokenhearted.

It never even occurred to me that I might end up breaking
a heart.

Y ou have got to be kidding me." I am standing on Charlie's doorstep at eight fifteen in the morning, and that's how I open the conversation. As much as Ryan's letters left me in tears, they also made me furious at Charlie for calling him behind my back in the first place.

I slept on it. Well, really, I stewed on it. And when I woke up this morning, I was somehow angrier, even more convinced that I had been the victim of a deep and ugly betrayal. So I drove over to Charlie's house and rang the doorbell. He opened the door, and that's what I said, "You have got to be kidding me."

Now he's just sort of staring at me, deciding what to say.

"You talked to Ryan, I guess," he says, as he leaves the door open and leads me into the living room. His tone is defensive and personally disappointed. He's wearing chinos and a white undershirt. I'm interrupting his morning routine getting ready for work.

"Excellent work, detective," I say. Now's not the time to explain my hacking habit.

"Look, I had a very good reason," he says.

"You don't get to decide things about my marriage," I say. "Leave Ryan out of this."

"It's not about your marriage, Lauren. Jesus."

Natalie has been sitting on the couch, her hands over her swollen belly. She's wearing thin sweatpants and a sweatshirt. "I'm going to go into the bedroom," she says.

"I'm really sorry," I say to her, somehow able to extract the anger from my voice long enough to speak politely to her. "I didn't mean to ruin your morning."

Natalie waves her hand. "It's totally fine. I thought this moment might come. I'll be in the bedroom."

Charlie gives Natalie a look that says both *Thank you* and *I'm sorry*.

When she's gone, I lay into him again. "Do you have no loyalty?"

Charlie shakes his head and tries to remain calm even while I let my voice fly. "Lauren, just hear me out."

I cross my arms and frown at him. It's my way of hearing him out and finding him guilty at the same time.

"Ryan is the baby's uncle."

"Through me!" I say. "He's the baby's uncle because I am the baby's aunt. By blood."

"I know. But still. It's an important distinction, don't you think? Not just your husband but also the baby's uncle."

"So what?"

"So . . . look around, Lauren. Do you see any other men in my life?"

I don't say anything, I just stare at him.

"We have no brothers," Charlie says. "Just me."

"OK," I say, agreeing with him in order to push the conversation forward.

"And clearly no dad," Charlie says.

"OK," I say again.

"And Grandpa's dead," he says.

"OK."

"All of my close friends are back in Chicago. I live with my fiancée. I spend most of my time with her, at work, or with my mom and two sisters."

I'm still angry, but I can recognize that this is not a line of conversation I can really disagree with. "OK," I say, this time more gently than all the previous times. I shift my body language to be less confrontational.

Charlie looks at me for a while, considering something. I can see him start to get emotional. He lowers his voice. "I'm having a son, Lauren. I'm having a boy."

Thoughts fly through my head so fast I can't choose one and hold on to it. That's great news! My family will be so happy! I didn't know they were finding out the sex of the baby beforehand! I'm so excited to have a nephew! A nephew!

"I'm going to have a nephew?" I say to him. The anger has retreated; it no longer bubbles on the surface. Part of it is the shock of finding out something I thought I wouldn't find out for a few months. Part of it is that my little baby brother, who clearly feels he has so much to prove, is getting a chance to prove it.

"Yeah," he says. I can see his eyes get glossy. "What do I know about raising a son? About being a dad? I have no idea. I have absolutely no idea. I mean, I know I'm going to figure it out but fuck, talk about making it up as you go along. My son needs an uncle, OK? I know things are strained between the two of you, I get it, but Ryan has had my back since I was fourteen. He was the first guy I really looked up to. And . . . I want my son to know him. I want him to be a part of my son's life. To be honest, I need someone to call and admit to that I have no idea what I'm doing."

"You have me," I say. "You have Rachel."

"You two don't have dads, either. We don't know anything about dads. And I'm sorry, this just . . . this isn't a thing a woman can help me with. It just isn't."

"OK," I say. I mean, what else can I say? I don't think I was wrong for being upset, but I think it would be juvenile and selfish to continue being upset in light of all this. "I get it. I wish you had talked to me first. But . . . no, I get it."

"Well, I did wait to talk to you, really," he says. "Because there is something that I would like to do, but I want your blessing before I do it."

"Uh," I say. "OK . . ."

"I'd like to invite Ryan to the wedding."

"Absolutely not." It flies out of my mouth like a bullet leaving a gun.

"Please think about it."

"No, Charlie. I'm sorry. Ryan and I said, in no uncertain terms, that we are not seeing each other or speaking until we have been apart for an entire year. That year is up at the end of August. Not July. And I haven't spent the last eight months resisting the urge to call him just to blow it all early. He won't want to break the deal, either, Charlie."

Charlie looks hurt by what I've said, and I'm not sure which part, exactly, is more hurtful to him. Is it that his own sister won't make an exception for his wedding? Or that I said the only man Charlie looks up to probably wouldn't want to come? Goddammit. You know, when you marry a man, you marry his family, and vice versa. They tell you that. But they don't tell you that when you leave a man, you leave his family. When your husband moves across town and starts dating someone named Emily, he breaks your brother's heart, too.

"Just let me invite him," Charlie says. "That's all I'm asking."

"Charlie, I really don't want him there."

"This isn't about you."

"Charlie—"

"Lauren, did it ever occur to you that my wedding is going to have family pictures? That we are going to put them around the house? That Mom is going to have one on her mantel? And years from now, you're going to look at them and see the hole this year has left in the family? You're going to taint my wedding with your bullshit because you can't see past it right now."

"There is not a hole in the family," I say.

"Yeah, there is. Ryan isn't just someone you love. He's a part of this family."

"Well, no one else seems to have a problem with it except you."

"Wrong again. Mom misses him. Mom told me a few months ago that she had to delete his number from her phone because it was too hard not to call him and check in on him and make sure he was OK."

"Well, Rachel's fine with it," I say.

"That's because Rachel thinks only of you. But I bet if you asked her, she'd say she wants to know how he is."

I can feel my pulse begin to quicken and the blood rush to the surface of my cheeks. I am starting to grow furious. "I made him a part of this family," I say. "And he's a part of this family on my terms."

"I know that you want that to be true. But it's not. You don't own Ryan. You brought him into this family, and you asked us to love him. And we do. And you can't control that."

I try to think of myself in a similar position, but the truth is, I can't. I don't know Natalie all that well. She will be a sister to me one day, but that takes time. It takes history and shared experiences. We don't have that yet. And she's the closest I've come. I was never all that close with Ryan's family, so I don't miss them. I don't know how I'd feel if I was Charlie in this situation. I've never been Charlie in this situation. And maybe that's the problem. Maybe I'm so very much *me* in this situation that I cannot see anyone else or anything else. And maybe I should take that as a sign that I might be wrong. That is, of course, most often the reason people are wrong when they are wrong, isn't it? When they can't understand anything but their own point of view?

I start to talk, to tell him that I will think about it. I open my mouth with the intention of saying, *You're right. I should give it some thought.* But Charlie speaks over me.

"This is so stupid. You two are getting back together in, what, August? What's a few weeks going to matter?"

"I have no idea if we are getting back together at all! I don't even know if—"

"What are you talking about? You said in the beginning that was the whole plan. You spend this time apart, and you get back together."

"Yeah, and you told me then that people rarely get back together. Most of the time, when people separate, it's just a stop on the way to divorce."

Charlie shakes his head at me. "Stop this. You're being dramatic. I'm sorry I said that. I was being a dick. Listen, I want him there. And it's my wedding, and I really do think of him as the baby's uncle, as my brother. Isn't that enough? Isn't that important enough?"

I look at him, thinking about what he has said. Son of a bitch. Life is not just about me. Even my marriage is not just about me.

"Go ahead," I say. "Invite him."

"Thank you," Charlie says.

"No plus one," I say. "Please."

"No plus one," Charlie says, placing his palms up and out in surrender.

"If Ryan is the man you're closest to, who is your best man?" I ask him. I'm suddenly heartsick thinking that my little brother has no best man.

"Oh," he says. "I was going to ask Wally, back in Chicago. But I'm not sure he's going to be able to come in the first place. Natalie and I discussed not having a wedding party at all, actually. I think that might be what we do."

"Not Ryan?" I ask him. I'm so late for work at this point that it's sort of silly to try to speed this up.

"I know what I'm asking you by inviting Ryan," he says. "It doesn't seem fair to ask for more."

So often I am convinced that my brother is a thoughtless jerk, and so often he proves that the thoughtless jerk is me.

"It's OK," I say. "Ask him."

Charlie holds back a smile. He manages to keep his face serious. "I don't want to put you in any more of a weird spot than I already have," he says.

"It's fine," I tell him. "You should do it. He'll say yes. I know he'll say yes."

"You think so?" Charlie asks, letting his excitement show just a little bit.

"Yeah," I say. "He will."

We hug, and Charlie looks at his watch. "Holy shit, I'm late," he says. "You know what? Fuck it." Charlie calls out to the bedroom. "Natalie, are you able to take the day off?"

"What?" I hear from the other room.

"Could you take the day off?"

"Um . . . I guess? I was going to leave early for a doctor's appointment anyway," she says, her voice getting closer as she joins us.

"How about you?" Charlie says to me. "Can you take the day off? We can go see a movie or something?" Natalie is now standing next to him, her arm draped around his waist, her head tucked into his arm. Look at them. Look at my brother. A pregnant woman at his side.

"Oh," I say. I start formulating an answer.

"Wait a minute," Charlie says. "If you and Ryan agreed not to talk for a whole year, how did you know I told him about the baby?" Charlie's voice isn't the least bit suspicious. It's curious and lively.

But I feel as if I've been caught red-handed, the criminal in the interrogation room under the hot lights.

"I should get to work, actually. I'm already an hour late, and traffic is going to be murder. You two have a nice, romantic day!" I say. I'm already heading for the door.

April 20

Dear Lauren,

Charlie called me today and said he spoke with you and that
it was OK with you if he asked me to be his best man.

What is happening in the world? I remember when he used
to beg me to play Grand Theft Auto with him when you and
I would visit on weekends from college. I didn't even like
that game, but I used to do it just to get him to shut up. And
the whole time, he would just talk about girls. The. Whole.
Time. And he was so stupid about girls. It baffled me. For a
boy living in a house with three women, you'd think he knew
how to talk to girls, but he just had no idea. And so I told
him about how I asked you out. I told him that whole thing
about how I pretended that it was you who was asking me
out. And how it's normal to be nervous, but you just have to
do it anyway, because the girls are usually nervous, too, and
they don't notice that you're nervous, and just stupid shit like
that.

And now he's getting married and having a baby. With
someone he really seems to like.

And you and I aren't speaking.

Thank you for saying it was OK. I miss your family a lot. That phone call from Charlie, it made my day. Hell, it might have made my year. This year has been so hard and so confusing, and when I heard Charlie's voice on the phone, it really reminded me of what I've been missing.

I'm looking forward to this wedding. If only because I know I'll get to see you again.

Love,
Ryan

Natalie is wearing a maxidress. She's the sort of pregnant that makes you want to offer your seat to her on the bus. Due in six weeks, she is glowing, but when you tell her that, she says, "It's sweat. Trust me. I'm sweating like the house is on fire."

I didn't tell anyone it's going to be a boy, so we stuck with yellow as the shower theme. My mother insisted on hosting it, and she's gone a little over the top. There are yellow balloons and yellow streamers. There are gifts wrapped in yellow. And a yellow cake, courtesy of Rachel. I think perhaps there is also an unspoken theme of ducks that I didn't get the memo about. The buffet table and the coffee table are covered in rubber duckies. Rachel even made a rubber ducky out of fondant and put it on the top of the cake.

"Guess it's more of a fondant ducky," I say when she shows us.

My mom laughs. "That's what I said, but she didn't seem to think it was funny."

"This cake is beautiful," Natalie says. "Rachel, I can't thank you enough. It looks professionally done."

I know that Rachel has baked this same cake five times, decorating it just this way, to be sure that she could do it. I know that she was up until the early hours of the morning getting the duck right. But she acts as if it was a breeze. "Oh, please," she says. "It's my pleasure." Rachel has on a cute short red dress with a square collar. She was wearing high heels for the occasion but kicked them off about ten minutes ago, well before anyone was even here. "Although I did take a picture of it for my portfolio." She's supposed to hear news on the loan any day now.

Mom comes out from the kitchen with a platter. "OK, you three girls will tell me if I've overdone it," she says. "But look! How cute, right?" My mother shows us a plate of cucumber sandwiches.

"It's not high tea, Mom," Rachel says. "It's a baby shower."

My mom frowns, but Natalie turns it right around. "They are adorable, Leslie. Really. Thank you so much. And my friend Marie, who is coming, is a vegetarian and always worries that there won't be things for her to eat. So it's perfect."

"Thank you, Natalie. I'm relishing this time before you feel as comfortable around me as my daughters do. This is when I still get compliments and not things like 'It's not high tea, Mom.'" My mother's impression of Rachel sounds absolutely nothing like Rachel and everything like Minnie Mouse.

Natalie laughs. "I really do like them, though!" she says.

"OK, Natalie," I say. "You've proven your point. She likes you best."

My mom laughs and puts the platter down and goes back into the kitchen to get more.

"Do you need help?" Natalie asks.

Rachel puts her arm out to stop Natalie from saying any more. "Relax," she says. "You're the pregnant one," she says. "We are the ones who should be offering to help Mom, and we aren't."

"Yeah, so don't make us look bad," I say.

Natalie laughs and sits down on the couch, crossing one leg underneath her and smoothing out her dress. "Well, since I have you two, I actually wanted to ask you a favor," she says. "As I know you know, Charlie asked Ryan to be his best man."

Rachel's jaw drops, and she whips her head at me. "What?" she says.

I shrug. "It's what Charlie wants. What was I going to say?"

"And you're OK with it?" Rachel asks. "How have we not talked about this?"

"It's fine," I say to Rachel. I don't want to get into it and complicate things in front of Natalie.

Natalie looks at me. "I want to say thank you for that," she says. "It has made Charlie really happy, and obviously, I'm not as well versed in the details of you and Ryan, but I would imagine it takes a big person to . . . just . . . thank you."

I nod at her. It's such a complex issue, with so many feelings involved, I fear that if I speak, even if only to say *You're welcome*, I'll start crying, and I won't even know exactly why.

"Anyway, Ryan is Charlie's best man, and it turns out his friend Wally is going to be able to make it to the wedding, so Charlie wanted him to be up there with him, too," Natalie says. "Which means I've got two spots on my side, and I'd love it if you two would be my bridesmaids."

"Wow," Rachel and I both say at the same time.

Rachel continues. "Are you kidding? That is so thoughtful of you."

"I know that it's short notice," Natalie says. "I wasn't sure what was happening with Charlie's side, but now that it's all settled, I really do think it worked out perfectly. I would love to have you two up there with me."

"Are you sure?" I ask. "I mean, our feelings won't be hurt if you have friends you'd like to ask."

"No," Natalie says. "I mean, I have people I could ask. I have girlfriends I love. But you guys are family. I love the idea of being a part of a big family. My family is just me and my parents. I'm excited to have sisters." Natalie tiptoes around the word *sisters* as if she's not sure that it's OK for her to be so presumptuous, and because of that, I feel the need to go overboard in letting her know that I absolutely do want to consider her my sister. That I want her to be a part of our family.

"We are excited, too!" I say, and then try to modulate my enthusiasm to seem less over the top. "Seriously, I feel lucky that Charlie has chosen someone so cool."

"Yeah?" Natalie says. "You'd be my sort of co-maids of honor, I guess. Since there isn't an official one."

"Works for us," Rachel says.

My mom comes back out with pigs in a blanket. "Check these babies out!" she says, laughing to herself. The three of us look at the tray and see that she's put food coloring in the "blankets." Some of them are pink, some of them are blue. "Since we don't know the sex of the baby yet. Get it?"

"So we are going to be eating the babies as an appetizer?" Rachel asks. I start laughing; I can't help it. Natalie tries to stifle hers.

My mom looks down at the plate, frowning. "Oh, no," my mom says. "Do you think people will feel like they're eating babies?"

"You guys are so mean!" Natalie says. "Leslie, they are great. It's a perfect baby shower thing."

"Mom, I was totally kidding," Rachel says, trying to take it back. My mom normally doesn't mind being made fun of, but today she's taking it at least a little bit seriously, and I feel bad about that.

She hasn't put the tray down. She's seriously considering not serving them. "No," she says. "It's weird. Shoot. I should have just left them not colored."

"No," I say. "Please. She really was kidding. It's perfect. It's just like those games where people melt candy bars in diapers to look like poop or bob for nipples, you know? Baby showers are supposed to be a little over the top. It's good!"

"You're sure?" my mom asks all of us.

"Positive," Rachel says.

Natalie nods her head. I walk over to my mom and put my arm around her. "Totally. You've done such a great job. It looks incredible."

"OK," she says, finally putting the tray down. "But I didn't get any nipples to . . . bob for. Is that bad?"

"No," I say. "It was just a suggestion. Is there more stuff in the kitchen? I'll come help you."

We head toward the kitchen, leaving Natalie and Rachel in the living room.

When we are out of earshot, I ask, "You doing OK?"

"Yeah," she says. "This is . . . it's a little stressful!"

"What can I help with?" I ask, standing at the counter, but it looks as if everything is under control.

"No, nothing," my mom says. "It's just . . . it's my first grandbaby."

"I know," I say.

"I always pictured myself throwing a baby shower for my first grandbaby."

"Sure," I say. "I can understand that."

"And I just figured . . ."

I wait for her to finish, but she doesn't. "You thought it'd be for me," I say.

It takes my mom a while to answer. "Yeah," she finally admits. "Which is fine. Your life is your life. I'm so proud of what you're doing with it."

"I know, Mom. But that doesn't mean it's not surprising. Or that things haven't worked out in a way that is stressful or confusing," I say.

"I'm so happy about all of this," my mom says. "I really am."

"But . . . ?" I ask.

"But," she says, taking the bait, "I don't know her. When I was shopping at the store and putting together the menu, I kept stopping and going, 'Does Natalie like olives? Does Natalie like cilantro?' I mean, some people hate cilantro."

"Yeah," I say.

"I just don't know her all that well yet," my mom says. "It's hard to throw a baby shower for someone you don't know that well yet."

"All that matters is that your heart is in the right place," I say. "Natalie is easy to please."

"Yeah, maybe," my mom says, staring at the plate of crab cakes in front of her. "Will you just go out there and casually ask her if she likes cilantro? I put some in the crab cakes, and some people just really hate cilantro."

"Sure, Mom," I say, just as the doorbell rings.

We can hear Rachel open the door, and a group of women's voices begin to chatter. The party has started. Natalie's friends and coworkers will start streaming in. The gift table will begin to pile up. Before you know it, we will be pinning the sperm on the egg and acting as if the Diaper Genie is the most fascinating object the world has ever seen. "You know, one day, it will be me," I say as I leave the kitchen. "And when it is, you can serve all the cilantro you want."

David is lying across my bed. His shirt is off. He's just in his underwear. We've been drinking.

It all started because David said he wanted to make me dinner, and he brought over a bag of groceries and took over the kitchen. And since he brought dinner, I figured I should open one of the bottles of wine that's been taking up space on the credenza. We each had a glass of red wine and then had another. And then another. And then we opened another bottle for some reason. Between the deliciousness of dinner and all the laughing, more drinking seemed like a good idea.

And here we are, stuffed and still drunk. We started kissing in bed. But his watch got caught in my hair, and we started to laugh. And since then, we haven't really recovered. We're just lying next to each other, both half dressed, holding hands and looking up at the ceiling.

"I think Ryan is going to want to get back together," I say to the air.

David doesn't move or look at me. He keeps his focus on the ceiling. "Yeah?" he asks. "Why do you think that?"

"Well, he said as much," I say.

Now he does shift toward me. "I thought you guys weren't talking," he says. David knows the deal. He knows the drill. At this point, he knows about the fights and the resentments. He knows about the lack of sex, the bad sex.

"He writes me letters sometimes," I say. I leave it at that. I don't feel like explaining it.

"Ah," he says. His hand is still in mine. He's starting to massage my hand in his. "Well, how do you feel about that?"

I laugh, because that *is* the question, isn't it? How do I feel about that? "I don't know," I say, and then I sigh. "I'm thinking that I'm not sure I feel the same way. Or, yeah, that's exactly it. I'm not *sure* I feel the same way. It scares me that I'm not *sure* anymore."

"Man," David says, looking back up at the ceiling. "I'm almost envious of you. I wish . . . God, I wish I could stop thinking about Ashley. I wish I could feel *unsure* that I love her or want her."

"It still hurts?" I ask, but I know the answer. I'm just trying to give him space to talk about it.

"Every day. It hurts every day. It kills me not to tell her everything going on in my life. And sometimes I just want to call her and say, 'Let's get dinner. Let's figure this out.'"

"Why don't you?" I ask. I roll onto my stomach, with my elbows out in front of me. Listening pose.

"Because," he says, his voice becoming animated and passionate, "she cheated on me. You can't . . . if someone cheats on you, I mean, the self-respecting thing to do is to leave that person. You can't be with someone who cheats on you."

Normally, I would agree with him. But it really sounds as if he's saying it because he's been told that's what he should think.

"I don't know," I say. "It was one time, right?"

"She says it was one time. But isn't that what all people who cheat say? Anyway, I'm not sure it matters whether it was once or a millions times." He turns over onto his stomach now, too. Our shoulders grazing each other.

"People make mistakes," I say. If I have learned one thing in all of this, it's that we're all capable of more than we think we are, for better or worse. Everyone has the potential to fuck up big when the stakes are high. "I threw a vase at my husband's head."

David turns to me. "You?"

I nod.

Yes, it was me. Yes, I am ashamed I did it. But it also wasn't me. That wasn't me. That person was so angry. I was so angry. I'm not angry anymore.

"The point is, everyone makes mistakes. And I have to think, the way you love Ashley, the way you talk about her, the way you can't get over her, I'm not sure that's all that common of a love. It might be the kind of love that can overcome this sort of stuff."

The fact is, I look at David, I look at how he yearns for his ex-wife, I look at how he is clearly unable to move on from her in any meaningful way, and I'm the one who's jealous. Not of her. Of him. I want to love like that. I want to feel as if I'm not OK without someone, without Ryan. But I *am* OK.

Things aren't perfect right now. But I'm OK.

That can't be good.

David and I keep talking. The conversation drifts in and out but always goes back to Ashley. I'm paying attention. I'm listening. But my mind is elsewhere.

I have something I need to do.

• • •

April 30

Dear Ask Allie,

I have been married for six years. My husband and I met eleven years ago. For most of my adult life, I have believed he was my soul mate. For most of our relationship, I have truly loved him and felt loved by him. But some time ago, for reasons that have only started to become clear to me now, we stopped being good to each other.

When I say that the reasons for this are starting to become clear, I mean I have realized that our marriage suffered from issues of resentment. We resented each other for things like how often we had sex, the quality of the sex we did have, the places we wanted to eat dinner, how we showed affection for each other, all the way down to basic errands like calling the plumber.

I've come to realize that resentment is malignant. That it starts small and festers. That it grows wild and unfettered inside of you until it's so expansive that it has worked its way into the furthest, deepest parts of you and holds on for dear life.

I can see that now.

And the reason I can see all of this now is that my husband and I recognized that we had a problem about nine months ago, and we decided to give each other some space. We agreed to a yearlong break.

The year is not over, and I already feel I have gained a great deal of perspective that I didn't have this time last year. I understand myself better. I understand what I did to contribute to the downfall of my marriage. I also understand what I allowed to happen to my marriage. When this trial period is over, I know I will be a changed woman.

The problem is that in our time apart, I have learned that I can lead an incredibly fulfilling life without my husband. I can be happy without him. And that scares me. Because I think, maybe, you shouldn't spend your life with someone you don't need. Isn't your marriage supposed to be the union of two halves of a whole? Doesn't that necessitate that they cannot be whole themselves? That they must feel as if they are missing a piece when they are apart?

When I agreed to this idea of taking time off, on some level, I thought I'd learn that it wasn't possible. I thought I'd learn that life without my husband was unbearable and that it would be so unbearable that I'd beg him to come home, and when he came home, I'd have learned a lesson about never undervaluing him again. I thought this was a way to shock myself into realizing how much I needed him.

But when the worst happened, when I lost him and he started dating other people, the sun rose the next morning. Life went on. If it's true love, is that even possible?

During our time apart, I've talked to anyone who will listen about my marriage. I've talked to my sister, my brother, my mother, my grandmother, my best friend, a man I'm seeing casually, and all of them have different ideas of what marriage is. All of them have different advice about what to do.

And yet I'm still lost.

So what do you think, Allie?

Do I get back together with the man I used to love?

Or do I start over, now that I know that I can?

Sincerely,
Lost in Los Angeles

I don't reread it. I know that I'll lose my nerve. I just hit send.
And off it goes, into the nothingness of the Internet.

I come into the office and head right to Mila's desk.

"I wrote to her, the advice columnist."

Mila looks up at me, smiling. "Well, I guess I have to take back all that stuff I said about it making you a loony."

"You don't think it means I'm crazy?" I say.

Mila laughs. "I find it easier to define 'crazy' by what rational people do rather than my own preconceived ideas. You did it. You're a rational person. Thus, it is not crazy."

My head cocks to the side. "Thank you," I say. I really did think she was going to think I was crazy. I'm glad I was wrong.

"So show me this woman, this Ask Allie," she says. "I want to read up on her. See what you've gotten yourself into."

I take over her computer and type in the Web address. The page pops up. The question at the top is the one I read last night. It's about a man who has been cheating on his wife for years and feels he finally needs to tell her. Ask Allie isn't very nice to him.

"Don't read that one," I say. "Or, I mean, you can, but read this one first."

I pull up the letter she wrote to a woman who placed her daughter up for adoption years ago and now wants to find her but doesn't know if she should. I really like the part where she tells her, *Make yourself available, make yourself easily found, should someone try to find you. Be open, be generous, be humble. You are in a unique position in which you cannot require love and acceptance, but you must give it if your daughter seeks it from you. It may seem hard, almost impossible, to love without the expectation of love in return, but once you have figured out how to do it, you will find that you really are a parent.*

"Let me know what you think," I tell Mila, and then I head back to my office.

Twenty minutes later, Mila is at my desk. "How have I spent my whole life not reading these letters?" she says. "Did you read the one about the gay son? I lost it right at my desk. I was tearing up!" Her voice changes as she sits down. "So what if she reads your letter? What if she answers it?"

"She's not gonna answer it," I tell her. "She's probably not even going to read it."

"She could, though," Mila says. "She might."

"I very much doubt it."

"You wrote to her about Ryan?" she asks.

"Yeah," I say.

"Did you mention the year-apart thing? That could be a good hook."

"You sound like my grandmother!" I say. "I asked her if she thought it made sense to start a marriage over or if . . ."

"If what?"

"If I shouldn't just start over on my own."

"Whoa," Mila says. "That's even an option? You're thinking about that?"

"I don't know what I'm thinking! That's why I wrote her."

"How did you sign it?"

"Oh, come on, that's the most embarrassing part," I say.

"Give it up, Cooper. How did you sign it?"

I sigh and resign myself to admitting it. "Lost in Los Angeles."

Mila nods her head in approval. "Not bad!" she says. "Not bad at all."

"Get out of my office," I say, smiling at her. "Are you free for lunch tomorrow? I need a second set of eyes on a dress fitting."

"What kind of dress?" Mila asks, her hand on the doorframe.

"Bridesmaid."

Mila raises her eyebrow. "What are the wedding colors?"

"Um," I say, trying to remember what Natalie told me. "Coral and pale yellow, I think."

"Sort of like persimmon and poppy?"

"I don't even know what you just said."

"Like grapefruit and lemon?"

"Sure," I say. "That sounds about right." Whatever happened to primary colors?

Mila nods her head approvingly. "Your sister-in-law's got style."

For some reason, I am personally flattered by her compliment. Natalie *does* have style. And she's going to be *my* sister-in-law. I get to have another sister. Maybe one day, we'll be so close that I forget that she was once new and unfamiliar. Maybe one day, I'll love her so much that I momentarily forget she's Charlie's wife or my nephew's mom. She'll just be my sister.

Rachel, Thumper, and I are supposed to go hiking this morning, but for the first time, we truly cannot find a parking space. We circle around the area for about thirty minutes before we all lose our patience.

"Brunch instead?" Rachel asks.

"Sure," I say. Eating brunch is exactly the opposite of hiking, and yet it feels like the natural move. "Where to?"

Rachel pulls up a list in her phone. "Are you up for checking out a bakery?" In her off time, Rachel has been going to every bakery she can find in Los Angeles, trying to figure out what she likes and what she doesn't. Slowly but surely, this bakery idea has become a real thing in her mind. It's something that is going to happen, sooner or later. The sooner or later depending on a small-business loan.

"Absolutely," I say. "Am I headed right or left?"

"Left," she says. "I want to check out this place in Hollywood I heard about. I read about it on a blog, like, a year ago and never made my way over to check it out. Apparently, they serve high-end waffles."

"High-end waffles? Like luxury waffles?"

Rachel laughs, pointing to her right to indicate that I need to turn here. "Like cream cheese waffles, peanut butter banana waffles, bacon waffles. You know, trendy waffles."

"That sounds like a dumb idea for a restaurant," I say. "Because what if I want eggs with my waffles?"

"Look, I just heard that the space was really cool, and I want to see it. We don't even have to eat there. We can eat farther down the block. Just take this until you hit Melrose, and take a left, and then we're gonna take a right."

"Aye-aye, Captain."

"Don't say that," Rachel says. She turns to Thumper, who is waiting patiently in the backseat. "Why does she talk like that, Thumper?" He has no answer.

When we get to Larchmont Boulevard, I park the car along the street, and Rachel, Thumper, and I head toward the store-front, but we can't find it.

"What number did you say it was?" I ask her.

"I don't remember," she says, trying to find it in her phone. She looks down at the screen and frowns, and then she looks straight ahead. We're standing in front of a glass storefront with a sign, "FOR LEASE," written across it in big red capital letters.

"This is it," she says, disappointed.

"It closed?"

"I guess so," she says. She stares into the storefront for a moment and then says, "If Waffle Time can't stay in business, how am I going to stay in business?"

"Well, you're not going to name your place Waffle Time, that's number one."

Rachel drops her arms and looks at me. "Seriously, Lauren. Look at all this place had going for it. Look at the foot traffic here. Everyone stops and walks around Larchmont. Parking is fairly easy. There's a parking lot right there for seventy-five cents. Where else is there a lot for seventy-five cents?"

"Well, it's seventy-five cents for a half hour," I say. "But I see your point."

Rachel puts her head to the glass and peers in, cupping her hands around her eyes to better her vision. She sighs. "Look at this place!"

I do the same, right beside her. There is an exposed brick wall on one side. A long L-shaped counter, a cash register on the small end of the L, built-in stools on the long side. There is a white, faded display case on the back wall. It looks adorable. With a couple of tables and chairs, I imagine it was a really nice place to get a luxury waffle.

"I could do it here," she says. "Right? I could try to lease this place."

"Absolutely," I say. "Does it seem like something in your price range?"

"I barely even know my price range," she says. "But no, not really."

It's been a long time since I've seen her this drawn to something.

I pull out my phone and take down the number on the sign. "You can call," I say, a hopeful tone in my voice. "It never hurts to call."

"No," she says. "You're right. It doesn't hurt to call."

There are two types of people in this world. There is the type of person who, when faced with this predicament, takes down the number but never calls, already assuming the answer is no. And there is the type of person who takes down the number and calls anyway, hoping for a miracle. Sometimes those people end up in the same place. Sometimes the person who calls ends up ahead.

Rachel will call. That is the type of person Rachel is. And that's how I know that her bakery has a real shot. That, and I think she will corner the baby shower market with those fondant duckies.

Friday afternoon, David calls me at work and asks if I'm free that night. "I have a surprise that has landed in my lap, and I'd love to take you," he says.

"Oh?" I'm intrigued.

"The Lakers are playing the Clippers in the playoffs," he says, excited.

"Oh, interesting," I say. Dammit. He wants to go to a basketball game? "I didn't know you were into basketball."

"I'm not, really. But Lakers versus Clippers? Two L.A. teams against each other on their way to the finals? That seems epic. And not the way people use that word now. I mean, an actual epic struggle for the heart of Los Angeles sports fans. Plus, these are great seats."

"OK," I say. "Cool. Go, Lakers!"

"Or Clippers," David says. "We'll have to decide."

I laugh. "I suppose we should be on the same team for this."

"Might make things easier," he says. "So I'll pick you up at your place around six?"

"Sounds good."

When he shows up at my door at ten of six, the sun is out and is only now considering the idea of setting. The heat, which in only a month or two will become as oppressive as a straitjacket, is merely mild and soothing, like a sweatshirt.

We get into the car, and David starts careening through the streets. He navigates with confidence. I am tempted, when he turns onto Pico, to suggest he take Olympic. I stop myself. It's not polite.

And yet Pico gets us there much, much more slowly than Olympic would have. The traffic is aggressive and bumper-to-bumper. People are cutting people off, sneaking into lanes they aren't supposed to, and in general acting like jerks. By the time we are downtown, circling around the Staples Center, I am remembering why I don't go to the Staples Center. I hate crowds of people. I hate congested parking lots. I don't really care about sports.

David pulls into a private lot charging twenty-five dollars to park.

"Are you serious?" I ask. I can't believe it. "Twenty-five dollars?"

"Well, I'm certainly not dealing with the bullshit of trying to get into one of those lots." He points down the street to men with bright flashing batons and flags, offering parking for fifteen. Cars are backed up for blocks to get in.

I nod my head.

We get out of the car. It takes us ten minutes just to cross the street to get to the Staples Center. A sea of people, some in yellow and purple jerseys, some in red and blue, swarms past us.

David takes my hand, which is good, because I have no idea where I am. We make our way into the stadium, entering through what look like the main doors. We hand over our tickets.

The ticket taker, a humorless forty-something man, frowns at us and tells us we are at the wrong door. He says we need to go to the left, around the building.

David is losing his patience now, too. "We can't get in this way?"

"Left and around the building," the man says.

So we go.

We finally find the right door.

We walk in. We are told that our seats are in section 119, which is nowhere near the door we came in. By the time we find our seats, they are inhabited by two teenage boys in Clippers jerseys. We have to ask them to leave, which makes me feel like pretty much the worst person in this stadium, since these boys actually care about this game and I don't care in the slightest.

But regardless, we sit down.

We watch the ball go back and forth.

David turns to me, the stress finally leaving his face. "OK," he says. "Let's root for the Clippers."

"Sounds good. Why Clippers?"

David shrugs. "They seem like the underdog."

It's as good a reason as any. When they score, David and I jump up. When a foul is called against them, we boo. We cheer for the guy trying to make the halftime shot. We pretend to be impressed by the Laker Girls. We stomp our feet in rapid-fire motion when the announcer tells us to make some noise. But my heart is not in it. I don't care.

The Clippers lose, 107 to 102.

David and I leave with the flow of the rest of the stands. We are pushed into the people in front of us. I trip on a stair. We break away from the crowd. We leave the stadium.

The sun set some time ago. I should have brought a sweater.

"Do you remember which way we came in?" David says. "It was this way, right? After we came around the building?"

"Oh, I thought you were paying attention."

"No," he says, his voice strained. "I thought you were."

I realize then that between parking in a random lot and walking all around the stadium to get in, neither of us has any idea where we parked.

And that's when I think, *Jesus Christ. I've done all of this,*

I've spent all of this time, done all of this work, just to end up back here?

Because while it may not look the same as trying to find your car in Lot C of Dodger Stadium, it sure as hell feels exactly like it.

And then I look at David, and I think that if all roads eventually lead here anyway, I'd rather it was with Ryan.

May 14

Dear Lauren,

I broke up with Emily. It wasn't really a serious thing, but I
thought it was better to be honest. I've been thinking about
you and me so much that it feels wrong to have another
woman in my bed. And it felt wrong to do that to her, too. So I
broke it off.

I've been thinking about our future. I've been thinking about
what life holds for us. I've been thinking of ways I can be a
better husband. I made a whole list! Good stuff, I think. Stuff
that is actionable. Not just things like "Be nicer" but actual
ideas.

I was thinking one of them could be that we have one night
a week where we eat some international food you like.
For instance, every Wednesday, we go out to dinner for
Vietnamese, Greek, Persian, Ethiopian, whatever you want.
And I'll never complain. Because the rest of the week, we
will compromise. But one day a week, we eat together
at some crazy place you love. Because I want you to be
happy, and you deserve to have tahdig or pho or a bahn mi
sandwich or any of those other things. Also, I'll only make
you go to the Chinese place on Beverly once a month. I know

you hate it. There is no sense in going there all the time just because I like the orange chicken.

See, honey? Compromise! We can do this!

Love,
Ryan

Rachel calls me when I'm at work, and I have plenty of work to do, but I pick up the phone.

"It's out of my price range," she says. "I went to look at it, and it's perfect. Completely perfect. But it's too much money. Like, not realistic for me but not so expensive that it's outrageous. It's just enough to torture me."

"I'm sorry," I say.

"Thanks. I don't know why I called you to tell you that. I think I just . . . I got kind of excited about the idea? And then I thought maybe this whole thing was going to become real?" She's saying all of these things as if they are a bunch of questions, but it's clear she knows them to be facts. "Yeah," she adds. "I think when I saw that space, I saw it all in my head, you know? 'Batter' written in script above the door. Me with an apron."

"You're calling it Batter?" I ask her.

"Maybe," she says defensively. "Why?"

"No, I like it."

"Oh, well, yeah. Anyway, I think it just seemed real."

"We will find you something," I say. "We can go out again this weekend and look at stuff."

"Yeah, OK. Are you around Friday night, actually? I kind of want to go when they are closed and just peer in. I feel like a spy when I do it to their face."

I start to laugh. "I can't Friday. I have plans."

"With that guy David? I feel like I barely know this guy. You never talk about him," she says.

"Yeah, I don't know, I guess there isn't much to talk about."

The truth is that I asked him to dinner because I want to tell him I think we should stop sleeping together. It's not that I don't care for him or like him. I do. And the night at the Staples Center was frustrating, but that's not it, either.

It's that I need to figure out how I feel about Ryan. I have to make a decision about what I want. And I can't do that if I'm distracting myself with David. David and I aren't going anywhere. And while I've never minded that about us, it's time to start making some life decisions. It's time to stop playing around.

"But I can do Saturday night," I say. "I'll be free Saturday night."

"Actually, forget it," she says. "Forget it. I'm calling the bank. That's where my bakery should be. I'm gonna see if I can increase the loan. I want to lease Waffle Time."

"You sure?" I ask her.

"No," she says.

"But you're going to do it anyway?" I ask.

"Yep," she says with remarkable confidence. And then she gets off the phone.

I asked David to meet me at a bar in Hollywood. We've been having a nice time chatting, but I think it's important that I don't mince words.

"I think we should stop seeing each other," I tell him.

He looks pretty surprised, but he seems to take it in stride. "Is this because I acted like such a dick at the Staples Center? I was just frustrated because we couldn't find the car," he says, smiling.

I laugh. "I just . . . Ryan and I are supposed to 'get back together' soon." I use my fingers to suggest quotations as I say it.

"Totally get it," he says. He puts his arms up in surrender. "I won't look at you seductively anymore."

I laugh. "You're such a gentleman," I say.

The bartender comes over and asks us what we want to drink. I remember him from years ago. Ryan and I came here once for a friend's birthday party. Ryan ended up having a few too many that night as the group of us were huddled around the bar. Around midnight, I grabbed the keys and told Ryan it was time to go home. After we said our good-byes and were headed for the door, Ryan stopped short at the end of the bar. He belligerently got the bartender's attention and said to him, "Excuse me, excuse me, have you ever seen a woman this beautiful?" pointing at me. I blushed. The bartender shook his head. "No, sir, I haven't." I remember thinking then that I was the luckiest woman in the entire world. I remember thinking, after all these years together, he thinks I'm the most beautiful woman in the world. I felt like one of the ones who had it all figured out. Now the same bartender is still serving drinks here, and I'm breaking up with another man.

"So what about you?" I ask David after we order. "What are you gonna do?"

"Me?" He shrugs. The bartender puts down David's beer and my glass of wine. "I'm no closer to figuring any of this out than I ever have been."

"For what it's worth," I offer, "I think you should call her."

"You do?"

"Yeah," I say. "I do. From everything you've told me, she was heartbroken to lose you. You said she dropped to her knees and begged you to forgive her, right?"

"Yeah," David says. "Yeah, she did."

"And you, you're heartbroken, too. After all this time. I think that means something."

David laughs. "You don't think it just means I'm mal-adjusted?"

I laugh, too. "Maybe. But even if you're maladjusted, you might as well be happy."

He considers it. "You remember she cuckolded me, right? I mean, I'm a cuckold."

I laugh at the word and then shrug. "So you're a cuckold. I mean, that's the reality of it. You leaving her doesn't change it. Maybe it's not what you wanted. But it's what you have. And you can be a cuckold on your own. Or a cuckold with the woman you love." I smile at him. "You're the one who told me that it's nice when you can let go of what you thought life should be and just be happy with what it is."

David looks at me. He really looks at me. He's quiet. And then he says, "OK. Maybe I'll call her."

The bartender comes by and drops off the check at the table. "Whenever you're ready," he says.

Our glasses are half full, but I think we're ready.

"So should I take from all of this newfound wisdom that you know what you want to do about Ryan?"

I smile at him, taking my last sip of wine. "Nope," I say. "Still not a damn clue."

When I get home, I wait for Thumper to come to me, and then I sit with him on the floor. I'm not sure for how long. At some point, I get up and open my e-mail. I start to try to write to Ryan. But nothing comes out. I don't know how I feel. I don't know that I have much to say. I sit there, staring at the blank screen, until the phone rings, jolting me out of my catatonic daze. It's Rachel. I pick up the phone and put it through to voice mail. I'm not up for talking at the moment.

A few seconds later, she calls again. It's not like her, so I pick up.

"Hey," I say.

"Have you talked to Mom?" Her voice is no-nonsense and rushed.

"No, why?" I immediately sit forward; my pulse starts to race.

"Grandma's been admitted to the hospital. Mom just got a call from Uncle Fletcher."

"Is she OK?"

"No." Rachel's voice starts to break down. "I don't think so."

"What happened?"

Rachel is quiet. When she finally does speak, her voice is meek and embarrassed. She sounds as if she's in pain and yet ashamed. "Complications from acute lymphoblastic leukemia."

"Leukemia?"

Rachel is hesitant to admit that I have heard her correctly. "Yes."

"Cancer? Grandma has cancer?"

"Yeah."

"Please tell me you are joking," I say. My voice is brisk and almost angry. I'm not angry at Rachel. I'm not angry at Grandma or Mom or Uncle Fletcher. I'm not even angry at acute whatever-it's-called leukemia. I'm angry at myself. I'm angry at all those times I laughed at her. All those times I rolled my eyes.

"I'm not joking," Rachel says. "Mom booked us flights leaving tomorrow morning. Can you go?"

"Yeah," I say. "Yeah, I'll make sure I can go. Is Charlie going?"

"We aren't sure. Natalie can't fly. He may drive up."

"OK," I say. I don't know what else to add. I have so many questions that I feel lost about which one to ask first. So I just go with the one I'm the most terrified of. "How long does she have?"

"Uncle Fletcher thinks only a few days."

"A few *days*?" I thought we were talking months. I was hoping for years.

"Yeah," Rachel says. "I don't know what to do."

"What time is the flight?" I ask her.

"Seven A.M."

"Is Mom meeting us there?"

"Mom's at the airport trying to get a flight out now."

"OK," I say. "I need to find someone to watch Thumper. Let me make a few phone calls, and I'll just come over once I have everything squared away."

"OK," she says. "I'm going to check in with Charlie. I'll talk to you soon."

"OK," I say. "I love you."

"I love you, too."

Part of me thinks I should call Ryan. He should watch

Thumper. But I also know that I have so much going on in my life right this very second that adding that complication on top of it seems messy. I won't be able to give Ryan the attention he needs in the midst of this. It won't do anyone any good. So I call Mila.

"I'm sorry it's so late," I say when she answers.

"Everything OK?" she asks, her voice muffled and tired. I tell her about my grandmother. I tell her about Thumper.

"Sure, absolutely. We'll watch him. Do you want to bring him over now?"

"Yeah," I say. "I'll see you soon."

I pack up his food and his leash. I put on shoes under my pajama bottoms. The two of us get into the car. I'm at her front door before I know it. I don't even remember how we got here.

Mila invites us in. She and Christina are in sweats. We whisper, because the kids are asleep. I rarely see Christina, but I am reminded now that she has such a kind face. Bright eyes, big cheeks. She gives me a hug.

"No matter what, we are here for you," she says. "Not just Mila but me, too." Mila looks at her and smiles.

"I should be back in a few days," I say. "He is pretty well behaved. If you have any trouble, just call me."

"Don't worry about us," Mila says. "You just worry about you. I'll take care of everything at work. I'll make sure everyone knows you need some time."

I nod and bend down to rub noses with Thumper. "I'll be home soon, baby boy."

When I walk out of the house, knowing I've left my dog, it hurts like a pinch. I get into my car and start crying. The tears stream down my face, clouding my vision. I can barely see. I pull over to the side of the street, and I let it out.

I'm crying for my grandmother. I'm crying for my mom.

I'm crying for Thumper. For Rachel and Charlie and me. And throughout all of it, I am crying over Ryan.

I know I will get through this, even though it will be hard. It will feel impossible, and yet I will do it. I know that. But the voice shouting in my ear, the feeling pulling at my heart and constricting my chest, says that it would be easier if Ryan were here. It would just be that little bit easier to have him by my side. Maybe it doesn't matter if you need someone during the everyday moments of your life. Maybe what matters is that when you need *someone*, they are the one you need. Maybe needing someone isn't about not being able to do it without them. Maybe needing someone is about it being easier if they are by your side.

I pull out my phone and open an e-mail draft.

May 30

Dear Ryan,

Grandma has been admitted to the hospital with leukemia.
She doesn't have much time. I keep thinking of all the times
I made fun of her behind her back for saying she had cancer.
The way we all treated it like some big family joke.

And I keep thinking that it would feel so good if you were
here with me. It would feel so nice to hear your voice. You
would tell me everything was going to be OK. You would hold
me. You would wipe away my tears. You would tell me you
understood. Just like you did when we lost Grandpa.

I'm leaving for San Jose in a few hours. We're going to
spend her last days with her there. This kind of stuff is why
I married you. I married you because you take care of me.
Because you make things seem OK when they aren't OK.
Because you believe in me. You know I can handle things
even when I feel like I won't make it through.

I know that I can do this without you. I've learned that this
past year. But I just miss you right now. I just want you near
me. You bring out the best in me. And I could use the best of
me right now.

I love you.

Love,
Lauren

I almost hit send. It seems important enough to actually send to him. But I don't. I choose to hit save. I put the car into drive, and I move forward.

part five

NOTHING
COMPARES 2 U

The flight was fine. It was fine in that there was no turbulence or delays. It's a forty-five-minute flight, so it's not all that torturous. But it was awful in that all Rachel and I did was say, "I really didn't think she had cancer," over and over.

When we get to the hospital, my mom is waiting next to my grandmother's bed. Uncle Fletcher is talking to the doctor. Mom sees us before we get into the room, and she steps outside to prep us.

"She's not doing great in terms of energy," my mom says, her face and voice both stoic. "But the doctors are confident that she's not in much pain."

"OK," I say. "How are you?"

"Terrible," she says. "But I'm not going to deal with it until I have to. I think the best thing for all of us is to buck up. Put on a brave face. Use this time to tell her how much she means to us."

Because we don't have much time left.

"Can we talk to her?" Rachel asks.

"Of course." Mom opens her arm and directs us into the room. Rachel and I sit down on either side of Grandma. She looks tired. Not the sort of tired after you've run a race or the sort of tired after you haven't slept. She looks the sort of tired that you might be after living so long on this earth.

"How are you, Grandma?" Rachel asks.

Grandma smiles at Rachel and pats her hand. There's no answer to that question.

"We love you, Grams," I say. "We love you so much."

She pats my hand this time and closes her eyes.

We all stand around for hours, waiting for her to wake up, seizing the moments when she's lucid and smiling. No one cries. I don't know how we all do it.

Around three, Charlie and Natalie arrive. Natalie looks as if she could burst at any minute. Charlie looks haggard and stressed. He looks at Grandma sleeping. "It's bad?" is all he asks, and Mom nods.

"Yeah," she says. "It's bad."

She takes Charlie and Natalie into the hall to talk to them. Rachel goes with her. It's just me, sleeping Grandma, and Uncle Fletcher. I never have much to say to Fletcher, and now, when it seems there is so much to say, I'm still speechless. He is, too. After a while, he excuses himself, saying he's going to find a nurse. As much as I have nothing to say to him, I also don't want him to go. I don't want to be alone in this room. I don't want to face this alone.

I walk up to the chair next to Grandma that Uncle Fletcher just vacated, and I sit down. I grab her hand. I know she's asleep, but I talk to her anyway. I'm not alone in this room yet, I realize. She's still here.

"You know, I wrote to Ask Allie," I tell her. "I wrote to her about Ryan and me. You were right about a lot of the things you said. About how I could have avoided this year altogether if maybe I'd valued some things differently. And yet I think I needed this year. I think it was in me, and it had to come out, if that makes sense. I think I needed extra time with Rachel. I needed to be able to focus on Charlie. I needed to explore some other things. Or, you know, maybe I didn't need to do it. Maybe there are a number of ways I could have handled my marriage, and this was just . . . this was the way I handled it. Anyway, I wrote to Ask Allie about it. I asked her what she thought I should do. You were right about her," I say, laughing under my breath. "She's good." It's eerily quiet in the room, so I keep talking. "Ryan was here when Grandpa died. And I remember the way he just held me and somehow made it better. Can just anyone do that for you? Can you be held by just anyone? Or does it have to be someone in particular?"

"Someone in particular," she says. Her voice is rough and scratchy. Her eyes are still closed. Her face barely moves when she talks.

"Grandma? Are you OK? Can I get you anything? Should I get Mom?"

She ignores me. "You have that someone. That's all I've been trying to say. Don't give up on him just because he bores you. Or doesn't pick up his socks."

"Yeah," I say. She seems too weak to keep talking, so I don't want to ask her questions. And yet there is so much I want to learn from her. Her eccentricities, the things that felt so silly and laughable before, now seem profound and insightful. Why do we do this? Why do we undervalue things when we have them? Why is it only on the verge of losing something that we see how much we need it?

"I wasn't actually positive that I had cancer," she says. "I hadn't been to the doctor in ages. I kept telling your mother and your uncle that I was going." She laughs. "But I never went. I figured if I did have it, I didn't want anyone trying to cure it. A few times, I walked out the door, telling Fletcher I was going to see my oncologist. I didn't even have an oncologist. I was playing bridge with Betty Lewis and the Friedmans." She laughs again, and then she fades out for a moment and perks back up. "The doctors say this type is fast-moving. Most likely, I just developed it. You guys weren't wrong to make fun of me all those years I kept saying I had it," she says, smiling at me, letting me know she knew what we were saying the whole time. "I was ready to die, and I think that was the only way I could admit it."

"How can you be ready to die?"

"Because my husband is gone, Lauren," she says. "I love you all so much. But you don't need me anymore. Look at all of you. Your mom is doing so well. Fletcher is fine. You three kids are doing great."

"Well . . ."

"No, you are," she says, patting my hand. "But I miss my mom," she says. "I miss my dad. I miss my big sister. I miss my best friend. And I miss my husband. I've lived too long without him now."

"But you were doing OK," I say. "You were getting out of bed. You were making a life without him."

My grandmother gently shakes her head. "Just because you can live without someone doesn't mean you want to," she says.

The words bang around in my brain, knocking into one another, bouncing off the edges of my mind, but they keep rearranging themselves in the same order.

I don't say anything back. I look at her and squeeze her hand. I often think of my grandmother as the old lady at the dinner table. But she's seen generations. She was a child once. She was a teenager. A newlywed. A mother. A widow.

"I'm sorry this has been so hard," I say. "I never thought of how difficult it must have been for you without Grandpa. It's a hard life."

"No, sweetheart, it's not a hard life. I'm just done living."

When she says it, she's also done talking. She falls back asleep, holding my hand. I rest my chin on her arm and watch her. Eventually, Natalie comes back in, needing to sit down.

"It's hard to stay on my feet so long," she says. "It's also hard to sit still for a long time. Or lie down for too long. Or eat. Or not eat. Or breathe."

I laugh. "Is this such a good idea?" I ask her. "I mean, you're due in, like, days, right?"

"I'm due Thursday," she says. Five days away. "But it was never a question. We had to come. This is where we need to be. I'd be uncomfortable sitting at home, you know? This way . . . this is better."

"Can I get you anything?" I ask her. "Ice chips?"

"You know I'm not actually in labor, right?" Natalie laughs at me, and I laugh back.

"Fair enough!" I say. It wasn't when she said she needed to be here for Grandma that she became a sister to me. It was when she made fun of me for offering ice chips. Big gestures are easy. Making fun of someone who's just trying to help you, that's family.

Charlie joins us. Uncle Fletcher comes in with a bag of Doritos. I don't even know if he went to get a nurse. Mom and Rachel come in. Rachel has clearly been crying. I look at her and see the red in her eyes. I give her a hug.

We stand around. We sit. We wait. I'm not exactly sure what we can do to make any of this better. Sometimes we are talking. Sometimes we are quiet. There are too many of us in this small room, and so we take turns walking out into the hall, walking down to the vending machines, getting a glass of water. Nurses come in and out. They change fluids. The doctor comes in and answers our questions. But really, there aren't many questions to ask. Questions are for when you think there is a way to save someone.

I feel a knot start to form in my throat. It gathers strength as it moves up to the surface. I excuse myself. I go out into the hall.

I put my back against the wall. I slide down to the floor. I imagine Ryan sitting next to me. I imagine him rubbing my back, the way he did when my grandfather died. I imagine him saying, *She's going to a better place. She's* OK. I imagine the way my grandfather might have done this for my grandmother when she lost her own mom or her own grandmother. I imagine my grandmother sitting where I am now, my grandfather kneeling beside her, telling her all the things I want to be told. Holding her the way that only someone in particular can hold you. When I'm her age, when I'm lying in a hospital bed, ready to die, whom will I be thinking of?

It's Ryan. It's always been Ryan. Just because I can live without him doesn't mean I want to.

And I don't. I don't want to.

I want to hear his voice. The way it is rough but sometimes smooth and almost soulful. I want to see his face, with his stubble from never shaving down to the skin. I want to smell him again. I want to hold the roughness of his hands. I want to feel the way they envelop mine, dwarfing them, making me feel small.

I need my husband.

I'm going to call him. I don't care about the pact we made. I don't care about the messiness of it. I just need to hear his voice. I need to know that he's OK. I stand up and pull my phone out of my pocket. I don't have any service. So I walk around the floor, trying to get a bar or two. Nothing.

"Excuse me?" I ask at the nurses' station. "Where can I get cell service?"

"You'll have to go outside," she says. "Once you get out the front doors, you should be OK."

"Thanks," I say, and I walk to the elevators. I hit the button. It lights up, but the elevator doesn't come. I hit it again and again. I've waited this long to call Ryan, and now, suddenly, I must talk to him this second. The urge has overtaken me. I need to ask him to move back home. I need to tell him I love him. He has to know right now.

Finally, the elevator *ding*s. I get in. I press the ground floor. The elevator drops quickly. It's so quick that my stomach doesn't fall at the same pace as my feet. I'm relieved when I touch ground. The doors open. I walk through the lobby. I walk through the front glass doors and step outside. It's a hot, balmy day. It seems so cloudy in the hospital that I've forgotten that it's actually very sunny and bright. I look at my phone. Full service.

It's loud out here in the front of the hospital. Cars are zooming by. Ambulances are pulling in and out. It occurs to me that I am not the only one losing someone right now. Natalie isn't the only one about to have a baby, either. Charlie's not the only man about to become a father. My mother isn't the only one about to lose her last parent. We are a family of people going through all the things people go through every day. We are not special. This hospital doesn't exist for us. I'm not the only woman about to call her husband and ask him to come home. I don't know why it feels good to know that. But it does. I'm not alone. There are millions of me.

A cab pulls up to the sidewalk, and a man gets out. He has a backpack. He shuts the cab door and turns to face me.

It's Ryan.

Ryan.

My Ryan.

He looks exactly the same as when I left him at our house ten months ago. His hair is the same length. His body looks the same. It's so familiar. Everything about him is familiar. The way he walks. The way he shuffles the backpack onto his shoulders.

I stand still, staring right at him. I can barely move. I'm not sure when it happened, but I have dropped my phone.

He walks toward the sliding doors and then stops once he sees me. His eyes go wide. I know him so well that I know what he's thinking. I know what he's going to do next.

He runs toward me and picks me up, grabbing me, clutching me.

"I love you," he says. He has started to cry. "I love you, Lauren, I love you so much. I've missed you. God, I've missed you."

My face hasn't changed. I'm still stunned. My arms are wrapped around him. My legs are wrapped around him. He puts me down and kisses me. When his lips touch mine, my heart burns. It's like someone lit a match in my chest.

How did he know I needed him? How did he know to find me?

He wipes my tears away. Tears I didn't even know were on my face. He's so gentle about it, so loving, that I wonder how I was able to wipe away my own tears all these past months. In an instant, I have forgotten how to live without him, now that he is here.

"How did you know?" I say. "How did you know?"

He looks me in the eye, preparing me. "Don't be mad," he says. His tone is playful, but the underlying message is serious.

"OK," I say. "I won't." I mean it. Whatever brought him here is a blessing. Whatever brought him here was right to do it.

"I've been reading your e-mail drafts."

I drop to the ground.

I laugh so hard that I lose control of myself. I laugh past the point where my abdomen aches and my back hurts. And because I'm laughing, Ryan starts laughing. And now we're both on the sidewalk laughing. His laugh makes mine seem funnier. And now I'm laughing simply because I'm laughing. I can't stop. And I don't want to stop. And then I see my phone, busted up and broken, from when I dropped it. And that seems hilarious. It's all so perfectly, wonderfully, amazingly, beautifully hilarious, isn't it? When did life get so fucking funny?

"Why are we laughing?" Ryan says, in between breaths.

So it turns out this is how I confess. This is how I tell him what I've done. "Because I've been reading yours, too," I say.

He cackles wildly. He's laughing at me and with me and for me. People are walking by and looking at us, and for the first time in my life, I really don't care what they think. This moment is too intoxicating. It has such a strong hold on me that nothing can bring me back to earth until I'm ready.

When we finally do get control of ourselves, our eyes are wet, our heads are light. I start to sigh loudly, the way people do when they are recovering from fits of laughter. I try to get control of myself, like a pilot landing a plane, slow and steady, readying to hit solid ground. Except instead of feeling the world under my feet, I take off again at the last minute. My sighs turn into tears. Laughing and crying are so intrinsically tied together, spun of the same material, that it's hard to tell one from the other sometimes. And it's easier than you think to go from being so happy you could cry to so devastated you could laugh.

The weeping becomes sobbing, and Ryan puts his arms around me. He holds me tight, right here on the sidewalk. He rubs my back, and when I start to wail, he says, "It's OK. It's OK."

I look at his left hand as it holds mine. He has his wedding ring on.

R yan and I get up off the sidewalk slowly. He grabs his bag. He picks up the pieces of my dropped cell phone and puts it back together.

"We might need to get you a new phone," he says. "This one appears to have taken a beating."

He grabs my hand as we walk into the hospital. We join the group of people waiting at the bank of elevators. When an elevator finally arrives, all of us cram into it, pushing against one another, spreading out against the three walls. Ryan never lets go of my hand. He squeezes it tight. He holds on for dear life. Both of our hands are sweating into each other. But he never lets go.

When we get to the eighth floor, I lead us off the elevator, and standing in front of us, ostensibly waiting for a down elevator, is Rachel.

"Where have you been?" Rachel asks. "I've been looking all over for you. I called you four times."

I start to answer, but Ryan answers for me. "Her phone is broken," he says, showing Rachel the pieces.

Rachel stares at him, her eyes fixated on him, trying to piece together why seeing him in front of her feels as if it makes perfect sense and yet doesn't make any sense at all. "Um . . ." she says. "Hi, Ryan."

He moves toward her and hugs her. "Hey, Rach. I've missed you. I came as soon as I heard."

Ryan's back is facing me, as Rachel's face is in my direct eye line. She mouths, *Is this OK?* half pointing to Ryan's back.

I give her a thumbs-up. That's all she needs. She just needs a thumbs-up. If I'm thumbs-up, she's thumbs-up. "I'm so glad to see you!" she says. She turns on the charm as if it has a switch, but it's real. She's being entirely genuine.

"Me, too," he says. "Me, too."

"We've missed you around these parts," Rachel says, giving him a sisterly light punch to the arm.

"You don't even know the half of it," he says. "What can I do? How can I help now that I'm here?"

"Well," Rachel says, looking at me now, "we've had a slight hiccup."

"Hiccup?" I say.

"Natalie and Charlie ran down to prenatal."

"Oh," I say.

"When is she due?" Ryan says. "It's soon, right?"

"Thursday," I say.

"Right," Rachel says. "Well, she thinks she has something called Braxton-Hicks."

"What is Braxton-Hicks?" Ryan and I both say at the same time. It's muscle memory, the way we can function as one unit so easily. It's such second nature to be two halves of a whole that after months of not speaking, we are now speaking as one.

"I don't know. Mom explained it. It's something where it seems like you're in labor but you're probably not."

"*Probably* not?" I ask.

"No," Rachel says. "I mean, she's not. But they thought it was best to address it. Apparently, the contractions feel just like real contractions."

"So it's painful?" Ryan says.

Rachel nods and tries not to laugh.

"What?" I ask.

"It's not funny," Rachel says. "It's totally not."

"But?"

"But when the first one came, Natalie grabbed her stomach and said, 'Holy Satan, fuck me.' Even Mom was laughing."

I start laughing along with Rachel. Multiple elevators have come and gone at this point, and we just continue to stand here.

"You guys are mean," Ryan says.

I start to defend myself, but Rachel intervenes. "No, it's just funny because Natalie is the nicest person I've ever met. Truly. When she said it, Mom laughed so hard she blew a huge snot bubble."

I start laughing again; Ryan does, too. My mother has appeared right behind Rachel.

"Rachel Evelyn Spencer!"

Rachel looks at me and rolls her eyes. "Mom heard me, huh?"

I nod.

"Sorry, Mom," she says, turning around.

"Never mind that," my mom says, her face growing serious. "We have a slight hiccup."

"Yeah, Rachel told us," I say.

My mom's line of sight focuses in on Ryan and then my hand, which is still holding his after all this time. "Good Lord, this is all just too much," she says. She sits down in one of the chairs along the hall and puts her head in her hands. "It's not Braxton-Hicks," she says. "Natalie is in labor."

"Please tell me you're joking," Rachel says.

"No, Rachel, I'm not joking. And this is a good thing, remember? We want this baby born."

"No, I know," she says, reprimanded. "I just mean it's a lot at once."

"Can I do anything?" Ryan asks.

My mom looks at him and stands up. She hugs him tight.

She hugs him the way only a mother can hug. It's not a mutual hug, like Rachel and Ryan had. My mother is hugging. Ryan is being hugged. "I'm just so glad to see your face, sweetheart," she says. "So glad to see your face."

Ryan looks at her for a moment, and I think he might lose it. He might actually start crying. But he changes course. "I missed you, Leslie."

"Oh, honey, we all missed you."

"How is Grandma Lois doing?" he asks. "Can I see her?"

"She's sleeping at the moment," my mom says. "I think we should split up. Some people need to go be with Natalie and Charlie, and the rest of us need to be with Grandma."

It's an impossible choice, isn't it? Do you want to be there for the last moments of one life or the first moments of another? Do you honor the past or ring in the future?

"I can't do this," my mom says. "I can't choose. My grandbaby or my mother?"

"You don't have to choose," I say. "Between me, Ryan, Rachel, and Fletcher, we've got everything. You can go back and forth."

"I suppose I'm going to get stuck with Uncle Fletcher?" Rachel says.

I look at her. The look on my face is an apology and a plea.

"Fine," she says. "Everyone has a life event but me. So I'll just go watch Grandma with Uncle Fletcher."

"Thank you," I say.

"When the baby is born, please come get me. Please? Ryan? Will you come get me? Switch with me or something?"

"Absolutely," he says.

"I'll go with you," Mom says to Rachel. "Keep us posted, please," she says to Ryan and me.

"OK," I say. "You got it."

"If she wakes up," Ryan chimes in, "tell her I'm here?"

"Are you kidding?" Mom says. "I don't know if we could keep the news in if we tried!"

Ryan smiles as I hit the elevator down button, and then I hit the up button. I don't know where we're going.

"Mom?" I call out.

She turns around.

"What floor?"

"Five."

The down elevator *ding*s. It's here. Here we go. We have been chosen to ring in the future.

It turns out that ringing in the future is not like New Year's Eve when you can count down from ten until the ball drops. Ringing in the future is a lot of waiting. It's a lot of sitting in uncomfortable chairs and walking back and forth to the vending machine. It's a lot of checking regularly with Charlie but not staying in the room itself.

"She's at three centimeters," Charlie says, when we find their room. He's talking to us while looking at Natalie, and it's clear he assumes we are Mom.

"You OK, Natalie?" I ask. She looks like crap. I mean, she looks beautiful, because beautiful people are beautiful even when they look like crap, but all the signs for looking like crap are there. Her hair is disheveled, her face is flushed. She's clearly been crying. And yet, somehow, she's entirely happy.

"Yep," she says. "I'm good. Just don't ask me during a contraction." She looks up at me and sees a strange man standing beside me. Admittedly, I should have thought about the fact that Ryan is a stranger and Natalie is in a hospital gown on a bed with stirrups.

"Uh . . ." she says, looking at him.

Charlie follows her eyes and turns around. His face lights up as if a lightbulb has just gone on above his head. "Ryan!" He steps up, dropping Natalie's hand, and gives Ryan a bro hug. There is a lot of back patting.

"Hey, Charlie!" Ryan says. When they are done hugging, Charlie stands next to him, and Ryan keeps his hand on Charlie's shoulder for just a second longer than a friend would.

They are closer than friends. Charlie starts to introduce Ryan to Natalie, but she starts cringing and gasping for air. Charlie runs to her. He's so quick it looks instinctual. This is a guy my mom has to beg to help with the dishes, but the minute Natalie is in pain, he's there. He's supporting her. Helping her. Being there for her.

"Can I do anything?" I ask. I am hesitant to offer ice chips again, but she did say that they were appropriate for labor. "Ice chips?"

Natalie laughs for a moment through her pain. It is, perhaps, the best laugh I've ever gotten in my entire life.

"Yeah," Charlie says, his hand being squeezed. "Ice chips."

Ryan and I leave to find some. The nurse tells us there is an ice machine at the end of a very long hall. We start walking.

"So I read about this guy David," Ryan says. "Is David still a . . . still a thing?"

"No." I shake my head. "No, not a thing."

"I want to kill him," Ryan says, smiling. It's a dangerous smile. "You know that, right? I've wanted to kill him for months. I sometimes dream about it. Notice I didn't call them nightmares." Our shoes squeak on the hospital floor.

"I'm not too fond of Emily, either," I say. For the first time in months, I allow myself to feel the rage I had when I found out he was seeing other women. I can feel it once again, the way it rises to the surface like a flotation device. The way it keeps bouncing back no matter how hard you push it down.

"Emily never held a candle to you," he says, when we finally get to the ice machine.

I grab a cup and put it underneath the machine. I could say more. I could ask more. But I decide to leave it at that. The machine grumbles, but it spits nothing out. Ryan slams the side of it, throwing his whole body against it. Chips start to flow out into the cup.

We walk back to Charlie and Natalie's room and hand Charlie the ice chips. He thanks us, and even though Natalie appears to no longer be in pain, I figure it's best if Ryan and I go to the waiting room.

"You'll come get us if you need anything?" I ask Charlie, and he nods.

Ryan makes a fist and gives Charlie a pound. "Good luck," he says.

The waiting room is mostly empty, save for a new grandparent or two. So we take a seat in the middle by the wall. Sometimes we talk about a lot of things. Sometimes we don't say anything. Sometimes we are quiet for a long time, and then the conversation takes off again when one of us says something like "I can't believe you don't like Persian food" or "I can't believe you bought me that beard trimmer to get me to shave my pubes. Definitely the most embarrassing thing I've ever read. I read that, and I literally walked straight into the bathroom and trimmed them." Ryan smiles, laughing. He gives a fake shiver. "Mortifying."

"I'm sorry," I say. "I honestly did not think you would ever read that."

"No, but it's good I did, right? A little pinch of embarrassment at first, but now I know. And henceforth my nether regions will be squeaky clean."

I look down at the ground. The hospital carpet is a pattern of diamonds. Diamond after diamond after diamond. I unfocus my eyes a bit and realize that if you look at it a different way, it's a large series of Xs. Or Ws.

"I think if I've learned anything about how to . . . fix this," I say, "it's that I really need to work on telling you what I want."

"Yeah," he says. "Same here. That's a big one for me. I was just going along with what I thought you wanted all the time, and after a while, I think I just grew pissed off about it."

"Yeah," I say, nodding my head. "I assumed that the way to be a good partner to you was compliance."

"Yes!" he says, eager in agreement.

"And so I never asked for the things I needed."

"You expected me to know them."

"Yeah," I say. "And when you didn't know them, or you didn't guess them, I just assumed you didn't care. That I didn't matter. That you were choosing you over me."

"I know exactly what you mean," he says. "Imagine if I had just told you I hate international food."

"Right!" I say. "I don't even care that much about eating Persian food or Greek food or Vietnamese. I really don't. I only ever cared about having dinner with you."

"So that's one of the things we have to do better, Lauren. We have to. We have to be honest."

"Yeah," I say.

"No," Ryan says, turning toward me, grabbing my hand, looking me in the eye. "Brutal honesty. It's OK to hurt me. It's OK to hurt my feelings. It's OK to embarrass me. As long as you do it from love. Nothing you could ever say out of love could hurt as much as it did to look into your eyes and see that you couldn't stand me anymore. I would rather be told to shave my pubes a thousand times than have you look at me the way you had been."

I want to roll around on the floor with him. I want to smell his hair. I want to kiss his neck. I want to sneak into one of those doctor "on call" rooms they have on soap operas and make love to him on the bunk beds. I want to show him what I have missed. Show him what he has missed. Show him what I have learned. I want to lose sight of where I end and he begins.

And we will do that. I know that. But I also have to remember that this is the beginning of the solution. This is the part where we do the work to fix our marriage.

"I love you," I say, my voice quivering. My muscles relaxing. My eyes filling with tears.

"I love you, too," he says, his voice breaking into a cry. It's a controlled cry. His tears barely make their way over the edge of his eyelid.

He kisses me.

And it is now that I understand the true value of the past ten months.

Sure, I have learned things about myself. I've learned what I want in bed. I've learned to ask for what I need. I've learned that love and romance don't have to be the same thing. I've learned that not everyone wants one or the other. I've learned that what you need and what you want are both equally important in love. I've learned a lot. But I could have learned these things with Ryan by my side. I could have sought out these lessons *with* him instead of *away* from him. No, the true value of this year isn't that I've learned ways to fix my marriage. The value of this year has been that I finally *want* to fix my marriage.

I have the energy to do it. I have the passion to do it. I have the drive. And I believe.

I want my marriage to work. I want it to work so bad that I feel it deep in my bones. I know the sun will rise tomorrow if I fail. I know that I can live with myself if we don't make it. But I want it. I want it so bad.

"So you'll stayed married to me?" Ryan asks. It has the weight and vulnerability of when he asked me to marry him, all those years ago.

I smile. "Yes," I say. "Yes!"

He grabs me and kisses me. He holds me. "She said yes!" he says to the waiting room. The few people in here just look at us and smile politely.

"I feel so good right now. I feel alive for the first time in years," he says. "I feel like I could conquer the world."

I kiss him. I kiss him again. He's so cute. And he's so handsome. And he's so smart. And funny. And charming. I don't know how I stopped seeing all of that.

"I never lost faith," he says. "I mean, in the back of my mind, I always hoped. You know that game people play in the car, when you see a car with one headlight out, you make a wish as you—"

"Flick the roof and say 'Pididdle,'" I say.

He nods. "I've only ever wished for one thing. Each time."

"Me?"

"Us."

"Even this whole year?"

"Every time."

We need each other. Whatever that means. We complement each other. We have great potential to make each other better. I was the one who had the strength to be honest about what we were doing to each other. I was the one who was brave enough to break this thing in half in the hopes of putting it back together. But when I lost faith, he's the one who had enough for both of us.

Ryan takes his hand out of mine for the first time in hours. He leans back and puts his arm around me. He pulls me in to him. The arms of the chairs make it slightly uncomfortable, and yet it is entirely comforting. I let my head sink into the crook of his armpit. I breathe in, sighing. He smells. He smells like Ryan. A scent pleasing in its familiarity and yet repulsive in its odor.

"Ugh," I say, not backing away. "You need to wear deodorant. Have you forgotten to keep yourself deodorized?"

"Smell it, baby girl," he says in an overly manly voice. "That's the smell of a man."

"The smell of a man is Old Spice," I say. "Let's invest in some."

That's when my grandmother dies. I mean, I can't be sure. I don't hear about it for another ten minutes. But when I do hear about it, they say it happened ten minutes ago. So I'm pretty sure it happened as I sat here, smelling Ryan's armpit, telling him to use deodorant.

It was supposed to happen after the baby was born. Or when I was with her. Or as she held my hand and told me the meaning of life. It wasn't supposed to happen when I was laughing with Ryan about Old Spice.

Some people love that about life, that it's unpredictable and unruly. I hate it. I hate that it doesn't have the common decency to wait for a profound moment to take something from you. It doesn't care that you just want one picture of your grandmother holding her great-grandchild. It just doesn't care.

• • •

My mom is crying when I get to Grandma's room. Fletcher is hugging her. Rachel is sitting in a chair by herself, head in her hands. Mom asked the nurses to move Grandma's body. It's gone by the time I get there. Thank fortune for small favors. I couldn't have handled that. I simply don't have it in me.

But the empty bed is hard enough. How can you miss someone so much already? My mind is full of all the things I didn't say. It doesn't matter how much I *did* say. There was still so much *left* to say. I want to tell her that I love her. That I will always remember her. That I am happy for her. That I believe she will find Grandpa.

Mom tells me that she told Grandma that Ryan was here. "I told her that he was with you, that he was taking care of you. To be honest, I couldn't tell if she heard me. But I think she did."

We all discuss plans, and we cry in one another's arms.

After a while, after we have squeezed too many tears out of our eyes, my mother tells us we need to "buck up."

"Chins up, people! Look alert! It's a big day for Charlie, OK? A big day for all of us. Grandma would not want this to be a day of sorrow. A baby is coming."

Rachel and I nod, drying our tears with tissues. Ryan has his hands on both of our shoulders.

"Fletch, you can stay here and take care of the details, right?"

Fletcher nods. He isn't crying in front of us, and I get the distinct impression that he's looking forward to being alone so that he can.

"And you come find me down on the fifth floor when you're ready."

My mom claps her hands together like a football coach, as if this is the state championship and we're down by six.

"We can do this!" she says. "There is plenty of time to think about Grandma, but right now, we need to be here for Charlie. We need to push this out of our minds and think about the beautiful little baby that's coming."

Rachel and I nod again.

"Yeah, coach!" Ryan says, giving my mom a high-five.

She looks at him, stunned, for a moment and then laughs. "For Charlie!" she cheers.

"For Charlie!" the three of us say, and Fletcher joins in at the last minute.

"I'll check in on you soon," my mom says to Fletcher, and then we all break for the elevator. When it comes, when we get in, when Rachel pushes the button for the fifth floor, when I feel the elevator drop, all I can think is that my mom has lost her mother today, and she's not crying. She's fighting to make this day right for her son. For her grandchild. Look at the things we are capable of in the name of the people we love.

Jonathan Louis Spencer is born at 1:04 A.M. on June 2. He weighs eight pounds, six ounces. He has a full head of dark hair. He has a squooshed face. He sort of looks like Natalie. If someone squooshed her face.

By sometime around nine in the morning, we've all held him. The nurse has taken him and brought him back, and now Jonathan rests in my mother's arms. She is rocking back and forth. Natalie is half-asleep in the hospital bed.

Charlie looks at me, proud papa written all over his face. "I've only known him for eight hours," he says to me, sitting in a chair, staring straight ahead at his baby boy. "But I could never leave him."

I grab his hand.

"It doesn't make any sense," Charlie says, shaking his head. "How our dad could have left. It doesn't make any sense, Lauren."

"I know," I say.

Charlie looks at me. "No, you don't," he says. It's not accusatory. It's not pointed. He is merely telling me that there is an experience in this world that he understands more intimately than I do. He's letting me know that as much as I think I get it, there is a world of love out there, a world of deep, unending, unconditional dedication that I know not of.

"You're right," I say. "I don't yet."

"I've never loved anything like this," he says, shaking his head again. He looks at Natalie, and he starts to cry. "And Natalie," he says. "She gave it to me."

My brother may not have been in love with Natalie when he asked her to marry him or when he decided to move back here. He may not have been in love with her when he brought his things into her house and started to make a life with her. But somewhere along the way, he learned to do it. Maybe it happened at 1:03 or 1:04 or 1:05 this morning. But there's no doubt it happened. You can see it in his eyes. He loves this woman.

"I'm proud of you, Charlie," Ryan says, patting him on the back. "I'm so happy for you."

Charlie closes his eyes, holding in the tears that want to fall onto his cheeks. "I'm gonna do this," Charlie says. He opens his eyes. He's not talking to me. He's not talking to Ryan. He's not talking to Rachel or Natalie or my mom. He's talking to Jonathan.

"We know you are," my mom says. She's not answering for herself. She's answering for all of us. She's answering for Jonathan.

I look at Jonathan's face. How can something so squooshed be so beautiful?

I look at Ryan, and I can tell what he's thinking. We can do this, too, one day. Not today. Probably not next year. But we can do this one day. Ryan squeezes my hand. Rachel sees it, and she smiles at me.

It's a good day. My mom, Charlie, Natalie, Jonathan, Rachel, Ryan, even me—we made this a good day.

"Wait," I say. "Is Louis for Lois?"

Natalie laughs. "It wasn't, but it is now!"

Charlie starts laughing, and so does my mom. If Charlie and my mom are laughing, then I'm right. It's a good day.

There is a funeral. And a wedding. And in between, a reunion.

At the funeral, Ryan holds my hand. Bill holds my mother. Charlie holds Natalie. Rachel holds Jonathan. Fletcher reads the eulogy.

I'm not going to lie, his eulogy is a little weird. But he does capture the heart of Grandma. He talks about how much she loved Grandpa. He talks about how lucky he felt to live in a home where his parents loved each other. He talks about how his parents are together again, and that brings him great solace. He talks about the right things my grandmother always said at the wrong times. He talks about how we all laughed when she said she had cancer, and he tells it right. He makes it funny and idiosyncratic instead of sad and rueful.

My mom stays quiet. She tries to keep the tears in and mostly succeeds. I am surprised to find that she does not lean on Rachel, Charlie, and me all that much. When she does cry, she turns to Bill.

Once the funeral is over, we all go back to Fletcher's house for food. We talk about Grandma. We coo over Jonathan. We follow Natalie around the room and ask her if she needs anything. She's the star of the family now. She's given us the crown jewel.

When I'm tired and I want to go, when I've had enough talking, enough crying, enough dwelling, I look over at Charlie and Ryan, talking to each other in the corner, each with a beer in his hand.

How did I forget that they are brothers in their own right? They do it so well.

When Ryan and I finally get back to Los Angeles, we don't go to our home or to his apartment. We go to Mila's house.

And waiting for us there is Thumper Cooper.

Ryan doesn't say anything when Thumper runs to him. He doesn't say *Down, boy* or *Hey, buddy* or any of the things you say to an excited dog. He just holds him close. And Thumper, normally excitable and rambunctious, rests comfortably and patiently in his arms.

Mila gives Ryan a hug of her own. "So you're back, huh?" she asks. She knows she'll get the details soon. She's just glad he's here. "Happy to see you," she says, smiling at me.

Ryan laughs. "Happy to be seen."

We thank Mila and Christina, and the three of us get into the car. We drive to our place. We get out of the car. I open the front door. We all walk in.

Here we are. Our tiny family. Nothing's missing anymore. We're home.

That night, Ryan gets into bed next to me. He holds me. He kisses me. He slides his hand down my body, and he says, "Show me. Show me how to do what you want."

And I do. And it feels better than it did with David. Because I am once again myself with the man I love.

We forgot, for a while, how to listen to each other, how to touch each other. But we remember now.

The next morning, I wake up and open the shoebox in the closet. I dig out my wedding ring. I put it back on.

The wedding is a month later. It's a hot July day. We're at Natalie's friend's beach house in Malibu. What this friend does for a living, I don't know. I would guess, judging from the fact that this house is quite literally on the beach and has one-hundred-eighty-degree ocean views from every floor, that it's something in entertainment. There is a bonfire scheduled for late tonight and a lobster bake picnic scheduled for after the ceremony. Drinks and dancing are on the roof deck. Remind me to start hobnobbing with Hollywood producers. I would like for this to become a regular thing.

The ceremony is starting in a few minutes. Natalie, Rachel, and I are finishing getting ready. Natalie is wearing a Grecian-looking dress, draped around her. Her face is flush. Her boobs are huge. Her hair is long and curled. She is wearing long earrings that are buried in her long, dark hair. Her eyes have so much life behind them.

"Does this look right?" Rachel asks, as she fastens the halter top of her "persimmon" dress behind her neck. I assure her that it does. I know, because mine looks exactly the same.

Natalie's mom is helping Natalie get her shoes on. I thought Natalie's parents would be lithe and vibrant like her, but they look entirely average. Her mom is round in the middle. Her dad is short and hefty. I'm not sure what it is about them that makes it clear that they are from Idaho, but they certainly don't seem to be from around here. Maybe it's the fact that they are some of the nicest, most sincere people I've ever met.

Natalie's dad knocks on the door to come in.

"Just a minute, Harry!" Natalie's mom calls out. "She'll be ready in a second!"

"I want to take a picture, Eileen!"

"Just a second, I said!"

Natalie looks at Rachel and me with a laugh. "Oh!" she says, the thought just coming to her. "The bouquets! I left them in the fridge."

"It's cool," I say. "I got it." I cross out of the room through the shared bathroom and head down the stairs to the kitchen, where I can see my brother standing with Ryan and his friend Wally just outside the sliding glass doors.

Charlie is dressed to the nines in a fitted cream suit. He looks sleek and handsome. He doesn't look nervous. He doesn't look shy. He looks ready. Ryan and Wally are wearing black suits with black ties. Outside on the beach, white chairs line either side of the aisle, facing the light blue sea. People are trickling in. They grab their programs. They take their seats. The minister is standing there, waiting. My mom is sitting in the first row on the right side. She is wearing a navy-blue dress. She's got Jonathan in her arms. Bill is sitting next to her in a gray suit. Mila and Christina are a few rows back. They are having a rare moment alone without their kids. I can see Christina look over and kiss Mila's temple. She smiles at her.

I grab the three bouquets from the refrigerator and shake them out over the sink.

"Any last insights?" I hear Charlie say. "Any words of advice?"

I should head back upstairs, but I want to hear Ryan's answer.

"All you have to do is never give up," he says.

"Simple enough," Charlie says.

Ryan laughs. "It is, actually."

I hear a pat on the back, I'm not sure who is patting whom, and then I hear a third voice, which I'm assuming is Wally's. "Dude, I have zero advice to give. Because I've never been married. But if it makes any difference, I think she's great."

"Thanks," Charlie says.

"You ready?" Ryan asks.

I hear them start walking, and I peek to see their backs as they walk out together, getting ready to take their places.

I run back up to the bedroom to find Natalie. All four of them—Natalie, her parents, and Rachel—are ready to go. I hand Natalie her bouquet and hand one of the smaller ones to Rachel. I keep the third.

"OK," Rachel says. "Here we go."

Natalie breathes in. She looks at her dad. "Ready?"

He nods his head. "If you are."

Her mom snaps a picture.

"OK, I'm going down first," her mom says. "I'll see you in a second." She kisses Natalie on the cheek and leaves before she can start crying.

"Hoo. OK. Here we go," Natalie says. "Any last tips?" She laughs. I assume she's talking to her dad, but she's talking to me. I am now a person people go to for marital advice.

I tell her the only thing there is to tell her. "All you have to do is never give up."

Natalie's dad laughs. "Listen to her," he says. "She's absolutely right."

It's ten o'clock, and the party is still going strong. When Natalie danced with her dad, I got misty. When Charlie danced with Mom, I broke down. The sun set around eight, but it's been a warm night. The wind off the beach is strong and cools us down. Charlie and Natalie put the baby to bed a few hours ago.

Rachel made the cake, and it is the hit of the night. People keep asking about it. Everyone thinks it was from a very expensive bakery somewhere in Beverly Hills. I correct one person who asks Rachel about it. I say, "It's from this great new place opening up called Batter," I say. "Location TBD."

"Location is on Larchmont Boulevard," Rachel says, correcting me. When I give her an inquisitive look, she tells me the bank approved the loan.

"When were you gonna tell me?"

"Well, I just found out, and I didn't want to steal the sunshine from Charlie's wedding," she says.

I whisper, "Congratulations."

"Thanks," she whispers back. "You can pretend you're hearing it for the first time when I tell everyone next week. You're good at that." She smiles at me to let me know she's teasing.

Mom and Bill dance the night away. Later on by the rooftop bar, I point to him across the room, eating shrimp cocktail. "So the romance is alive and well, huh?" I ask Mom.

She shrugs. "I don't know," she says. "Maybe it's OK to stick around a little longer than the honeymoon phase."

"Wow," I say. "I'm impressed. Are you thinking about letting him move in?"

She laughs at me. "I'm thinking about it. All I'm doing is thinking. Have you seen this, by the way?"

"What?" I say, turning my head to look where she's pointing. Over in the far corner of the dance floor, Rachel is now dancing with Wally.

"Interesting, no?"

I think about how Rachel would want me to answer. "Yeah," I say, shrugging. "We'll see what happens."

"Yes, we will."

The music changes. You know the party is reaching its peak when the DJ plays "Shout."

Ryan runs up to me. "Baby! We gotta dance!"

I put my drink down and turn to my mother. "If you'll excuse me," I say.

"Certainly," she says.

We run into the crowd. We surround Charlie and Natalie. We join Rachel and Wally. We sing our hearts out. And because "Shout" is the type of song that brings everyone onto the dance floor, Mom and Bill hop in just as Natalie's parents make their way into the circle. Soon Mila and Christina join us, and even Uncle Fletcher can't resist. We dance together, twisting side-to-side, crouching lower and jumping higher as the song plays on, forgetting to worry about whether we look silly, forgetting to worry about anything at all.

I look at the people in this circle with me—my family, my friends, my husband—and I am overwhelmed with hope for the future.

I don't know if everyone is as thankful for this moment as I am. I don't know if everyone here understands how fragile life and love can be. I don't know if they are thinking about that right now.

I just know that I've learned it for myself. And I'll never forget it.

A few months later, it's a Wednesday night. My night to pick whatever dinner I want. I decide to order from the Vietnamese place down the street and then think better of it. Ryan has had a hard day at work. I'm going to order us a pizza.

But before I do, Ryan waves me over to his computer.

"Uh . . . Lauren?" he says.

"Yeah?" I say, walking toward him.

"Remember when you said you wrote to that woman?"

"What woman?"

"Ask Allie?"

I sit down next to him. Thumper is at his feet. "Yeah," I say.

"Well, it looks like she wrote back to you. Are you 'Lost in Los Angeles'?"

• • •

Dear Lost in Los Angeles,

I'm going to let you in on a little secret. It's a lesson learned by those who have faced the most miserable of tragedies, and it's a secret that I suspect you yourself already know: the sun will always rise. Always.

The sun rises the next day after mothers lose their babies, after men lose their wives, after countries lose wars. The sun will rise no matter what pain we encounter. No matter how much we believe the world to be over, the sun will rise. So you can't go around assessing love by whether or not the sun rises. The sun doesn't care about love. It just cares about rising.

And the other little piece of information that I think you need to know is that there are no rules in marriage. I know it would be easier if there were. I know we all sometimes hope for them; cut-and-dried answers would make the decisions easier. Black-and-white problems would be simpler to solve. But there simply isn't a rule that works for every marriage, for every love, for every family, for every relationship.

Some people need more boundaries, some people need fewer. Some marriages need more space, some marriages need more intimacy. Some families need more honesty, some families need more kindness. There's no single answer for any of it.

So I can't tell you what to do. I can't tell you if you should be with your husband or not. I can't tell you if you need him or want him. Need and want are words we define for ourselves.

Here is what I can tell you. All that matters in this life is that you try. All that matters is that you open your heart, give everything you have, and keep trying.

You and your husband reached a point in your marriage where most people would give up. And you didn't. Let that speak to you. Let that guide you.

Do you have more to give your marriage? If you do, give it everything you've got.

Much love,
Allie

. . .

I print out the letter and put it in the shoebox in the closet. It's the first thing you see when you open it now; it's on top of all the keepsakes and mementos. I think of it as the last piece of advice my grandmother ever gave me.

Ever gave us all.

And I intend to follow that advice.

I don't know if Rachel's bakery is going to succeed.

I don't know if Charlie and Natalie will stay together.

I don't know if my mom will move in with Bill.

I don't know if Ryan and I will celebrate our fiftieth anniversary.

But I can tell you that we are all going to try.

We're all going to give it everything we've got.

ACKNOWLEDGMENTS

This book is dedicated to my mother, Mindy, and my brother, Jake, because I would not be able to write about family without them. Thank you both for being so supportive and encouraging. The same goes for Linda Morris, an extraordinarily exceptional grandmother. And much thanks to the rest of the Jenkins and Morris families.

Thank you to the Reid and Hanes families, including but certainly not limited to the Encino clan of Rose, Warren, Sally, Bernie, Niko, and Zach. Words cannot express my gratitude for your unyielding and sincere support. I could not have married into a more loving family.

I am lucky enough to have far too many supportive friends to name and that alone makes me immensely grateful every day of my life. In addition to the wonderful friends I thanked in my first book, special attention must go to the early readers of this one: Erin Fricker, Colin Rodger, Andy Bauch, Julia Furlan, and Tamara Hunter. I am also hugely thankful to Zach Fricker for answering every medical question I have with a curmudgeonly zeal.

Carly Watters, my cheerleader and first line of defense, I'd be a starving artist without you. You also consistently prove that Canadians are the nicest people in the world.

Greer Hendricks, you make every book infinitely better in ways both big and small. Your expertise and intuition are invaluable. Sarah Cantin, you make being a professional writer feel easy. To the copy editors, cover designers, and publicity team at Atria, thank you. Atria feels like family I only see on the Internet.

I've been blessed with fellow authors who have shared their audience and time with me: Sarah Pekkanen, Amy Hatvany, Sarah Jio, Emma McLaughlin and Nicola Kraus, and many more. Thank you all so much. I feel so lucky to be the recipient of your kindness and support.

To the woman who opened up her heart to me and confided the story of her own beautiful and fragile marriage, I cannot thank you enough for your time and trust.

Special thanks go to my pit bull, Rabbit Reid, for being the apple of my eye. Rabbit, you can't read and you don't speak English, but I think you know how important you are to my every day. I also owe a great deal of thanks to Owl Reid, a dog so noble and good that I honestly believe I'm a better person for having known her. If anyone is thinking about getting a dog, give pit bulls a chance. There is no love quite like it.

And lastly, my husband, Alex Reid: This book is as much yours as it is mine. Every sentence I write is as much yours as it is mine.

AFTER I DO

TAYLOR JENKINS REID

QUESTIONS AND TOPICS FOR DISCUSSION

1. Read through Lauren's flashbacks of her and Ryan's relationship, leading up to the night of the Dodgers game. At what point did you notice a shift in their dynamic? Discuss with the group.

2. Early in the novel, Lauren playfully says of Ryan, "He always loved making me say the things he wanted to say." In what ways does this become a loaded assessment of their relationship?

3. Turn to page 125, when Lauren and her mother are discussing marriage. Lauren says that she doesn't want to fail at her marriage, which her mother dismisses: "If you stay married for a number of years and you have a happy time together and then you decide you don't want to be married anymore and you choose to go be happy with someone else or doing something else, that's not a failure." Do you agree with her?

4. Even though the underlying question of the narrative is whether Lauren and Ryan's marriage will survive, Ryan himself is not an active character for the majority of the novel, and we spend much of our time with other people in Lauren's life. How does observing Lauren in these dynamics enhance our understanding of her? And did you have a favorite supporting character?

5. What do you think Lauren gets out of her relationship with David? Is the fact that he is separated from his wife integral to their dynamic?

6. Did Rachel's revelation on page 225 surprise you? Do you have any relationships like hers and Lauren's in your

life—where the similarities are so clear that the differences can be ignored, sometimes to a fault?

7. Discuss the theme of communication within the novel. To what degree do these characters struggle to express themselves, and how do they find alternative ways of doing so when straight dialogue doesn't suffice?

8. Turn to page 236 and re-read the conversation that Rachel and Lauren have with their mother about romance and long-term relationships. Do you understand Ms. Spencer's perspective that "I don't need a life partner . . . I want love and romance." Can romance be kept alive by forestalling a greater commitment, or is it "the nature of love," as Lauren suggests, for relationships to "become more about partnership and less about romance"?

9. Discuss the role that sex plays in Lauren and Ryan's relationship, and how it relates to the feelings of resentment that she describes on page 272. If romance is, in fact, destined to evolve into more of a partnership, what happens to sex in that equation? Is romance required for a mutually fulfilling sexual relationship?

10. Even though Lauren and Ryan don't have children, the potential demise of their relationship still has collateral damage. Turn to page 257, and the conversation that Lauren has with her brother about inviting Ryan to his wedding. Do you think Lauren has a right to an opinion here? Do you agree with her statement that "I made him a part of this family . . . and he's a part of this family on my terms"?

11. Thinking about Ryan, Lauren says: "We have spent enough years together to know how to work in sync, even when we don't want to." To what extent is a long-term relationship defined by whether the other person is

someone with whom you know how to endure the tough moments of life? Find examples within the novel to support your opinion.

12. Lauren gets relationship advice from a variety of people throughout the novel. Did any of it in particular resonate with you? Pick a favorite line and share why you connected to it with the group.

13. Speaking of advice: the Ask Allie column plays a large role throughout the book. Was Lauren able to take any wisdom from Allie's old columns that perhaps a closer friend or family member couldn't have said to her directly? What did you think of her final letter to Lauren?

14. Consider the romantic partnerships that Lauren has to look to as models: her mother and Bill, Charlie and Natalie, Mila and Christina, even her grandmother and deceased grandfather. What does she take away from each of them?

15. Discuss the portrayal of compromise in the novel, and compare how it is depicted in romantic relationships versus within family dynamics. Do you think of compromise differently when it comes to family members, as opposed to romantic partners? Why or why not?

ENHANCE YOUR READING GROUP

Read Taylor Jenkins Reid's debut novel *Forever, Interrupted* as a group. How are these love stories different? Having now read two of Reid's novels, what can you identify as distinct qualities of her writing style?

The e-mails that Ryan and Lauren write each other but never send prove to be very cathartic to both of them. If you could write to someone you've been romantically involved with (in the past or currently), knowing that they might read it but that they couldn't confront you about it, what would you say?

The book makes the point that "marriage" is a word that has many different definitions. Whether you are married or unmarried, what does marriage mean to you?

What's the best piece of advice you've ever been given about marriage and family?